P9-ECZ-721

THE
WOLF'S EYE

THE WOLF'S EYE
Stories from Northwestern Ontario

edited by
Charles Wilkins

THUNDER BOOKS
The Thunder Bay Publishing Cooperative
1992
with the support of
The Thunder Bay Public Library

The copyrights © for all stories in this book are held by the individual authors.

Canadian Cataloguing in Publication Data
Main entry under title:

The Wolf's Eye: an anthology of stories from Northwestern Ontario

ISBN 0-9696339-0-4

1. Short stories, Canadian (English) - Ontario,
Northern.* 2. Canadian fiction (English) - 20th century.* I. Wilkins,
Charles.

PS8329.5.05W65 1992   C813'.0108971311
PR9198.2.052W65 1992   C92-094738-7

Book design: Kathy Lucky
Cover: Dan Diamond, Charles Wilkins

Published by the Thunder Bay Publishing Cooperative, with the support of
the Thunder Bay Public Library, 285 Red River Road, Thunder Bay,
Ontario.

"A Canadian Tale: 1955" by Elizabeth Kouhi first appeared in slightly
different form in *The Northward Journal*. Reprinted by permission of the
author. "This White Wail, This Loud Blur" by Claude Liman is reprinted
from *Skiing* magazine by permission of the author. "Travels with Uncle
Edgar" and "A House in the Country" by Bill MacDonald are reprinted
from *The Whales of Superior* (Porphry Press) by permission of the author.
"The Bridge" by Jake MacDonald is reprinted from *The Bridge Out of
Town* (Oberon Press) by permission of the author.

**This book is distributed by: Singing Shield Productions,
104 Ray Blvd., Thunder Bay, Ontario, Canada. P7B 4C4
Phone 807-344-8355**

All orders and inquiries should be directed to Singing Shield Productions.

*This book is dedicated
to the writers whose
talents inspired it*

*and to the
Friends of the Thunder Bay Public Library*

AUGUSTANA UNIVERSITY COLLEGE
LIBRARY

Acknowledgements

The editor would like to offer his sincere gratitude to the following people, who in their own ways, large or small, have contributed to the making of this book: Marg Joblin, Pat Shaw, Lisa Shaffer, Julie Perrier, Grace Magisano, Barbara Philp, Tuula Maki, Gilbert Bede, Cathy Ridley, Sue Douglas, Ty Kaipio, Joe Arena, Mary Ann Vic, Maria Morgado, Carol Everett, Elinor Barr, Diana Stephenson, Christina Stricker, Jamie Nicol and Jess Vamplew.

With special thanks to Irma Weinrauch for patiently tending the lines of communication between editor and authors.

To Lori Ann Kauzlarick for her observant proofreading.

To Dan Diamond for his generous assistance with production and design.

To Karen Harrison, who saw the importance of *The Wolf's Eye* when she arrived as Chief Librarian at the Thunder Bay Public Library, and has provided enthusiastic, ongoing support.

To Kathy Lucky for her magnificent effort at the desk-top unit, and for her design expertise.

To Barbara Koppenhaver for so many things... but especially for providing devoted moral support from beginning to end.

To Rosalind Maki who has been an indispensable editorial advisor and consultant, as well as contributing mightily to the production and to the content of the book.

To Gerald Graham for his generous promotion over the airwaves.

To the Board of the Thunder Bay Public Library for its valued endorsement.

And to Betty Carpick for her ongoing participation in the roadshow.

Thanks are also due to The Canada Council Explorations Program; The Reflections '92 Program of the Ontario Ministry of Communications and Culture; the Thunder Bay Writers Guild; Sweet Thursday Books; and to The Friends of the Thunder Bay Public Library... all of whom have provided generous financial backing.

Contents

Preface

The Thunder Bay Public Library and the Thunder Bay writing community have had a close relationship for many years, with the library actually fostering the creative process through Writer-in-Residence Programs and Reading Grants and our frequent writers' workshops. *The Wolf's Eye* is the culmination of that relationship.

It is wonderful to read these stories, written by and for this northwest corner of Ontario, but neither limited in interest nor provincial in any other way. Not only will the valuable contribution of our local authors be preserved in this work, but *The Wolf's Eye* will encourage the creative development of those writers not published this time.

It is my great hope that this anthology will help us look at and think about ourselves in a way that only regional writing can: by exploring the impact that our unique position in space and time has on who we are and what we say. The geography and special character of the Thunder Bay area is a strong thread linking these stories to each other, and us to *The Wolf's Eye* and its authors.

Karen Harrison, Chief Librarian
Thunder Bay Public Library
September, 1992

Introduction

As I write, I am seated at a half-ton oak desk in the recesses of the Thunder Bay Public Library — Waverly branch. For the past year, I have been the TBPL's writer-in-residence, entrusted more or less with helping the city's writers in any way I can. Or think I can.

I arrived in Thunder Bay with my family at the beginning of October, last year, to take up my current position, and within weeks of this writing will come to the end of my term.

Along the way, I have frequently been asked what exactly I *do* as writer-in-residence (I have sometimes sensed a sneaking suspicion that I spend my time lolling around the stacks, burning off taxpayers' money).

For one thing, I edited the book you hold in your hands — an enjoyable task. I also spent a good deal of time reading manuscripts — fat, thin, dull, fascinating — and giving what I hope was helpful advice to the people who wrote them. Editorial advice not being a very precise science, I suppose that some of what I dispensed was less than helpful, perhaps even useless — though not so bad, I trust, that it violated the physician's first maxim: never do anything that'll make the patient sicker than he is.

I have conducted seminars, visited schools, and expounded at length over the local airwaves. On one occasion, for the first time in my life, I took to the pulpit (invited), addressing the local Unitarians on the modest topic, "The Meaning of Literature."

More importantly, time and again, I have used my position
to disseminate the basis of my philosophy of writing: that if the
work is going to be any good it must in one way or another
approach the mysteries at the core of human experience.

My office here at the library is by no means what Coleridge
had in mind when he spoke of ''caverns measureless to man.''
In fact, it is a teensy cinder-block cell, poorly lit and increas-
ingly crowded with obsolete computer parts. And yet it holds
very happy associations for me — some of them represented by
the decor on the walls. To the right of my desk, for instance, I
have taped several letters from kids at local schools I've visited
('' ...I think you are the best awther I know, espexially your
drawings of hot vazleen. I really glad you are gong to let us buy
you book at cost... '' [sic], etc.

On another wall are a number of design sketches for the
cover of this book, a most satisfying symbol of my year.... And
a list of the phone extensions of the staff of the library. I cannot
think of my year in *any* terms without reflecting happily on the
pleasure of associating with the Thunder Bay Library staff.
They are among the most considerate, friendly, helpful and
dedicated people I have met.

On another score, my time in Thunder Bay has given me a
powerful affection for the geography of Northwestern Ontario.
If I lean back on my chair and stretch my neck — or if I look out
the front windows of the house where my family and I have
lived for the past year — I can see perhaps a hundred square
miles of Lake Superior, the ''majestic and inscrutable body of
water'' referred to on the back cover of this book. I can see deep
forests, old mountains and, in the distance to the east, emerging
from the lake, the legendary Sleeping Giant (those of you who
know Thunder Bay will understand that I am talking about a
mountainous land formation, the tip of the Sibley Peninsula,
that sits ten or twelve miles off the city waterfront). In the

foreground below me, the inner harbour is alive with ships and sailboats and gulls.

In human terms, Thunder Bay is surely the warmest of our frigid Canadian cities. From the day we arrived here, Thunderbanians have gone out of their way to make us feel wanted and comfortable and well fed.

And as I teeter on the brink of irrelevance — or of turning this introduction into shameless civic bumf — let me refocus it by highlighting one further pleasure of my year as writer-in-residence: that I have met a far greater number of talented, devoted writers than I would ever have thought possible in a relatively small city such as Thunder Bay. I've met so many, in fact, that when the time came to put together a volume of their stories — as I felt I must if I was going to do them justice — I realized that *two* volumes would be needed to accommodate the profusion of fine work.

The Wolf's Eye is the first of those volumes (the second will be along shortly and promises to be every bit as good). *The Wolf's Eye*, in fact, is the first *ever* collection of stories from this region. Indeed, it has occurred to me that Northwestern Ontario, an area roughly the size of Saskatchewan or Alberta, is probably the last substantial patch of the Dominion to draw attention to its indigenous writing in this way.

As intensely pleased as I am with the book, I cannot say its creation has been easy. Along the way, my cohorts and I have had to: found a publishing company; raise $20,000; read hundreds of manuscripts; figure out how the print trade operates — as well as enacting all the other painstaking chores and observances necessary to producing and selling a book.

Has it been worth it?

Most certainly.

The Wolf's Eye, I hope, will be a pole-star for the advancement of fiction publishing in Thunder Bay. It is proof that, with a little ambition and faith, books such as this *can* be published here. What's more, it gives voice to an impressive group of talented new writers — John Pringle, Bonnie Blake, Pat McLeod, Rosalind Maki, Jen Thompson, Marianne Jones, to name but a few — as well as raising the readership and profile of experienced writers such as John Futhey, Elizabeth Kouhi and Bill MacDonald, among others.

From the point of view of *readers* in this area, *The Wolf's Eye* provides a first opportunity to see their landscape, history, concerns, careers and spirit — in short, to see themselves — reflected in a broad range of contemporary writings.

My hope is that the book will also help bury a notion held by some local readers, that *real* writers come from somewhere else. Real writers, talented writers, come from Thunder Bay and Atikokan and Minaki, as well as from Toronto and New York. (Writers such as Claude Liman, Elizabeth Kouhi, Joan Skelton, Penny Petrone, Ruby Slipperjack, Bill MacDonald, Elinor Barr, Pat Barclay, George Kenny, and Hazel Fulford proved this long before the appearance of *The Wolf's Eye*.)

We have good reason to be proud of our writers. And they to be proud of themselves.

Impossible though it is to predict the fate or appeal of a book or its components, I am convinced that a number of the stories in *The Wolf's Eye* will eventually take their place in the permanent canon of fine Canadian writing.

We are all beneficiaries.

My sincere appreciation to the Thunder Bay Public Library for appointing me writer-in-residence and thereby providing me the opportunity and time to work on this book.

May it be the first of many.

Charles Wilkins
November, 1992

Slim Pike and the Windipogo
(from the novel *Tales from Windigoostigwan*)
John Pringle

No ONE KNEW WHERE SLIM PIKE came from originally. Some say he was in the army, some say prison. If you happened to ask directly about his origins, he'd just snicker and say: ''I came out'a the swamp, jest crawled out'a the mud somewheres back in there, heh, heh, heh.''

Maybe Slim Pike *was* born somewhere back in the sprawling network of streams, ponds and cattails that lie at the east end of Lake Windigoostigwan. There's a lot of life in the wetlands. You'll see more birds, reptiles and mammals in one hour back there than you'll see the rest of the day anywhere else. Perhaps even the Windipogo was born back there. If it was, Slim Pike would know.

Slim lives in a peculiar house near the mouth of a creek that flows into the lake from the swamp. There's a small beach nearby, with a stand of black ash trees behind it. The house is fastened to the roots of the trees, and it straddles a junction of two shallow streams. When Slim wants a meal or snack, he drops what he's doing and sits hunched over the water that flows through his kitchen. Occasionally his hand darts out and he captures a minnow or a water beetle and pops it into his mouth.

I suppose the weirdest thing about Slim Pike — other than the fact that he eats raw fish and insects — has to be his clothes. They are made entirely from fish skin — specifically, pike skin. He must have caught some huge pike in his time to have made the suit he wears. His coat is green and scaly, cut tightly to his body with sharp tails tapering into two symmetrical V's. The leggings and vest match the coat, except they are embossed with black and gold thread.

As his name suggests, Slim Pike is a thin man with angular features, dead grey eyes, and a protruding bottom jaw like that of a jackfish. He even smells of fish because he slicks his hair back with pike slime. Worse than that, his teeth are filed down to points that slant backwards into his mouth.

It was Slim who stole Sam Bombay's bone-handled razor. He had always admired the razor, and one moonless night in March he glided down the lake on his cedar skis. When he reached Sam's, he quieted the dog Rufus with a moose bone, crept into the house, and made off with Mr. Bombay's prized possession. Slim said that he needed a razor to scrape his fish skins and trim his clothes.

It was really jealousy. Sam Bombay had opened a bait shop of such prosperity, it made Slim Pike grind his teeth in rage and exclaim, "If that old railroad bum can open a baitshop then I'll open a tailor shop and we'll see who makes the most money!" An evil flash of fire flickered in those dead grey eyes.

QUIETLY, SURREPTITIOUSLY, SLIM PIKE built a tailor shop out near the highway about three miles east of the Bombay Baitshop. The building went up so quickly it took everyone by surprise. No one had ever imagined Slim Pike to be the

enterprising type, so when he erected a glossy sign that read
THE SLIM TRIM TAILOR SHOP, most residents of Thornapple
and the vicinity were skeptical.

"I wonder what that slippery rascal is up to," muttered
Clarence Johnson as he paddled by one day. "I think I'll
stop in and see."

As Clarence entered the shop, Slim Pike deftly slid Sam
Bombay's razor under a large fold of pike skin.

"Good morning, Mr. Johnson." Slim's smile showed his
pointed teeth, making Clarence shudder.

"Morning, Slim, how's the fish hide business?"

"Well," purred Slim Pike in an unctuous voice, "I'm not
breaking any records right away, but I expect business will
pick up soon when I show my latest designs." Slim held up
the garment he was working on — a pike skin suit a lot like
his own, but with bass dorsal fin epaulettes, pickerel eye
cuff-links and a high-neck collar trimmed exclusively from
the belly of ling cod.

"Would you care to make an order, Mr Johnson? I could
measure you right now if you like? Your underwear appears
a trifle worn."

Clarence Johnson, who dressed exclusively in red one-
piece longjohns, said, "Er, no thanks, Slim, I'm real happy
with my wardrobe. To tell ya the truth I don't know how
anybody could wear the stuff you make — it's too weird for
me, and I don't think that these businesses of yours and
Bombay's are going to do the lake any good either."

"Oh?" said Slim, raising his slimy eyebrows in mock
surprise. "How so?"

"Too many people catching too many fish, polluting the
water, throwin' their garbage around, water skiing, racing
their boats, makin' a ruckus — where did the nice quiet days

on the water go? Now everybody's out to make a buck and that's about all. This should be a place to come and enjoy nature, sure, catch a few fish if you like, but this commercial stuff all of a sudden, like Sam Bombay and his Windipogo contest.''

''Windipogo?'' asked Slim with a mischievous smile. ''Do you believe in the creature, Mr. Johnson?''

''Course not,'' replied Clarence, a little too quickly.

''Well, I do, and some day... '' Slim picked up a pair of scissors, and still smiling went, ''Snip! Snip! Snip!''

Clarence's eyes narrowed and he felt his face flushing.

''The most precious skin on the lake, Mr. Johnson, and it will be mine, heh, heh, heh. Are you sure you wouldn't like to make an order?''

''You're crazy, Pike, you'll never own what doesn't exist. This business of yours is going nowhere and I'm going to do what I can to stop you and Bombay from ruining Windigoostigwan!''

''Nobody's ruining anything, Mr. Johnson. I'm just trying to make an honest living, a simple tailor, that's all. And as for your non-existent Windipogo, there's a rumour going around that you made quite a catch a couple of weeks ago... hmmmmm? Or is that something you'd rather not discuss?'' At this point Slim Pike began to giggle and snip his scissors in the air.

Slim, it should be known, had hunted the Windipogo for years — long before Sam Bombay offered a prize to anyone who could catch the legendary creature, and long before Clarence Johnson accidentally captured it and released it this summer.

Slim had swum the lake, surface and depths, drawn charts and maps and diagrams, and was obsessed with the thought of bringing home the creature's precious skin.

Clarence had had enough of Slim Pike for the day and headed for the door. The fact that even a rumour was circulating about his run-in with the Windipogo was disturbing. These days, about the only chance the poor creature had against tourists and against predators like Slim Pike was the preservation of the mystery that had always surrounded its existence.

"Goodbye, Slim," said Clarence. "I suggest you go back to the swamp; I hear there's a shortage of snakes back there — you'd fit in well."

"Bye bye, Windipogo Johnson!" chortled Slim, and as he did, his elbow knocked the pike skin hiding Sam Bombay's razor, sending the latter to the floor.

Clarence saw the razor and said, "Well now, isn't that interesting," and he swung out of the Slim Trim Tailor Shop.

"That sleazy fish will never sell anything," he mused as he walked down the hill to his canoe. "All the same he's up to no good. I wonder if I should tell Sam about that razor?"

Inside the shop Slim stared at the stolen razor and cursed. But he needn't have worried, for the immediate future was secure. Despite Clarence's predictions, the Slim Trim Tailor Shop began a booming business. Residents of Thornapple and fashion-conscious people from far abroad flooded to the shop to buy piscean apparel. Slim was overwhelmed by the demand, but had it not been for his apprentice, the business never would have prospered.

THE APPRENTICE WAS AN INSECURE young man named Petey the Greedy, who wanted everything and lots of it. As a child his most obvious craving had been food. He had demanded so much milk from his mother that she grew thin and weak while Petey blossomed fat and strong. His poor parents were obliged to purchase a large cow to satisfy their child. But by the time Petey was weaned, both his mother and the cow resembled war refugees: thin, tired and very sad.

Petey the Greedy was too busy eating to notice. He ate fresh food, canned food, frozen food, boiled, baked, barbecued, braised food, roasted, steamed, raw food, your food, my food, everybody's food, and still he wanted more food.

One day, his father came home from fishing with three fat trout which he put in the sink while he changed his clothes. When he returned, his son had eaten two of the fish raw and was trying to steal the third from the cat!

"Stop, Peter, you'll get worms!"

"Worms?" answered Petey. "Where are they? I'll eat them, too!"

When he was a little older, his parents took him to a restaurant for lunch. Petey ate his food and asked for more. His parents said, "No, Peter," so Petey ate his napkin. His father was furious over this to the point where he couldn't eat. So Petey ate his father's dinner, which upset his mother. She was still very thin and tired and she started to cry and had to leave the table. So Petey naturally cleaned up her plate and then began to gnaw on her salad bowl.

His father hollered, "NOW YOU STOP THAT!"

A man sitting behind Petey and his father, disturbed by the commotion, turned and said, "Please, if you don't mind, I'm trying to enjoy my meal."

Petey stared out the window, a look of horror on his face. "Look, Mister, your car is on fire!"

When the poor man turned his head Petey grabbed his plate and gobbled down everything on it, including the steak bone.

A fist fight ensued between Petey's father and this fellow who lost his steak, and soon the whole restaurant was involved in the brawl. As the battle raged and Petey's mother cried, Petey ran from table to table wolfing French fries, soup, hamburgers and milkshakes, until he was so engorged that he collapsed in a swollen heap.

The next day his father put an ad in the paper. It read: "Greedy child needs a home. Take him away. Take him today. No money down."

WHEN SLIM PIKE APPEARED AT their door inquiring about the ad, the sight of him was enough to give Petey's parents second thoughts. But when they considered how only that day their son had gobbled the goldfish, a house plant, most of the neighbour's vegetable garden and half of his father's leather coat, not to mention five full meals and numerous snacks, the decision to say good-bye to Petey was not so difficult. Besides, his new guardian, despite his outlandish clothes, was very polite and assured them that "Peter," as Slim called him, would assume the apprenticeship of a tailor and live in the country where he would be well fed and cared for.

It was a sight to see, the rotund figure of young Peter waddling off hand in hand with this strange lean creature in the fish-skin suit who had bribed the boy with promises of ice cream and cake. Petey's parents waited until their son had rounded the corner, and then fell into each others' arms crying with hysterical relief.

On the train back to Windigoostigwan Slim Pike explained to Petey what his new life would be like — in fact, described it as a deal: if Petey did so much work he would be allowed so much food. Fish would be the staple, along with beetles, bugs, birds, plants and anything else he could lay his hands (or teeth) on. Petey's work would be to catch these creatures and deliver their skins to the Slim Trim Tailor Shop. As a bonus he would be entitled to a percentage of the shop's profits. There was great potential in Petey's greediness — it just had to be directed and cultivated.

Under Slim's guidance, Petey became a master fisherman, hunter and gatherer. Each day he'd set out for the shallow bays to check his nets and traps, filling the boat with pike, pickerel and perch. He had set-lines down deep to catch trout, ling and white fish, and fine mesh traps for minnows, salamanders, beetles, crayfish and newts. He attracted leeches and snapping turtles by throwing fish carcasses into a large mesh trap, which he left in the shallows. He used a long-handled net to scoop sleeping mud turtles off of logs, and captured frogs and snakes with his bare hands.

The drying racks behind the tailor shop were covered with skins, while inside Slim worked steadily, filling orders for customers who were just as greedy as Petey and himself.

"Why don't you use furs?" many of Slim's customers inquired.

"If it's furs you want, then furs you shall have!" responded the thin man with the pointed teeth.

So Petey became a trapper, and the hides of wolves, foxes, bears, beavers, muskrats, mink, marten, lynx, deer, moose, rabbits, weasels, squirrels, chipmunks and mice piled up in heaps around Slim Pike's work table.

"What about some feathers?" asked the customers.

Eagles, ospreys, sparrows, robins, crows, juncos, waxwings, grosbeaks, jays, snipes, hawks, gulls, woodpeckers, ducks, geese, swans — anything that flew fell victim to Petey's gun. The feathers were bagged and delivered to Slim while the remains went into the great black stew cauldron that bubbled continuously over a slow fire.

Petey the Greedy grew in proportion to the amount of game he destroyed. Slim clothed him in fish-skin suits, collared with furs, embroidered with feathers, and urged him to gather more. They would become rich and travel the world together, amassing fame and admiration wherever they went. Slim could see it now, and he filled Petey's head with stories of silver and gold. Petey was no longer just a greedy little boy. He had become a monstrous salivating beast, constantly chewing and swallowing, belching and farting, a fixed grin on his greasy face. As he went about his business, a swarm of flies buzzed around him, feeding on the spoils. He was so fat that he panted in a wheezing rasp; you could hear him coming from a distance, followed closely by the droning of flies.

Needless to say, Clarence Johnson and Sam Bombay were outraged over this terrible carnage inflicted upon the wildlife of Windigoostigwan. They agreed to have a meeting to plan how to stop it.

WHEN CLARENCE ARRIVED FOR THE meeting at the Bombay Baitshop, Sam was just rowing up to the dock, his youngest son Billy Bombay swimming frantically behind. Clarence walked down and helped moor the boat.

"Morning," said Sam in a gruff monosyllable. "Jest teaching young William how to swim. He picked it up real quick."

"I've noticed all your children swim extremely well," said Clarence. "How do you do it?"

"Easy. I jest haul 'em out inta the middle o' the lake and chuck 'em overboard — they learn real quick that way.

Never lost any of 'em yet.''

Clarence looked at young Billy but didn't say anything, as he'd decided to put aside his differences with Sam in order to stop Slim Pike and Petey the Greedy. Sam Bombay and his wife had their own way of raising children and Clarence wasn't about to interfere.

At that moment Mildred Bombay appeared and invited the men in for a cup of labrador tea.

The Bombay children were playing about the room. Bradley Bombay, the eldest, was drinking raw molasses out of a jar. The molasses was slow, so he had his elbows propped on the table with most of his face in the jar. His sister Bernadette was skipping a rope and singing, while the youngest, a slight fellow with thick glasses, named Borneo, played his violin. Billy came in dripping wet and stood by the wood stove to warm up.

"Would ya like to see my scar?" asked Sam, as Clarence sat down. Before his guest could answer, Sam had his shirt up and his pants down, displaying a jagged red line that ran from his belly to his neck.

"Operation?" asked Clarence.

"Yep. I been havin' such terrible gas lately that Mildred insisted I go to the doctor and have him open me up. The doc wouldn't do it at first, then Mildred threatened him with a beaver tail, and I let one go in his office that stunk so bad I nearly kilt everybody. But anyways, to make a long story short, they opened me up and couldn't find nothin' except the usual stuff and I still got bad gas! Ya know, I've had it ever since I had my razor stolen all them years ago and I drank that potion. I don't know if it's the anger over losin' the razor or if it was the ingredients of the potion, but I tell ya, I'm gettin' tired of sleepin' outside.''

"Sam, they don't wanna hear about yer operation or yer gas," said Mildred as she poured the tea.

Clarence cleared his throat and said, "Actually I've got some news for you about that razor." He proceeded to tell the Bombay family about what he'd seen when he visited Slim Pike. When he finished, the whole family stared hard at him with their eyes narrowed. Bradley had put down his molasses, Bernadette had stopped skipping and singing, and Borneo's violin rested in his lap. "Why didn't you tell me this before?" said Sam Bombay in a voice that barely disguised his rage.

Clarence looked him in the eye and replied, "That's what I've come to talk to you about. You know I've never liked the idea of your Windipogo contest bringing all the tourists to the lake. They have no respect, all they want is money; they want to catch the most beautiful, mysterious part of Windigoostigwan and turn it into gold. And what's worse," he went on, "is that slippery crook who came out of the swamp has turned Windigoostigwan into a killing zone. And what for? So he can feed that monster he calls his apprentice, and so he can make more money than you or I or anyone else. When all the animals and fish are gone, then what?" Clarence fell silent for a moment, narrowed his eyes, and said, "Slim Pike has got to be stopped, before he catches one more fish or bird or..."

"Or the Windipogo?" asked Sam.

"Or the Windipogo," agreed Clarence.

"Ya know, Johnson, I underestimated you. I figgered nobody'd ever catch that critter, yet you went and done it. Never claimed a prize for it neither. What'd you do with them pictures you took anyway, burn 'em?"

"How did you know about that?" said Clarence gravely.

"'Cause I ain't stupid, that's why. I known about that old sea serpent since the old days. I also know how smart he is and that he's been around a long time."

"And how do you know *that*?"

"'Cause I can FEEEL it!" Sam whispered, leaning forward in his chair, his eyeballs bulging. "I can FEEEL it when there's a mist on the lake or when I stand real still in the middle of a black spruce swamp in the dead of winter and I ain't had a thing to eat for three days. I can FEEEL it when the moon shines down through the white pines or when the lake licks at the shoreline when there ain't no moon or when ya wake from a silver dream and the loons are flocked up and singing to ya in the middle of a hot August night. I can FEEEL it when the lightning cracks and the hailstones bite, when the trees sway and the leaves come rippin' off the branches from an arctic wind, or when the snow devils go whirling across your tracks and the ice moans and the ravens turn somersaults when its forty below zero! It's the spirits talkin' to ya then, that's when ya gotta listen!"

There was a sudden dampness in the room and the Bombay children shifted uneasily towards their father. One of the windows trembled slightly.

Sam's black eyes swung to it, staring wildly. "It's here! It's here now!" he said in a hoarse whisper.

In the distance a train whistle sounded. A rumbling freight was approaching.

"It's in this room!" Sam rose to his feet, his head back, eyes on the ceiling. "I can FEEEL it!"

The room had definitely become colder. The draft in the wood stove sucked more air, making a whooshing sound. All eyes were on Sam. He was swaying back and forth in a trance now, his entire body trembling. Mildred Bombay closed her eyes and moaned.

"They been killin' ravens!" wailed Sam. "They been killin' owls!" He fell to his knees, his fists clenched over his eyes, and stayed there as the train thundered by, shaking the house and flickering the lights.

BEFORE THE SOUND OF THE retreating train subsided, Mildred Bombay had poured the tea and helped Sam to his chair.

"Ravens." She shook her head. "Owls. They've gone too far. We'll help you. That silly Windipogo Contest sign is coming down, too. Ain't that right, Sam?"

There was no question about it, and Sam knew it. "We'll take the sign down," he said wearily. Then an edge of anger came into his voice. "When that razor-stealin' snake starts killin' ravens and owls and everything else, we gotta put a stop to him!"

There was a silence in the room as they drank their tea. Mildred broke it.

"Sam, you should go and consult. Go and see Ayeesha. She'll tell us what to do."

Sam looked at his wife and nodded.

"There's something else, Sam," she added.

"What's that?"

"Bring the kids."

"Hmmmmm, yeah, good idea.... What about him?" Sam motioned at Clarence with a toss of his head.

"Yes," was all Mildred Bombay said.

"Who's Ayeesha?" Clarence couldn't help but ask.

Borneo Bombay spoke for the first time. "She's the guardian spirit of the Windipogo," he said, "and she listens to this!" and he held up his violin and smiled.

AYEESHA THE WATER SPIRIT, protector of ancient energy and healing light, lives in the caves far below the surface of Windigoostigwan. Her domain is not confined to the water, however. Her force is felt in the wind and seen in the stars. She is in a clear blue sky or the red clouds at sunrise. She is a presence that is felt behind the curtains of the visible world by those who care enough to know her.

Sam and Mildred Bombay knew of her through dreams and visions. It had been a long time since Sam had listened to her guidance, but his wife had kept in touch. Mildred told them where she could be found, and they journeyed to a narrow point that extended far out into the lake. Ayeesha was not there when they arrived — she had to be summoned with music.

After building a small fire and collecting enough wood for the night, Sam unwrapped his drum and began a slow hypnotic rhythm. At a signal from his father, Borneo began to play. The music was eerie, echo-like, with a distant quality that seemed to carry them out of their senses into the mystical realm of the imagination. They sat entranced, each in his separate world yet united by the wonder of the music and the beauty of the flames reflected in the lake.

Bernadette and Billy fed the fire just enough to maintain a constant size, never too big, never too small. Bradley prepared a drink from herbs and roots given to him by his mother who took the cup from him and passed it around. When they all had sipped, she sat across from her husband and closed her eyes in concentration.

For several hours the music continued, gaining strength and resonance, rising and falling in natural frequencies that matched the night breezes and the lapping of waves against the ancient shoreline. While the music played, Clarence found himself thinking about the Windipogo. What was it? Something that had survived from millions of years ago? Was it magic, or just another animal like the rest of them? What were any of them? Were they all magic, or part of someone's dream from far away? And what were they doing here anyway? Clarence looked up at the stars and wondered: If I could travel beyond them, would I ever come to the end? What would be at the end? What was beyond it?

And then Ayeesha came. Like a whirling kaleidoscope of colour and energy, she swirled from the water, at first shapeless and translucent, until she materialized in such terrifying beauty that it made Clarence clutch Sam by the arm.

Her eyes held Clarence's immediately in a reptilian gaze, and he shuddered before she passed on to Bernadette. Those eyes flickered without blinking, around the circle until they rested on Sam Bombay. There they stayed a long time.

Finally Ayeesha spoke. "You have been a fool! A greedy fool who hasn't listened like you used to. I gave you a gift once when you showed me your faith. Now you have thrown it away and replaced it with poisonous thoughts that have polluted you and brought treachery and destruction to the waters."

Sam looked very uncomfortable, and when Ayeesha said "polluted" he belched with his mouth closed so that his cheeks inflated.

"You have not dreamed of me for two years because of your greed," continued Ayeesha. "You have not listened to your wife or your children who dream of me frequently. You have sought power to use it arrogantly without regard for others, and now you seek to exploit what lies beneath these waves. What I gave to you the night you danced long ago was not to be abused. You have weakened me and my kindred with your foul thoughts. I can no longer protect what you do not respect!''

She turned to Clarence and her countenance softened. ''I greet you,'' she said. ''Although you have never seen me before, I feel that you know me, especially since you released a great spirit from your hooks. It took courage and wisdom to do such a thing and I thank you.''

Clarence glowed like a fool in love as Ayeesha turned her attention to the Bombay children. She rose and held each one's head in her hands for several seconds, kissed their foreheads and then knelt in front of their mother. ''You have listened,'' she said, ''and now you have called.''

''We have called you to give us guidance,'' said Mildred confidently. ''There is a great hunger at Windigoostigwan. There is a terrible killing, so much blood.''

''They's killin' owls and ravens,'' murmured Sam.

''It must be stopped,'' said Mildred. ''We are asking for your help.''

''There is a great evil in the swamp,'' said Ayeesha, her head held high, ''but it can be destroyed. At this moment they are setting a net for the great creature you call the Windipogo.''

''What can we do to stop them?'' said Clarence.

''Give me the strength of your faith. I will do what I can.'' She rose to go.

''Ayeesha!'' cried Sam in alarm.

Ayeesha looked into Sam's face for a long time and then took his head in her hands and kissed him as she had the rest of them.

Sam had a gentle smile on his face when she whirled into her colourful liquid cloud and disappeared. She had given him another chance.

The night was quieter now. The wind had dropped and the stars seemed to crackle with a soothing energy. In the distance across the lake, up among the pines, a horned owl hooted and then swooped to another tree for a better view of the rising moon.

THE WHOLE TIME SLIM PIKE and Petey the Greedy were killing and skinning countless animals, fish and birds, they were also scheming about how they were going to someday capture the Windipogo. When their bloody day's work was done, Slim would lead Petey back down the path to the cabin that straddled the creek in the stand of black ash. Before they retired to bed, Slim would tell Petey a story: ''Yes, Peter, it was a good day's work,'' he'd say, ''but we must not forget the greatest prize of all, the hide of the monster that lives in the depths — a hide so precious it will make us rich for the rest of our days. That ancient skin is like the finest silk, supple and smooth, with a texture so rare it thrills the fingers to touch it. You see, Peter, there is a great and holy power in the Windipogo's skin. If a man or a woman wears it, no harm shall ever come to them — not age, not fire, not disease, not hunger. To wear the skin is to live forever!''

Petey puzzled over this and said, ''If the Windipogo has such power, how will we ever catch it?''

Slim chuckled gleefully, his stained teeth glistening in the candlelight.

''Because, dear Peter, there has been a shift in power! The Windipogo and its spirits are only strong if they have the faith of the people, and the people are changing, Peter! The natural spirits are shrivelling like dry leaves, because no one listens to them anymore. No one dreams them true! People's dreams have turned to gold, Petey! Our gold! We must simply make their dreams come true!'' Slim jumped to his feet and capered about the room. He grabbed a bag of coins, jingling them in one hand while he snipped his long-bladed scissors in the other.

Petey giggled until the entire cabin shook from the weight of his jiggling belly.

When they'd settled down and were stretched out in their beds, Slim revealed to Petey how they were to catch the creature with the precious skin.

THE NEXT MORNING THE WORK began. The first job was to construct a long smooth ramp of planks that angled gradually up from the lake. It had to be strong, with high sides, and had to taper to a ''V,'' the narrow end of which would drop into a deep pit at the top of the hill. While Slim built the ramp, Petey dug the pit. When they were finished, they greased the ramp with pike slime so that it was as slippery as frogs' eggs.

Slim wanted to test the ramp, so he had Petey slide down it into the lake. When Petey hit the water he created a wave — a tide — that swamped a passing boatload of tourists.

At lunch Petey ate a beaver, three muskrats, a five-pound lake trout, a jar of pickled salamanders and a partridge in a pear tree. He ate the tree, too. Slim Pike dined on minnows and frog legs and explained to Petey how they were going to pull the Windipogo from the lake.

That afternoon they wove a giant net, and the next day they pushed out from shore in Slim's small skiff. They intended to string their net across a narrows in the lake. However, with the weight of Petey in the bow, they hadn't gone far before they'd swamped and were forced to swim to shore. For Slim this was no problem; he swam as smoothly and silently as a jackfish. Petey tended to float like a cork, bobbing lazily on the surface in no particular hurry to go anywhere. Watching Petey bob on the surface gave Slim an idea: he would use his fat apprentice as a floating buoy to set their huge net.

Hooking Petey up to a guy rope, Slim winched him across the narrows, instructing him to release the weighted folds of the net so that they sank to the bottom. Slim had made sure the net was strong, constructing it of moose hide, rope, tamarack roots, and fishing line. He anchored it on the south side to a huge red pine beside the railroad tracks, and on the north side to an old white pine.

When they were finished Slim sat back and chuckled. ''Now all we have to do is wait, and when we get him, pray that the net and trees hold him until the next train comes.''

In normal times the Windipogo would never have been foolish enough to become ensnared in Slim Pike's net. But, as Ayeesha said, these were different times; the balance of power was no longer with the spirits of the lake. If some faith *had* been restored that night around the fire, was it enough to save the ancient creature from Slim's deadly plan?

IT WAS IN THE EARLY MORNING before sunrise that the ropes holding the net tightened around the trees and made them shudder, sending the squirrels chattering in alarm. Slim Pike sprang from his bed, shook Petey the Greedy awake and placed Sam Bombay's stolen razor in Petey's hand. ''We have him, Petey, and I hear two trains coming, too! Be quick! Take the razor and run to the north shore. When I give the signal, cut the rope!''

Petey ran off as quickly as he could, his bulk crashing through the bushes, snapping off trees, sounding like a herd of moose gone berserk. Slim ran up the path to the red pine by the railway tracks. The net was pulled taut, and the huge tree swayed and strained as if under the force of a hurricane wind. The eastbound freight was already into the siding and slowing down. Slim quickly tied a thick length of rope to the net and spread it out so that the looped end lay close to the tracks. When the eastbound train stopped to let the westbound go by, he hooked the loop over the hitch of the caboose and signalled to Petey to cut the rope on the far side. But where was Petey?

Well, you have to remember that Slim had awakened Petey so suddenly that he hadn't had time for breakfast. So Petey had stopped along the way to pick blueberries and had begun to hunt a delicious-looking partridge, when he heard Slim shrieking from across the lake for him to cut the rope. Petey reluctantly left the partridge and lumbered up the shore to the white pine. He got there just in time, for the train was picking up speed and the net tightening.

When Petey reached up and slashed the rope with Sam Bombay's razor, he was standing in the wrong spot. The rope snapped free, whipped around his legs, and in an instant, the train was pulling both the Windipogo *and* Petey the Greedy across Windigoostigwan!

The Windipogo, tangled, and thrashing furiously, put up a terrible fight, and the puzzled train engineer had to apply full power before he could get any speed up. When he did, the Windipogo came sliding up the ramp like greased light-ning and plopped into the pit just as Slim cut the rope that connected the net to the train. ''We have him!'' screamed Mr. Pike, dancing ecstatically. ''We'll have him for break-fast! We'll roast his liver! We'll tan his hide! We're rich! Hah haaaah!''

As Slim stepped to the edge of the pit, drool slid from his jaw and his eyes glistened with a savage joy. He bent closer to look at his prize. The lump in the net squirmed and wiggled. A leg appeared, a rather plump one, then an arm, a belly, and finally a round face. The face's jaws were moving, chewing. Petey the Greedy blinked at Slim and then belched.

There was nothing else in the pit.

Slim Pike's face twisted into such a scowl of rage and disappointment it made Petey dive back under the net. Slim opened his mouth, and a terrible scream arched out across the sky. It was an unearthly sound, wretched and forbidding, tapering off into a spittle-crackling rasp.

Slim knelt by the pit, his head slumped on his chest. If he had had the strength to look up, out at the lake, he would have seen a large tail break the surface, wave a sassy good-bye and disappear.

If he had looked even closer, he would have seen a spiral of coloured mist suspended above it, shimmering, and then dissolving in the bright morning sun.

Snakes and Ladders
Rosalind Maki

JUST SAY IT. TELL HER. But she looked so formidable staring at him from the living room doorway, her square German jaw thrust over the collar of her fur coat. "What's wrong?" she asked. "Are you sick? Why are you wearing your overcoat?"

God, she looked good. Those high cheek bones; Nordic blue eyes; sleek blonde hair. She could have been a model or a movie star. Instead, she was a high school history teacher.

"Neil?"

"Well, Lorraine, you can forget about taking Heather to Disney World in March. I'm out of a job." He watched for her reaction, saw her eyes widen, go grey.

"What?" she said.

"They made more staff cuts. I'm one of the cut-ees."

"Oh, Neil. No." There — her eyes had softened: concern. She was moving quickly across the room, sitting beside him, taking his hand. Neil gripped her hand and squeezed his eyes shut.

"What happened?" she asked. "I mean, how did they tell you?"

He stood up, went to the window. Posted on the snow-bank like Alpine guerrillas, the Henderson twins fired snowballs at passing cars. "Clean and quick. They called me —"

"Who? Those two from Toronto?"

"Yeah. Steckman and his over-paid flunky. They called me upstairs. They're using Crane's old office. I'd barely sat down when they started on about soft markets, vanishing profits, cost cutting, reorganization. Before I knew it they were shaking my hand, telling me what a great job I'd done. We're very sorry, nothing personal, Neil, blah, blah, blah. Happy New Year." He slammed the edge of his fist against the window. "Sixteen goddamn years down the tubes."

Lorraine picked up the manila envelope from the coffee table where he'd tossed it when he came home. "What's this?" she asked.

"Severance, vacation pay, pension forms. I was the best purchasing agent they ever had. Simpson doesn't know a dryer felt from a brass tea kettle — they keep him. I wonder how he'll hide his computer phobia with me gone."

Lorraine emptied the envelope onto the table, then took a Hershey Kiss from the crystal bowl. She peeled off the foil, slipped the chocolate between her teeth. "This is quite a bit of money. What does it work out to — six month's pay? You'll have another job in six months."

" There won't *be* any jobs in six months." — he was shouting now — "Everybody's cutting back!" Her eyes stopped him. He knew the look; she used it on waiters and store clerks, and probably her students. "Sorry," he said. "It's just, oh, the thought of starting over."

Lorraine unwrapped another Hershey Kiss. "It won't be so bad, Neil," she said in a voice thick with chocolate. She reached behind her neck and pulled her hair tight against the silver barrette. "It's your turn to pick up Heather from Brownies." She looked at him and said, "I'll go."

NEIL CHANGED HIS CLOTHES, then mixed himself a Scotch and water. He took his drink into the family room, sat on the floor against the couch, closed his eyes. He could still see Turner leaning into his office, his hand hooked onto the door frame, his shirt sleeves rolled to his elbows. As casual as a kid on a round-about.

"Could you stop by the office when you have a minute, Neil?"

"Sure, Bob. I'll finish this and I'll be right up."

"No hurry."

He hadn't hurried. After he'd given the report to Marie for typing, he stopped in accounting to pay Paul for his hockey tickets. When he reached the office, they were waiting: Steckman behind the desk, Turner perched on the credenza.

Why hadn't he seen it coming?

On the table beside him, the phone rang. Neil opened his eyes. He let the machine answer, listened to the message. *Neil, Paul here. I just want... look, if there's anything I can do... well, you know. Have you heard Gunnar's gone? Mackenzie too. And Walker. Mac says he'll sue. Everybody's pretty tense around here.... Call me, eh?*

Mac gone, and Gunnar? His wife had their third kid Christmas Day. Only Paul left. And the four of them were going to be running the place in ten years. What a joke.

That evening Neil went out to the mill. He drove slowly at first, scraping strips of frost as delicate as peeled skin off the interior of the windshield. He turned north onto the expressway and was overcome by a sense of desolation. Ahead lay neither road nor trees nor sky — only darkness. Without the green glow of the dash to fix him in place he would have dissolved.

He drove into the mill yard, past the long steel buildings that housed the paper machines. A pall of vapour hung over the parking lot, pressed down by the cold. He pulled up outside the gatehouse, a small brick building honeycombed with bright frosted windows. As he walked by the door, the security guard, Frank Payne, stepped out.

"Evenin', Mr. Carpenter," he said. He was a small man, about fifty, but even in his bulky company parka there was a menace to him. A man you wouldn't argue with in a bar. Neil told Payne he was going up to his office. The guard shook his head and waved a clipboard, said he'd been given a list; no one on it was allowed in.

"Why?" Neil asked. "Are they afraid someone'll steal a box of pencils?" He moved toward the main door, but the guard stepped in front of him, so close Neil could see the frost furring his nostrils.

"Look. I just want to clear out my office. You can watch if you want."

Beyond the guard's shoulder, Neil saw the office building's closed double doors, and beyond that the darkened reception area. He was out, finished. Persona non grata. The realization struck him with such force it seemed to tear something loose in his chest.

He turned to leave, then stopped. "When we're all gone and the machines are rusting hulks, guys like you will still be here. Right, Frank?"

Dolly Carpenter poured her son a cup of coffee and assured him that his dad would be home any minute. "He's lined up in express with all the other retired husbands and their four cans of Minute Maid."

Neil half-smiled at his mother's remark as he gazed around

the kitchen — the lemon yellow walls; the electric clock hung so high you almost wrenched your neck reading the time; the stiff, ruffled curtains; the beehive cookie jar his mother had made one winter in ceramics class; the sharp odour of Javex — everything so keenly familiar from his place behind the table where he'd sat for so many years.

His father Jack came in stomping the snow off his boots, and hung his parka and cap on the hook behind the door. "What are you doing here, Neil? Day off?"

Dolly set a cup of coffee on the table in front of her husband who watched Neil expectantly. Neil shifted in his seat. When he was twelve he had spent half of one night shivering on the floor of a lighted phone booth in Ignace, beside the Trans-Canada highway, afraid to call home. An accidental runaway, trapped earlier that day on a westbound freight he had hopped in the Neebing yard on a dare. How do you tell your parents you're stranded someplace you shouldn't be?

He ran his finger along the crack in the table and said, "I've lost my job."

His father rubbed his hand back and forth across his forehead; his mother settled onto the empty chair, pressed her hand over her mouth. Jack spoke first: what happened? who else? how many? why you? what do they think they're doing over there? Neil wanted to leave, he had no intention of dissecting the whole brutal mess on his parents' kitchen table.

For some reason he thought of his father's lunch pail, its place at the end of the counter beside the bread box now occupied by the Cuisinart they had given Dolly for Christmas. Flat black with worn clasps and handle, the lunch pail had represented to Neil the truncated rhythm of their family life, a mill worker's life: six-day tours — graveyard, evening, day — that wound through the days and weeks (it seemed to Neil he was always asking, Is Dad home?) until long-awaited, the four-day weekend arrived. Then Neil and his sister were scrubbed up and hauled through family picnics, fishing trips, duty visits to fussy old aunts, jaunts to Duluth, the Carpenters appearing together in public like any normal family.

Now, expected, the remark Neil has steeled himself for: "If you were in a union, they couldn't have done this to you. Take. Take. Take. That's all they know. I've always said they'd run that place into the ground." They, the bad guys, the men in black hats.

NEIL UNDERLINED Career Objectives for the third time, then printed GET A JOB. He crumpled the page in his fist, started a clean sheet, wrote Achievements. He chewed on the end of his pen, a silver Cross that Lorraine had given him for his fortieth birthday, and reread his university transcripts. His marks didn't seem as impressive now as they had when he was twenty-two. Hunting for them had turned up a letter of recommendation from the manager of the local Safeway where he worked as a stock boy during high school. *Neil Carpenter has proven himself a loyal and capable employee.* The edges of the letterhead were yellowed and crisp. High acid content, Neil thought as he tore it to shreds.

He moved from the kitchen table into the family room, put his feet up, drew another line under Achievements. He decorated the page with intricate patterns of loops and swirls.

The carton containing his possessions, his personal effects, from the office sat in the corner by the fireplace where he'd dropped it Friday night when Paul came to get him for the Flyers game. He hadn't gone, he'd faked a cold. No way he was going to let those pencil pushers from accounting pity him. He could see it — the shuffling feet, the leaden lapses in conversation, the slippery eye contact — treating him as though he were contagious. No way.

He dragged the carton to the couch, turned back the flaps. On top, Heather's school picture, then his framed certificates, desk clock, coffee mug, a roll of Certs, his Day-Timer Planner. He flipped the book open to January 14. This morning at seven he should have been on the plane to Toronto.

By the end of January his days had taken on the semblance of routine. He rose when Lorraine was showering, started the coffee, roused Heather, made breakfast, packed lunches, while Lorraine rushed around in her bra and slip — her silk armour. He helped Heather into her snowsuit, a quick kiss and off they went, slamming the door. He watched his daughter run up the walk to meet her friends while his wife hopped into her red Mazda and zipped down the road waving — to him, the husband, the provider, the man of the house, left behind in the prickly silence, in his bathrobe and slippers, unshaven, drinking his third cup of coffee.

Afterwards he would make himself some toast, stretch out on the couch with his pillow and the afghan, half his attention on the yellow legal pad, the other half on *Canada A.M.* Usually he drifted off to sleep before the show ended, then woke in time to fix himself a sandwich, find out what was happening on *All My Children.* One Thursday at noon Lorraine came home and caught him sleeping.

''What's this?'' she asked, standing over him, the scent of winter clinging to her fur coat.

''I don't feel well. I've got this weird feeling in my gut. Maybe I should see a doctor.'' He struggled to sit up, blinked himself awake.

She toured the house, came back and said, "The kitchen isn't cleaned up, the beds aren't made."

"What are you doing, checking up on me?"

She bent down and picked up his dirty dishes. "How's your resumé coming?" she asked. Trapped in the flue, the wind rattled the damper like a convict banging a tin cup.

Neil dragged the legal pad out from under the newspapers. "I can't remember when I got that first promotion."

"There's hardly anything here. Neil." She pronounced his name with two syllables. Ne-il.

"Are you going to give me a detention?"

She flung the legal pad into his lap. "What's your problem?"

"Damn it, Lorraine, it's not easy remembering everything you've done, all the positions you've held, your duties, your little successes. Turning it all into ACHIEVEMENTS." He extended his arms, imitated hefting a slab of marble. "And resumés are only the first round. If they're sufficiently impressed, they invite you for an interview. Do you have any idea what *those* have become? They're an art, Lorraine. A bloody art. No more friendly chat with some benign grandfatherly type who asks you where you're from, what your dad does for a living, if you played football in high school. Now it's INTERVIEW BY COMMITTEE. Professional interviewers, trained to root out your personality flaws, decide if you suit the corporate team. And who will I be competing against? Young hot shots right out of university. And do they have serviceable, run-of-the-mill BAs? No, they've all got MBAs."

"Neil, you've got fifteen years experience. And you're a supervisor."

"*Was* a supervisor."

"That's worth an MBA any day. And the company gave you an excellent reference. It's not as if you were fired."

"Ha!"

Lorraine's eyes went hard. "I have to get back to school. We can't both be out of work. And throw that robe in the wash, you've got marmalade down the front."

ON MONDAY, AN OVERNIGHT STORM closed the schools. Neil wandered restlessly from room to room, watching the wind manoeuvre the snow into drifts. They'd had another fight. About the Florida trip. Now she wouldn't speak to him. He could hear her on the phone talking to her mother. Had to be about him.

He had been in love with her since high school. They had attended different schools, but he'd always known who she was: one of the rich kids from the hill. He first spoke to her when they were in university.

Second year, the students' union sponsored a dance in the Great Hall. Neil was in charge of tickets and advertising. The band was hot, the crowd hotter — you could feel the floor vibrate. He got stuck working the door until after eleven. Whenever he had a chance he would look for her. Those days she wore her hair halfway down her back, parted in the middle. After his relief arrived, he downed three quick beers. Then he asked her to dance.

As he led her out into the middle of the floor, she asked him his name.... Hello, Neil Carpenter, she said.

The band played a Tim Hardin song he knew by heart. *If I were a carpenter and you were a lady, would you marry me anyway, would you have my baby?*

A memory worn as smooth as a creek stone: He had

pulled back, looked into her face, found her smiling an amused kind of smile. But her eyes smiled too, and he knew everything would work out.

Right.

Neil reread the Help Wanted ads in the *Chronicle-Journal*. In a single column between ''Waitress Wanted'' and ''Babysitter In My Home'' he found a small item: ''Business Experience? Expanding international corporation seeks highly motivated, responsible individuals for managerial positions. Top Salary. Competitive benefits. Accepting applications, conducting interviews at the Prince Arthur Hotel, Room 205, Wednesday, February 4.'' A possibility.

Heather tiptoed into the family room holding a box behind her back. She leaned against the arm of his chair. ''Play a game with me, Daddy.'' Her eyes roamed his face — she wouldn't look him in the eye. Six-year-old guile.

''Alright. What should we play?''

''You pick.''

Neil tried to make her look at him. ''How about... Scrabble?''

She grinned, catching the joke. ''You know that's too hard.''

''Life?''

''No.''

''Balderdash.''

''Daddy!''

''Well, you said I could choose.'' Neil brought his face close to hers, made her look into his eyes. ''I think you should pick the game.''

She smiled shyly as she displayed the box under her chin. ''Ta-Da. Snakes and Ladders.''

They set up on the kitchen table. Heather rolled a five,

climbed a ladder to the second row. Neil rolled a four, fell short of the first ladder. A snake tail dangled harmlessly by his token. On his next turn, he advanced into the middle of the board where the longer snakes lurked.

A five took Heather up the tallest ladder to the top of the board. She moved her token deliberately, touching each rung. ''Are we going to have to move?'' she asked, handing him the die.

''Why would we move?''

''Because we're poor now.''

Neil rolled a six, barely escaped the jaws of a sly yellow snake.

''We're not poor.''

Heather cupped the die in her hands, blew on it for luck — a pint-size crap shooter taking on Vegas.

''April's daddy doesn't have a job and they're poor. The snow in their front yard is covered with dog poo.'' She screwed up her face.

''Don't worry. I'll get another job.'' She stared into his eyes. He took the die, tossed it quickly to get her mind back on the game. A four. He counted out the spaces slowly, landed in the mouth of the Monster Snake.

''Oh, Daddy,'' she cried and buried her face in her arms.

''It's just a game,'' he laughed. ''The snakes are for sliding on.'' He ran his token up and down the red snake's back. ''It's fun. See?'' She shook her head, unconvinced; wisps of red hair escaped from her ponytail. Neil pulled her onto his lap. ''It's just a game.''

A different kind of memory: Steckman rocking slightly in Crane's black leather chair, scratching the back of his hand, the rough scales of eczema. And Neil, dismissed, retreating to his office, a hollow sack of skin.

BEFORE COMMITTING HIMSELF TO the hotel stairs, Neil checked the lobby which was empty except for the housekeeper, who shoved a droning vacuum over the maroon carpet, and a man in a grey suit who glanced up from his newspaper.

On the second floor mezzanine a woman seated behind a long cloth-covered table intercepted him. "Good morning, I'm Barbara," she said in a clipped voice. She handed him a fistful of paper, said, "Our application, and an aptitude test. Use this pencil to blacken the box that corresponds to your answer." She flipped through the pages, pointing out the small rectangular boxes with a red artificial nail.

He followed her to the end of the hall where she let him into a small banquet room that smelled of stale sweat and cigarettes. "I'll be back shortly," she said.

Neil removed his overcoat, laid it carefully over the back of a chair. He dusted cigarette ash off the table, straightened his tie, took out his Cross pen.

The application was headed Starcor. Had he heard of it? Name, address, education, past positions in chronological order, outline of duties, salary. He finished quickly, even included his Safeway job. The aptitude test was standard. Math and logic problems, personality stuff. He had barely set down the pencil when Barbara returned and took the forms.

He waited at the window. Across the bay lay the Sleeping Giant, its cliffs snow-blasted, its flanks assailed by ice. So easily discerned now, but Neil had been six before he could recognize the man-shape in the rock.

He hadn't told Lorraine he was going to apply, thought it wiser to check out the situation first. This way he could avoid explaining, rationalizing, if things didn't work out. He buttoned his suit jacket, gave a quick tug to his shirt cuffs and thought of Turner and Steckman. He'd made a fool of himself, actually begged them to reconsider. As if they cared. He was nobody, just an expense to eliminate. They sat there, Crane's office ringing harshly with his pleading, they in their tailored suits, Neil in shirt sleeves. As though he'd dropped in to make a social call.

He dragged his hands over his face and turned to see a gaunt silver-haired man sailing across the room, his arm extended. "Mr. Carpenter, I'm Bob Taylor. Glad you came down. Let's go into my office, shall we?"

The room was narrow, a lone bed under a mauve flowered spread against one wall. A steel desk had been set up in front of the window. Taylor pushed aside a room service tray that held an empty mug and a dirty plate. He switched on the dresser lamp. "I must apologize for the room. We requested a suite. This is what they gave us. Coffee?"

"No thanks."

As they sat down, Neil on a black vinyl stacking chair, Taylor behind the desk, the older man said, "I can't help telling you, Neil, I was excited when I read your application. We don't always get men of your experience applying."

"Well, I... there aren't a lot of jobs out there, unless you're willing to wait on tables or drive a cab."

"It's this rotten recession. Give your best years to a company and suddenly you're out on the street."

Neil was impressed by Taylor's style: navy suit, striped shirt, silk tie. More like an executive than any executive Neil had ever met.

"I expected to see more people applying," Neil said.

"Oh, they're here. There's three of us interviewing today. When we go to Winnipeg next week, there'll be six. To tell you the truth, Neil, I didn't expect as many applicants as we've had. You're my fourth interview this morning.'' He reached out, flipped open a file folder. ''I suppose you're wondering what Starcor is all about.'' Outside, a pigeon flopped breast-deep onto the snow-covered ledge, then whirred away. ''Well, we're an American company, head office New York. Mainly manufacturing for the big chain stores — major appliances, plumbing supplies, small motor equipment like snowblowers, lawn mowers. We build to a store's specs, slap on their brand. That's why our name may not be familiar to you. Profitable way to do business, let me tell you. Guaranteed market, and the stores handle all the warranty and service work. In fact, business is so good, we're opening four plants in Canada.''

Neil shifted forward. ''What positions do you have open?''

''Everything. We have to staff from manager to maintenance, from the top floor to the cellar. That's why I'm sure you'll fit in, Neil.''

Neil outlined his education and experience, passed Taylor his letter of reference from the mill. ''This is just a photocopy. I have the original at home if you need it.''

''Good, good.'' Taylor slid the letter into the file folder. He reached back, stretched, then clasped his hands behind his head. He smiled. ''We'd like to make you an offer. Manager, Purchasing. How does that sound?''

''Sounds great.''

''Seventy-five to start. And we'd like you to begin a.s.a.p.''

Neil exhaled audibly. ''Well, I'd have to talk to my wife first. There's a lot to consider.''

Taylor's face went dark. He focused on a spot over Neil's head. ''You realize, Neil, I can't hold this offer open indefinitely. We do have an agenda.''

''Where would I be working?''

"You'd be working here. Didn't I mention, one of our plants will be built in Thunder Bay. The feds, your provincial government, E.D.C., they're all involved. And the city's guaranteed us a parcel of land in... what's that open stretch just west of here?"

"Parkdale?"

"Parkdale. Right," he said, stabbing the air. "I'm surprised your local news media hasn't picked up on this. Must be keeping it quiet — speculators and all."

"There's not even a road into Parkdale yet."

"Well, there will be an interim period for training before the plant is built. We'll want you to work out of our Chicago office for a while. Of course, you'll need a work permit and other documents so you can work in the States."

"Chicago? I hadn't... "

"Our legal department will arrange everything. All I'll need from you is a cheque for six hundred dollars to cover costs."

"Six—"

Taylor held up his hand. "I know it may seem like a lot to someone who's out of work, but consider it an investment, Neil, an investment in your future."

The man with the silver hair formed his mouth into a smile, and ran the tip of his tongue over his lips.

"WHY DID YOU HAVE TO invite them?" Neil asked, sipping scotch and staring out the kitchen window. Across the street the Hendersons, fighting the wind in toques and scarfs and fur collars, climbed into their Toyota and headed off to church.

"We invite them every year, Neil. She's the only grandchild on both sides." Lorraine shot chunks of lettuce into the salad bowl.

"It seems to me that just this once... God, you must have spent a fortune. Prawns. Artichokes. Lobster tails. How long do you think the money's going to last, Lorraine? Do you want me to end up on pogey? ...And this Florida thing."

"If you don't like it, don't come. Cash in your ticket."

She plucked vegetables from the cold water in the sink with coarse reddened hands.

He looked at her and said, "No one ever calls you Lori, have you noticed? Always Lorraine."

"That's my name."

"It's because you're tough, you handle things." He spun the ice cubes in the bottom of his empty glass.

"I hope you left enough liquor for the rest of us," she said.

"Why? Did you eat all the chocolates?"

Neil stationed himself on the raised hearth, his back against the brick. He drained his glass, set it on the floor, ignoring his mother who stared at him through the top of her bifocal lenses. Dolly sat on the couch to the left of Wilson Sommers, criminal lawyer, crown attorney, Lorraine's dad. Ev Sommers sat on his right. And Wilson, sitting large beneath the watercolour of scarlet lilies, his arms outstretched along the back of the white leather couch, possessed the whole room. Neil was waiting for his father-in-law to check his watch. Lorraine's parents rarely visited. They preferred to hold court on Sommers turf, where Wilson could play the magnanimous host, work the crowd like a politician. *Glad you could come. Did you get a drink? Great to see you. Excuse me a minute.*

In the corner by the window, Jack Carpenter reclined in the Lazy-Boy, and served up his political insights and weather predictions — *In like a lion, out like a lamb.* The recliner had been a housewarming gift from Neil's parents, arriving one Saturday afternoon on the back of a Sears truck, upholstered like an encyclopedia salesman in brown plaid.

Snow from the roof rained down past the window; Heather somersaulted across the dove grey carpet through the patchy winter sunlight. Wilson Sommers managed a glance at his watch.

"So tell me, son, how's the job search coming?" his father-in-law asked. All eyes shifted to Neil. "Any luck?"

"I'm still looking." Neil was surprised at how flat his voice sounded.

"Putting out feelers?"

"I'm looking." Neil picked up his glass. "Anyone want another drink?"

He stood at the buffet that served as a bar, his back to the room. His father said, "I blame the government. Too many corporate hand-outs, tax write-offs. No control. It's the little guy who's left holding the bag."

"It's not that simple, Jack," said Wilson.

Neil pressed his thumbs against his eye sockets. He felt foggy-headed, and it wasn't the liquor. He hadn't been sleeping well. For weeks now, ever since his run-in with that old ferret, Bob Taylor, he had been waking at four a.m., eventually moving down to the couch to escape Lorraine's ragged breathing, the pressure of her body. At fifteen he'd spent a week camping at Kakabeka with Chips and Fiorito, the three of them squeezed into a two-man tent, wrestling their nightmares and each other's sweating bodies. After four days of fishing for walleye that refused to be caught and surviving on canned spaghetti and burnt marshmallows, they rode their bikes back of Conmee township, scouting the gravel roads for abandoned barns and houses. Eventually they found themselves on a bushed-in road without power or phone lines. Ahead, barely discernible in the mixed light and shadow, they spotted something — a greasy blanket? broken bale of hay? As they approached, crows scattered. It was the body of a dog, headless. At first, unable to gaze on it fully, they stared at the back end which was whole, the fringed tail jauntily outstretched, the grey legs posed delicately in an attitude of running. Fiorito was the first to really look. "Must have been done with a power saw," he said. The stump was ragged, black with thickened blood and squirming feasting flies; it oozed fresh blood where the crows had picked. The stench made Chips throw up. Fiorito insisted they drag the body into the ditch, cover it with branches and ferns. All the while the crows in the trees lifted their wings and nattered in their rusty-hinge voices.

"Well, at least they didn't close down the mill completely," his father was saying. "Folks in town can be thankful for that."

"Damn it, Dad, I wish they *had* shut the place down."

"Well, that's mighty mean-spirited of you, Neil," his father said sharply.

Returning to his place on the hearth like a chastised household pet, Neil stepped over Heather who was undressing Barbie and Ken in the middle of the floor, and came face to face with Lorraine carrying a tray of vegetables and dip. She stepped back to let him pass, allowing him more room than he needed. As she set the tray down everybody leapt, scooping up dip on broccoli heads and carrot sticks. Lorraine took a piece of celery to the hassock and sat opposite Neil but didn't look at him. She wore a dull green dress of some silky material, the skirt long and droopy. It was a dress she knew he had never liked.

Squatting on the low stool, she chewed the celery into nothingness. She rested her elbows on her knees, picked at her nails. A strand of hair trailed in front of her eyes which were outlined in black like cartoon eyes. Self-absorbed, she gnawed a strip off her thumbnail. How ugly she looks, Neil thought. He wanted to hit her.

Dinner was laid out buffet-style. After serving themselves everyone withdrew to the living room, ate from plates balanced on their laps. Neil poked at his food.

When he carried his plate through to the kitchen he found Lorraine in the dining room putting candles on the cake, which was shaped like a Smurf and decorated with blue and white icing and shredded coconut.

She looked up, said, ''Switch on the coffee, will you?''

It was the first time she'd spoken to him since their parents had arrived. He felt almost grateful. He had a sudden desire to confess to her about his encounter with Starcor. Scamcor. He wondered how to begin. Perhaps he could say, ''You won't believe what happened to me.'' Instead he said, ''Do you need anything else?'' But she had turned her back and seemed not to hear.

In the kitchen scraping the dishes into the sink, he picked up the sulphurous odour of matches, heard Lorraine summon the family into the dining room, then Dolly and Ev's oohs and ahs over the cake.

''I hate coconut,'' his father grumbled.

''Well then, I guess you're going to have to pick it all off, Jack,'' said Lorraine. His father laughed.

How does she get away with it?

''Daddy, hurry up, the candles are disappearing.''

Neil stared out at Wilson's white Cadillac glistening beneath the street light in front of the house. He shoved a half-eaten cherry tomato into his mouth, followed with a scrap of ham. His field of vision shortened and he caught his reflection in the window. His face seemed to float beyond the glass, half-formed and strange, ghostly, a prawn entering his mouth.

''We'd better start singing. There won't be any candles left for Heather to blow out.''

''You start us off, Dad.''

''*Dad-dy.*''

He spit the prawn into the sink, grabbed his jacket from the back closet and went out through the garage. When he reached the street, he broke into a run. Down the middle of the road, against the wind. His heels punched wedges into the packed snow; the blood drummed in his ears; his breath cast clouds in front of his face. He ran through intersections without stopping, without looking right or left. Halfway into the fourth block, sucking air, he had to stop. He fell backwards against the hood of a grey Buick. The cold air scraped his throat. He was afraid he had torn his lungs. He spat into the snow, expecting to see blood, and at that moment the street lights blinked out and the houses around him fell dark.

Neil straightened up. He felt strangely pleased. He envisioned in the houses up and down the block men and women, suddenly blind, gasp then curse. He saw them jump to their feet and, clawing the blackness with tentative desperate strokes, blunder into chair legs, sharp tables, doorways; hunt for flashlights and candles — *Where are those bloody matches?* All the while they fret about tomorrow, how they'll ever manage to get up what with the radio-alarm not working, and if by chance they should, they'll wake to cold floors, cold showers, cold cereal, going without that first jump-start cup of coffee. People who only seconds before had entrusted their well-being to the power company, R-20 insulation, gas heat, annual check-ups, clipping A&P coupons, rotating their radial tires, tithing, a secure job, the empathy of neighbours, permanence of love.

Neil stepped in front of the Buick and drove his heel into the headlamp which shattered with a satisfying crunch. The barking of a dog sounded in the next alley. He flipped up his collar, shoved his hands into his pockets and, straightening his back, stared in the direction of home.

Travels with Uncle Edgar

Bill MacDonald

TWO DAYS BEFORE HE DIED, I went to visit Uncle Edgar in the hospital. The tumour he'd been battling for the past year, and which he'd hoped to defeat with thought-waves, had turned out to be an invincible opponent.

It was a cloudy, blustery August morning, and the harbour was full of whitecaps. He lay looking out his window, watching the clouds and the dancing waves.

Consuela, his day nurse, came in to check his intravenous, and asked him what he was looking at.

"Whales," said Uncle Edgar.

"*Whales*?" said Consuela. "There are no whales in Lake Superior!"

"There are this morning," said Uncle Edgar. "Belugas."

Glancing across the bay, I could see what he meant.

At first Consuela refused to look, but then she went and stood at the window, and when she turned around she said, "How do you know they aren't dolphins?"

"*Dolphins*?" said Uncle Edgar. "There are no dolphins in Lake Superior!"

HE TOLD ME HE'D BEEN thinking about his old friend Tyrone Weatherwax, wondering what had become of him. I'd never met Tyrone, although Uncle Edgar and I did try to go and see him last fall, just after receiving the first bad news about the tumour.

We'd gone for a walk down at the marina, because he said he wanted to see the *Peninsula* and the *Donald Mac*. It was a cool, gray September afternoon, threatening rain, and the harbour was all but deserted. Still, it was where he wanted to be, and we walked all the way to Woodside's and back.

"Uncle Edgar," I said, "would you like me to drive you to Rochester for a second opinion?"

"Second opinion?" he said scornfully. "Why the hell would I want a second opinion? What I'd like to do is go and see my old friend Tyrone Weatherwax."

And so we did. Or at least tried to.

The last time he'd seen him, Tyrone was living in St. Cloud, Minnesota, where he spent his winters in a one-room cabin on the banks of the Mississippi, his summers on an old boathouse named Angelica, cruising up and down the river between Belle Prairie and Coon Rapids, drinking Southern Comfort and taking friends out fishing.

But when we got to St. Cloud, no one knew where Tyrone was, or even if he was still alive. His cabin on the riverbank was in disrepair, with broken windows and a tree down across the front porch. His houseboat was still there, but half sunk in the mud and full of bullet holes, as though someone had been using it for target practice.

So we headed back up Highway 23 in the rain.

AT SANDSTONE, WIND AND DARKNESS overtook us, and Uncle Edgar said he didn't like the look of the weather. The words were scarcely out of his mouth when the car suddenly lost power, and in pouring rain, we coughed and sputtered to a stop at the side of the road.

"Out of gas?" said Uncle Edgar.

"Can't be," I said. "We filled up in Mora."

"It's been that kind of day."

Sitting there in the dark, with the wind whistling around us and dead leaves landing on the windshield, I could think of better places to be, such as the Jolly Fisher in Duluth.

"Try 'er now," said Uncle Edgar.

I did, but nothing happened.

"Could be the battery," said Uncle Edgar.

"Or the alternator."

"Or the carburetor."

During a lull in the downpour, we saw a dimly lit farmhouse off to our right, and decided the best thing to do was go for help.

"I'll stay here," said Uncle Edgar. "You go knock on the door."

"I'd feel better if you came with me."

When we got out of the car, we saw that it was not a farmhouse after all, but a ramshackle old service station, with a dilapidated sign: Broderson Bros. Garage & Truck Stop.

"How appropriate," said Uncle Edgar, turning up his collar and preparing to make a dash for it through the puddles.

It did seem like an amazing coincidence, although by the look of it, there hadn't been many trucks stopping lately. The lopsided gas pumps were *Out of Order*, and the only vehicles in sight were a few rusted wrecks sitting on their axles.

"I have a feeling this is going to cost us," said Uncle Edgar, patting his pocket.

The first door we knocked on turned out to be the entrance to a disused garage, whose dark confines smelled strongly of wood rot and mouldy rubber.

"Be funny if there was no one home," said Uncle Edgar.

But there was. Having heard us rapping, an old man now opened a door in the adjacent building, and stood there peering out at us. "What you boys want?" he growled, moving his head from side to side, trying to get us in focus.

"Our car quit," said Uncle Edgar. "Damn thing died on us, right in the middle of the road."

"Probably the rain," said the old man, and seemed about to close the door, as though a diagnosis was all he thought we needed.

"My nephew and I were wondering..." said Uncle Edgar.

"This here your nephew?"

"He owns the car. Damn thing died on us."

"I don't sell gas no more."

"We're not out of gas," I said. "The tank's half full."

"Where you boys from?"

"Canada," I said.

"I thought so," said the old man.

"We're on our way home," said Uncle Edgar. "We went to St. Cloud to see my friend Tyrone Weatherwax."

"I don't sell gas no more," said the old man, bobbing his head up and down, studying us through his bifocals.

"Are you Broderson?" said Uncle Edgar.

"George," said the old man, lest we mistake him for his brother.

"Damn car died in the middle of the road!" said Uncle Edgar.

"You should get a better car!" croaked George.

"Or stay home in weather like this," I said.

Finally, with the rain coming down in torrents and drenching us, George stepped back and motioned us in. "No use standing out there getting soaked," he said, as though it had been our choosing. "Man could catch pneumonia! What kind of car you boys driving?"

"A '72 Chevy," I said.

"I can't do nothin' for a '72 Chevy!" said George.

His lodgings could best be described as a boar's nest. One had the feeling that during its last days of viability, Broderson Bros. Garage & Truck Stop had infiltrated the living quarters, and the two entities had become almost indistinguishable. Not that oil changes or brake jobs were done in the kitchen, necessarily, but greasy old car parts littered the premises, and there were tools everywhere. Sparkplugs sat on the pantry shelves; fanbelts hung on doorknobs.

And yet, the place had a certain unpretentious homeliness to it, a sort of masculine authenticity, that made one feel comfortable. It looked and smelled like a man's domain, with equal emphasis on mechanical and culinary endeavours.

With the door closed against the elements, George gave us one last cursory inspection, seemingly unperturbed at the pools of water dripping off us. He stirred up the fire in his cookstove and added a few pieces of split birch.

"You boys look like drowned rats," he said, rummaging in a cupboard. "You boys look like you could use a snort."

But his rummaging did not produce a snort, only two dusty cans of Grain Belt beer, which he opened with a flourish and handed to us, indicating that we should draw our wooden chairs closer to the stove. "I was sure I had a jug here someplace," he muttered.

And then, without asking us whether we'd had supper, he

began frying pork chops. I didn't notice a refrigerator, so wondered where he'd been storing them. The room was soon full of blue smoke, but very snug and comfortable, with the rain pounding on the roof and George stoking the fire and frying pork chops. When the latter were well scorched he emptied a tin of beans over them and pushed them to the back of the stove to simmer.

"Do you have a telephone?" Uncle Edgar asked him.

"I do," he said. "Out in the garage. Never had one in the house."

After proclaiming the disadvantages of having a telephone in the house, he dished up supper: pork chops, beans, and Grain Belt beer. For dessert he opened a tin of plums, referring to them as "apples of discord."

"So your friend in St. Cloud wasn't to home?" he said.

"No," said Uncle Edgar, bearing down with a dull knife.

"I spent some time on the Mississippi in my younger days. Had a place in Guttenburg. Worked on a tugboat out of La Crosse one year. Ran aground in Dubuque."

We chewed in silence for a time, listening to the rain and the crackle of the woodstove.

"I wonder if we should try the car again?" I said.

"What for?" said George. "If she wouldn't run before, why should she run now?"

"He has a point," said Uncle Edgar.

"Best stay the night," said George. "Put you up in a bunk bed, nothin' fancy. Come mornin', if this rain stops, we'll take a gander at your '72 Chevy."

I glanced at Uncle Edgar, wondering what he was thinking. We should have been in Duluth by now, or Lutsen or Grand Marais. And here we were, in some defunct service station, with an old codger who *might* know how to fix our car. But Uncle Edgar didn't look impatient. He looked re-laxed.

"Little grandson got killed here last summer," said George, gathering up the dishes. "His father was takin' down that big elm tree used to stand out front, cuttin' off the limbs with a chainsaw, and we was all off at a safe distance, except the boy's dog got loose and went runnin' across the yard, and damned if the biggest limb didn't come down just as he ran after the dog. We was all yellin' at him to stand clear, but the limb got him on the head... Jesus!"

"Amen," said Uncle Edgar.

"So now I'm here alone," said George, as though having explained everything. "We been closed since I-35 went through."

We played three-handed cribbage till midnight, listening to stories about the Mississippi and Wisconsin rivers, and about how I-35 had caused the demise of Broderson Bros. Garage and Truck Stop.

Sometime during the evening a shaggy white cat saun-tered in, with pink eyes and matted fur, and though George spoke to it and called it Snowball, he said it was as deaf as a post. "What good is a cat that can't hear?" he said.

And he told us about being a locomotive driver on a slow train between Alexandria and Monticello, hauling tourists in summer, freight in winter, back in the days of coal-fired steam engines, when railroaders still wore striped overalls.

"Maybe your friend in St. Cloud is dead," he said to Uncle Edgar.

"Maybe he is," said Uncle Edgar.

"Or maybe he just went south for the winter."

WE SLEPT WRAPPED IN BLANKETS on bunk beds at the back of

the room, where George's brother used to sleep. Before turning in, George stoked the woodstove and said he had a feeling the rain would let up by morning. "If it doesn't, I'll phone around and see if I can find us a tow truck."

"We'd be obliged," said Uncle Edgar.

"You boys in a hurry?"

"No," yawned Uncle Edgar. "Not anymore. We have all the time in the world."

Which I thought was a brave thing for him to say, especially after the kind of day he'd had.

In the morning, I woke to the sounds of Uncle Edgar coughing and George Broderson banging stove lids. Sure enough, the rain had stopped, and the sun was making an effort to break through.

"It's your fuel pump," said George, seeing me awake.

"How do you know?" I said.

"Because I went out and took a look at it. I figured that was your problem last night, from the way you described it."

"Can you fix it?"

"Well, I sure as hell don't have no fuel pump for a '72 Chevy! But I reckon after breakfast, I could phone around and find you one."

Which is what he did, after frying up a panful of eggs on the woodstove and serving them on the same plates we'd used for supper. We accompanied him out to the garage where the phone was, alongside a smudged and well-scribbled calendar from 1963, depicting a nude girl pushing a lawn mower. After six or seven calls he found a neighbour who had a demolished '72 pickup truck in the back yard with the same engine as ours, still in possession of its fuel pump.

"Seein' as how you boys ain't in a rush, he'll bring it

over after he does his chores,'' said George. ''Before sun-down.''

He arrived about an hour later, a thin, red-faced farmer named Treblehorn, with grease on his cheeks and newly skinned knuckles. We stood around the car while he and George removed the faulty fuel pump and installed the new one. There was a heated argument about whether or not the lines should be bled, which I gathered turned out to be unnecessary, because after pouring a little gasoline down the carburetor, Treblehorn got in and turned the key and started the engine with a tremendous roar.

''Good as new!'' he shouted, jumping out and putting a bony arm around Uncle Edgar's shoulders. ''I see you boys are from Canada. I been to Canada a couple times, me and the missus. ''Couldn't afford to live there, though.''

The thing was, he would only take ten dollars for the fuel pump, and nothing for the labour.

''Glad to help out,'' he said over the roar of the engine. ''These days, guys like old George and me never get a chance to help out!''

WE LEFT IN THE EARLY afternoon, under a gray fall sky.

Walking us to the car, George said, ''I'm sorry you boys couldn't find your friend in St. Cloud. But if you're ever back this way, and I'm still here, come and set a spell. Don't get many visitors anymore.''

Like Treblehorn, he refused payment, too, and said if we persisted in offering him money, he'd be insulted. ''I didn't *sell* you nothin'!'' was the way he put it.

And so we thanked him and shook hands and drove off.

Near Duluth, Uncle Edgar said, ''There's something I'd like you to do for me.''

"What's that?" I said.

"Find out what happened to Tyrone. If he's not dead, get word to him that I tried."

"All right."

He was silent for several miles, and then he said, "There's something else. I want you to take a boat trip to the Saguenay for me, and look for whales."

"Look for *whales*?"

"It's something I always wanted to do."

"But you still can!"

"No," he said softly. "Not now. But I want you to. I want you to go and look for belugas, and grays, and humpbacks, and think of me looking over your shoulder, seeing what you're seeing, hearing what your hearing. Will you do it?"

"I suppose so."

He closed his eyes and put his head back. "Nice fella, George Broderson. We must send him something."

We stopped for gas and hamburgers at Two Harbours.

Getting back into the car Uncle Edgar said, "I hope they don't expect me to go gentle into that good night. I intend to rage, *rage*, against the dying of the light!"

"Sounds very Irish," I said.

"Dylan Thomas," he said. "About as Irish as you can get!"

HE WAS BURIED IN MOUNTAIN View Cemetery on a warm August afternoon, and everyone said it was the kind of day he'd have chosen.

On the weekend they held a wake for him at Silver Islet, at Great Aunt Edna's house. There were a dozen of us out on the veranda that evening, watching the moon come up. The lake was like a millpond, the air so still you could hear the conversations of people going by in rowboats.

As usual, my aunts and uncles began to sing:

In the evening by the moonlight,
You could hear those voices singing.
In the evening by the moonlight,
You could hear those banjos ringing.
How the old folks would enjoy it,
They would sit all night and listen,
As we sang in the evening by the moonlight.

Before long we could hear other people joining in, people who had been out strolling, people drifting by in canoes, resting on their paddles close to shore.

Someone said it was not a time for sorrow, but a time for remembering childhood, and being thankful for old friends.

We sang ''Red River Valley'' and ''Home on the Range,'' which had been Uncle Edgar's favourites, and ''The Erie Canal'' and ''The Eddystone Light,'' and I think he would have been pleased, looking over our shoulders, seeing what we were seeing, hearing what we were hearing, listening to all those voices floating on the warm night air.

Sweet William

Bonnie Blake

IT IS COVERED WITH A LAVENDER FLOCK, as pretentious as cheap parlour wallpaper. Arnold's broad shoulders are squeezed into the narrow space, like an overgrown child hiding in a cupboard. A long white lily lies beside him. Arnold would have preferred a bit of colour. Mary Preston — no, not Preston anymore — chose the too-small coffin and the flowers.

There is nothing childlike in Arnold's lined face. Nothing left of my twelve-year-old younger brother who made the trip to Halifax such a long time ago.

THOSE THREE DAYS WITH AUNT BESSIE dragged and jerked like cement-dulled skates. She had the voice of a fox-frightened hen and I never knew when she'd descend on me. "Thomas, there's no need to snap off half the bean when you clean it. Thomas, why didn't you empty the slop bucket 'fore it got too heavy to lift? Thomas, the wood's low again." Peck, peck, pecking.

We both rushed to the door when we heard the wagon approach. I knew the news was good the moment I saw their faces.

"Arnold's not retarded," Mother announced even before

she had her coat off.

"Well, we all knew *that*," confirmed my aunt as she prepared the tea.

Aunt Bessie had continually said Mother was fooling herself thinking Arnold was anything but brain fried, but no one pointed that out now.

"So, what's the problem?"

"It was the scarlet fever," explained Mother, as she fixed the hair pins in her auburn bun. "His mind's just fine."

"He's deaf," announced Father.

"Deaf?" said Aunt Bessie. "He hears me call him to supper."

"He is too," said Mother. "Not completely, but enough so's he doesn't understand most of what's said. He knows when it's mealtime, and if you're calling in his direction, what else could it mean?"

Everyone studied Arnold, who looked from face to face.

"Why's he talk so peculiar?" asked Aunt Bessie.

"Partly because he hasn't heard proper speech since he was three, but mostly because his vocal chords are damaged. Even if he remembered how to say a word from when he was little, it wouldn't come out that way, and he wouldn't know because he can't hear it right."

"Well, Lord love a duck!" announced Aunt Bessie as she crossed her bulging arms.

"If that isn't enough," said Mother, "he probably has bad eyes too."

"So what's to be done?"

"We're going to get him a hearing aid and glasses if he needs them," said Father. "Can't do a thing about the vocal chords. But his speech will improve enough for people to understand."

Everyone stared at Arnold, the eighth wonder of the world. I punched his arm so he'd know I was happy.

"The doctor said there's absolutely nothing wrong with this boy's mind," said Mother. "He may be a bit slower than some, but only because he probably hasn't heard eighty percent of what his parents and teachers have been saying for the last nine years. Imagine that! It's a miracle he's gotten on as well as he has."

Mother burst into tears. Arnold looked bewildered as everyone hugged him and each other in turn.

That Sunday we didn't mind being quiet and spending our time praying, praising the Lord. Mother made sure we were up before the rooster on the Holy Day. Had to meet the Lord shining clean and ready to receive His word. We all trooped down to St. Michael's Presbyterian and, throughout the service, Reverend Fraser seemed to be thanking the Lord just for us.

OUR NEIGHBOURS, THE PRESTONS, were Roman Catholic. But George Preston only attended services at Christmas and Easter. The rest of the family attended in fits and starts — or whenever the children needed clothes from the church poor box. Mary was our age, and sometimes her dresses hung right to the ground. Our school buddies called her "Mother Mary" and "Mother Hubbard." Arnold didn't know what they were saying. Just as well.

Mary had always snubbed us, especially Arnold who she felt provided a reason to snub a MacDougal. Our farm was twice the size of Prestons' and her father George wasn't too successful. Rumour had it he kept a stash of whiskey in the barn. He had seven children and two others in the Catholic Cemetery.

Arnold used to hunch over the plants by the pump, clipping flowers for Mary Preston, his long calloused fingers ignoring the thorns. Even standing, his lanky body hunched, it was as if he were sinking into his own chest. The neighbours had to admit, though, he had a talent for growing things.

The boys at school weren't impressed; they still called him dummy. After the scarlet fever, Arnold probably hadn't heard what they were saying. If he spoke, they laughed and mocked his speech. He blinked his big grey-blue eyes and turned away. Irene knuckled her little hands on her skinny hips and told them to leave off.

Irene's been my lady for as long as I can remember. I told her once when she took a fancy to the minister's son to give it up, I'd keep after her 'til the last dog was hung. She laughed and said, ''No doubt, Thomas.'' But she didn't laugh when the boys bullied Arnold.

Mary Preston just giggled and dug at the dirt with her shoe. She was a tall, broad girl, with stringy brown hair, a long nose and pale blue eyes. O' course, that's not how Arnold saw her.

It was the school teacher, Sarah West, who talked Mother into taking Arnold to Halifax. Mother's voice was insistent when she talked to Father. So unlike her. I listened through the stove pipe hole from my bedroom above the kitchen.

''Miss West says he understands very quickly when people show him what to do. She thinks there's something else wrong. That he's not ...''

''Retarded?'' finished Father.

Father was always one for facing facts. ''Admit your mistakes and take your punishment,'' he'd say in his deep soft voice. His face was large and tanned, white-lined where the crows' feet danced around his eyes. He was tall and broad-shouldered with large, strong hands.

"I know it's hard," Father continued. "He was such a bright little one. But that scarlet fever overheated his brain. He'll never be normal."

"He is normal," countered Mother. "He doesn't have to be like everybody else to be normal. I want him to be happy. He's clever with his hands and good with the animals. Once he caught on to numbers he learned his sums and tables real quick. I think Doctor Kinlock was wrong. I want to take him to Halifax." She paused a moment and said, "He's twelve, Jack. We've got to find out for sure before he's all growed up and it's too late."

At last, Father gave in. They'd visit Aunt Bessie the following day. If she could take care of me, Bert could handle the farm.

THE DAY ARNOLD GOT HIS hearing aid everyone talked in such loud, excited voices he probably could have heard us without it. It was a bit smaller than those little Walkmans they have today and sat in his chest pocket with a thin cord running to the plug in his ear. For weeks, Arnold walked around looking astonished at every sound. The thing whistled and crackled with any quick movement, but Arnold couldn't stop smiling. I figured it wouldn't be long before he'd be talking up a storm, but he became even quieter.

"I talk stupid," he told me once.

I guess he never knew how he sounded.

"So what?" I said. "Say intelligent things and no one will take notice."

He must have heeded my advice. He moved to the front row at school and soaked up every word Miss West spoke.

But his ears still flamed when she called on him. Even when he had the answer, he stood staring at his feet until she let him sit back down.

One chilly afternoon, Miss West asked Ed Irvine a question about King George. Irvine was a fat bully with scaly skin and no eyelashes, who took pleasure tormenting the little ones. Ed picked at his warty hands.

"Stand up, Edward," ordered Miss West. She repeated the question.

Before Ed could mumble something, Arnold shouted out the answer. There was a surprised silence, then the students burst into laughter. Arnold looked around. I smiled at him so he'd know they weren't laughing *at* him. "Yes, Arnold, that's right," said Miss West. She smiled and ignored that he'd failed to raise his hand. "You're certainly enthusiastic about the royal family."

Ed glared as he sat down.

I was away the next day. Just a little cough, but Mother insisted on smothering me in a mustard and garlic plaster and keeping me in bed. While I was going up in flames, Ed and his buddies cornered Arnold by the well. Tommy Turner, who didn't join in but was too cowardly to stand up to Ed, told me about it.

"Turning into a smart mouth, eh, MacDougal?" Ed sneered.

Arnold shook his head no.

"What's the matter? Can't talk? Or maybe this ain't turned up enough." He poked the hearing aid with his finger. The box crackled and whined in a high pitch. Arnold jerked the plug out of his ear. The boys laughed and taunted him.

I don't know how they made him do it, especially since he

AUGUSTANA UNIVERSITY COLLEGE
LIBRARY

was feeling good about school. But, that afternoon, Arnold climbed into the crawl space under the roof. The trap door was near the teacher's desk and was always left partly open. When Miss West passed underneath, he dumped a box of crushed chalk and chalk dust on her.

There was no chance Miss West would favour Arnold again. He was so ashamed, he didn't say a word when Father took him to the woodshed.

A couple of weeks later, Arnold received his first pair of glasses. We made a day of the trip into Dartmouth, leaving right after chores. Arnold sat in stunned silence for the return trip, his mouth and eyes big open circles.

After supper, he stood by the front window. I joined him and we stared down the lane. "I never knew you could see the mailbox from the house," he whispered. I swallowed hard and asked him what he could see before.

"A blur of trees and dirt. Now I can even see the clouds."

Arnold was looked upon with some envy by the other students. Mary Preston stared wistfully. Not many parents would spend that much money on a hearing aid and glasses for their young one. Our family esteem rose.

Arnold still talked oddly and had gaps in understanding, but he was always smiling and polite. Few took pleasure in calling him dummy anymore. He tore right through the senior second reader. Even the nickname "four eyes" faded.

On the last day of school before summer holiday, when Arnold was fourteen, he stopped to gather purple irises from the garden. He stood them in a McCormick's Assorted Candies tin.

"Who's that for?" I asked as we walked to school. "Got a girl?"

Arnold blushed, but he didn't answer. He left them anonymously on Miss West's desk. "Oh, I love flowers," gushed Mary Preston, as all the girls crowded around to smell them.

Arnold smiled and fingered his shirt cuff. I'd noticed him staring at Mary when he thought she wasn't watching.

Off and on that summer, I saw Arnold arranging blue and red sweet William in a peanut brittle can. They weren't for Mother, and I thought it was strange that he would bring Miss West flowers now. Maybe he still felt guilty about dumping the chalk.

One evening, I followed him down the west lane out to the Preston farm where he left the flowers on the splintery back steps.

The next summer, Arnold continued to deliver flowers: yellow chrysanthemums, pale blue carnations, lavender, and fire-engine red roses. Once he came racing back up the lane, as if the bull had gotten loose.

"What's the matter?" I teased. "Mary see you?"

She had, of course, and he looked stunned. Both of us confronting his secret in the same day was just too much.

"So, what did she say?" I pressed.

"Nothing."

Neither Arnold nor Mary mentioned the flowers come September. When Mary saw him watching her, she would smile quickly, then turn away. Arnold would get this hopeful, confused expression. It was his last year at school. He was doing an adult's work on the farm.

The following summer, a week before Commonwealth Day, I saw him cutting deep pink hybrid tea roses.

"Why don't you just give them to her, instead of leaving them on the doorstep? She won't eat you."

Arnold flinched, then shrugged.

"Go on. Just knock on the door."

"Can't do that," he muttered. "Too many kids."

"Wait outside for her. She's got to come out to do her chores. Give them to her then. What's the point of bringing her flowers if you never talk to her?"

"What do I say?"

"Just talk to her like you talk to me. It isn't so hard once you get started. I talk to Irene about all sorts of things."

Returning, Arnold strode into the yard as if he'd just completed a cross country march. There was a big sweat mark on the back of his shirt, although it wasn't a hot day.

"Well?" I demanded.

"I asked her if she was going to the box social."

"Is she?"

Arnold nodded. "I asked her to put a rose on her lunch box so's I'd know it was hers and I could bid on it." His eyes looked like blue ponds through the thick glasses. He shifted his feet and the hearing aid whistled. "I'm going to eat lunch with her," he whispered.

At the appointed day, Mary wrapped her lunch box in pink tissue paper and put the pink rose on top. I saw her carrying it in. The flower was wilting.

Women's Auxiliary tablecloths covered the sawhorses and sheets of wood. There were fancy embroidered linens, orderly cross-stitched ginghams, and crocheted pineapples. We laughed and elbowed one another, circling the riches, guessing which box belonged to which girl and the possible contents — juicy fried chicken, spicy cooked ham, cool cucumber sandwiches. I made a big show of being interested in this box or that one.

"Aren't you going to buy Irene's?" Arnold whispered.

"Of course. I'm just having a bit of fun with her."

"Irene's a nice girl," Arnold said.

I laughed. "I know. She made potato salad and smoked salmon slices. I wouldn't pass that up now, would I? You know which one you're bidding on?"

"The pink one with the rose," said Arnold with his shy smile.

"What if it belongs to Ed's ugly sister?"

"Oh, no. It belongs to the prettiest girl here."

I laughed again. "Then it may cost more than you can afford."

Paul Smith and Murray McDonald decided to challenge my bid. Irene wouldn't have given them the time of day. There was also a new man bidding, name of Jack Seagrum. He sold combines and was spending the holiday with his sister and her family. I wondered how a young girl might feel having to eat her lunch with him. They watched when he bid. He had a moustache like Errol Flynn and wore fine clothes. He bid on most every box that was auctioned. It seemed as though he was helping to raise the price and not interested in winning. Then a pink tissue-wrapped box was held up.

"Isn't that the one you wanted?" I asked Arnold.

"No. There's no rose."

When the bidding closed, Jack leapt onto the platform to claim his prize.

"And who's the lovely lady that made this lunch?" called the auctioneer.

Mary Preston stepped forward. She smiled at Jack, who bowed graciously in return. Arnold turned pale, and his face sagged, as if someone had punched the air out of him.

A few days later, Mary told Arnold to stop bringing her flowers. Jack Seagrum was seen at the Preston farm every night.

In the weeks that followed, Arnold let the weeds twine their pervasive way through the rose bushes. I couldn't bear to see them choking, so I cleared them one morning after milking.

"You weed the roses?" Arnold asked at supper.

I admitted to it.

"No need," he said.

"They shouldn't be left to die. Plenty of girls like roses."

Arnold's head jerked up. He met my look, then shook his head slowly. "Give them to Irene," he muttered.

MARY LEFT TOWN WITH Jack Seagrum. Some say Old George threw her out because she was in the family way. Arnold took up tending the roses again. He gave some to Mother. I gave some to Irene, but most ended up in the compost heap. He planted few annuals.

We lost track of Mary Preston. Mother passed on during the bitter winter of '49. Father died under the hay wagon a year later. I married Irene and brought her to live on the farm. She tried to matchmake Arnold with several women, but gave up when he barely spoke.

On our seventh anniversary, Arnold took care of the two young ones so we could drive to Dartmouth. We went for a restaurant meal and caught the motion picture *A Streetcar Named Desire.*

When we arrived home late that night, Irene made tea for the three of us. The two newest MacDougals were asleep upstairs.

"You'll never guess who we saw in town," cried Irene, as she sipped her tea.

My kick missed her and hit the table leg.

"Mary Preston. Remember her?"

Arnold's cup dropped to the saucer with a clink. His tea splashed.

"Seems the wonderful Jack Seagrum's run out on her and the three little ones."

"Th-three!" stuttered Arnold.

"I'm pretty sure they never did marry either. Those poor kids. What a burden, being, you know... My children are so fortunate to have a father like Thomas."

I had to forgive her.

"How Mary's going to support them alone on a second cook's pay and no one to help—"

"'Cuse me," muttered Arnold. He stood, dumped his tea into the slop bucket and went upstairs.

At breakfast, he announced that he was going to Dartmouth.

I gave him my best look of discouragement while Irene showed great interest in her tea. He looked steadily back at me.

"For how long?" I asked.

"A week, maybe more. I'll stop by Ferguson's and hire his boy to help out while I'm gone."

"No need. We can manage for a week."

"Might be more, Thomas. I'll pay him."

What could I say to a grown man who'd been alone while I was raising a family?

They were married in Dartmouth. Irene and I were witnesses. Mary carried a bouquet of lilies, baby's breath and sweet William from our garden.

Arnold saw a lawyer and changed the children's names to MacDougal. I didn't like the idea much, but it wasn't just my name. He brought them to live on the farm. Suddenly the house was filled with shrill voices.

Irene coped with the crowding as best she could, bless her heart. She tried to make it seem like their home as well.

Arnold built an extension off the back and divided it into two rooms. Mary's children worshipped him, particularly little Bobby who followed him around like a newly hatched duckling.

All summer long there were flowers in a Blue Ribbon coffee can on the kitchen table. It hurt me to have to show Arnold the empty vodka bottle.

"It's just one bottle," he said.

"It's the third one I've found. Mary's been odd lately."

"The women have been giving her a rough time. They snub her at church. Say she doesn't belong there."

"I see."

"It's none of their damn business. She's my wife. She's got nothing to be ashamed of."

I told him that the night before last I'd found her asleep at the kitchen table. "Bobby was outside alone after dark."

"I'll take care of Bobby. It's none of your damn business either!"

He glared at me, his eyes as sharp as sickles. I shouldn't have interfered between a man and his wife.

The next day at supper, Mary left the kitchen twice. Each time she returned, she seemed more irritated. When Bobby spilled a glass of milk, she slapped him.

"I'll get it," said Arnold.

"I'll get it," mimicked Mary, copying his stumbly speech.

The kitchen clock ticked in the silence. The children looked at their plates. Bobby sniffled.

The families started eating meals separately. Irene and I let them eat first, but that had its drawbacks. Arnold would join Mary for a few drinks afterward and their voices would get louder and louder.

"Why don't you answer me?" we heard Mary say one night. "I know why. 'Cos you got nothing to say. Nothing from nothing."

Arnold's voice was a low rumble.

Irene told me it upset her stomach listening to them while she ate. Her pregnancy was a good excuse to switch. She said she was too hungry to wait, so she and I and our two young ones began eating first.

It wasn't much better. Sometimes they started drinking before supper.

"What's the matter with you? Turn that damn thing up if you can't hear me!" Mary yelled.

"I hear you."

"I hear you! I hear you! Then why don't you ever understand me?"

I could see Arnold from where I sat. He sighed and turned down the volume on his hearing aid. It whistled shrilly, and Mary leapt to her feet. She ran into the kitchen and began smashing the plates on the floor, one after another, in a steady rhythm. Irene jumped up but I grabbed her arm. They were Mary's dishes.

A few days later, Mary let a soup pot boil dry on the stove. Irene was frightened. The next morning the house still smelled of smoke.

The following week, they left. There were farming jobs in Manitoba.

THE NEXT CHRISTMAS I received a card with a note inside. I read it to Irene.

"I broke my leg last month and been bedridden. Mary's

working as a cook. Doing all right but it'll be a bare Christmas. Hope you're doing well. God bless. Love, Arnold.''

We looked at each other, and I said, "I'll send him what I can."

I never expected to be heading west myself. But soon after, our littlest one developed asthma. After a few close calls, the doctor advised that we move off the farm to a drier climate — the Maritimes were too wet and cold.

I got a job in a grain elevator in Port Arthur, Ontario. I used to think that some of the wheat coming through might have been cut by Arnold.

I never was much good at letter writing. Arnold neither. We exchanged cards at Christmas, but they didn't really say much. We went to visit once. Mary's hair was mostly grey and her clothes stained with grease spots. Arnold was quieter than ever, and he stooped like an old man. The prairie wind never stopped blowing.

I'M SURPRISED THEY LEFT Arnold's coffin open. I thought he'd be smashed up. Mr. Rantz, the mortician, did a good job.

Four men came out to the funeral from the first farm he worked on, and others from other places. I could tell they respected him. He always was a hard worker — fair and honest. More than one said they could count on him. The lad who drove the combine didn't come. Must have been a hard lesson.

I thought Mary'd be hysterical, or maybe falling down drunk, but she preened under all the attention. Kept telling everyone how Arnold used to bring her sweet William from his garden when they were still in school and how he always managed to get her flowers on her birthday, even between jobs.

Bobby, her oldest, has all grown up into a shaggy-haired young man. He seldom speaks. Reminds me of Arnold in a way. But Arnold wouldn't have approved of the glares he gives his mother. He said he could tell I was Arnold's brother; we look alike.

The cemetery is one of those modern places with flat headstones you can mow over. No one's allowed to plant flowers on the graves. I'd brought some sweet William seeds, though I doubt they'd have survived in the dry wind anyway. Arnold's the first in four generations not to be buried down home.

When Mary and the others had said their goodbyes to Arnold, I stepped forward and said to Mr. Rantz, "One moment please, I'd like to take this white lily."

"Would you like me to remove his glasses?" whispered Mr. Rantz.

I looked at Arnold and thought of the day he'd brought his first pair of glasses home — how he'd gone to the front window, able at last to see clearly what the world had to offer.

"Leave them where they are," I said, and I stepped back, turning the lily in my hands.

The Bird

Jen Thompson

A SLEEK RED CAR SPEEDS SOUTH toward the border, its tinted windows flickering with the black and gray of aspen trunks. Through the shadows the ghost-like passengers, a man and a woman, toss back their heads in laughter.

They have escaped for one long weekend together, on the promise of a kiss, and his hand, exploring hers, trembles with anticipation.

Approaching them around a curve in the road, an over-burdened pulp truck slews its logs, like shadows made solid, through the glass. Their heads fly back.

Moments later, crumpled red metal lies scattered among the daisies in the ditch, and the car horn drones on and on.

THE CALL CAME IN AROUND FOUR-THIRTY as Clayton Leister was sawing up logs for the wood stove. His red and black hunting jacket looked like a bandage against the line of white birch. He'd started tossing sawn chunks up against the house when the phone connection he'd rigged up to the back shed began hammering away.

He sheathed his chain saw and stashed it under the back steps. Clay was retired now from the Forestry fire fighters, but he was still captain of the local volunteer boys, CPR instructor, and Santa Claus for all the Christmas parties. He squeezed the cigarette from his lips and stubbed it on the steel toecap of his boot. As he reached the receiver a ball of tar rose up to the back of his throat. He held back the door and spat into the wilting petunias, so as to avoid Aila's crushed white gravel path and the painted Snow White.

"Clay Leister. Where's the fire?" he hollered into the mouthpiece.

It was the widow from the house on the hill. The family had moved in last June. Ran out of water in July. Clay had helped them dig in a new well. Husband was a lawyer. Drove a red Audi, but it never seemed to be parked there. Come September it wasn't parked there at all. The woman was buying a van, second hand, from Aila's cousin. Winter was coming. Clay had known somehow that a woman on her own with youngsters, in that house, would soon be calling for help.

"What kind of bird, Mrs. Roberts?" Clay scrubbed his fingernails on the grey stubble of his chin. "Dead. I'll be up in five, don't you touch a thing."

Clay scouted around his workbench. Nails. Trowel. Wire. Screws. Squirrel crap. Cigarettes. He tapped a fresh one from the packet, propped it under his top lip, and lit it for his climb up the hill.

The late October sun had turned the grasses and fallen leaves a mellow orange hue that was easy on the eyes, but Clay squinted from the stitch in his chest as he climbed the rubbly road. The crisp air stung his cheeks and bit at his fingers, but he wouldn't button his jacket, nor stoop to lace his boots. Not in October for pity's sake. The aspen trunks were stark against the sky. You could spot a moose before it smelled you when the forest thinned like this.

The Roberts place was a thing of modern design, angular with wooden shingles and slabs of plate glass that made caves of the shadows within and mirrored the woods without. Birds would fly straight into the windows, then plummet with broken necks onto the doorstep.

Clay found the Roberts woman on the front deck, huddled with her fair-haired daughter and a little red-haired boy. At their feet lay the dead bird, a clump of mottled brown and grey feathers with its neck twisted skyward. The eyes were glassy black holes. There was no blood.

"Been dead a while?" Clay asked, surprising them.

"I suppose so," said the woman. "I didn't hear it hit. I usually do."

"Daddy used to bury the dead birds." The daughter tilted her jaw at Clay. "What are you going to do with it?"

He smiled at the defiance in her eyes. "Well, I don't know," he said, crouching. "It's a partridge. Look at its pretty feathers."

"Daddy did not use to bury dead birds," the little boy said softly.

Clay turned the bird over in his hand.

"I thought it was a game bird," the woman whispered. "I thought you might want to take it. You helped us with the well." Her eyes ran over the fanned wings. "It seemed a waste to bury it. I didn't know what to do with it."

"I'll show you," said Clay. He spread the bird's wings wide and placed a boot on each one.

"Jeffrey, go inside," the woman said without looking away.

Clay gathered the two scaly feet into his right hand.

"Emma, take your brother in." The woman raised steel in her voice. "You don't have your coats on."

The boy ran inside, to watch from the window. The girl stayed.

In one fluid movement Clay wrenched off the legs, entrails dangling, and tossed them into the scrub. He snapped off a wing and placed it gently on the step. Snapped off the other, and spread them into a fan.

"Pretty, aren't they?" He smiled at the orderliness of the feather patterns, but the girl clenched her mouth tight shut.

Then he slipped his yellowed fingers up under the fluffy grey down of the bird's breast.

"Like a glove," the woman said absently.

And he pulled the clean pink breast from the feathered pouch. The head dragged out the heart and Clay flung them into the dogwood bush. He gave the still-soft flesh a little squeeze as he handed it to the woman.

"Been dead about an hour," he said. "You can see the bruise where she hit."

"Above the heart," the woman said, fingering the purple.

"It'll taste like chicken, only a bit more gamey." Clay wiped his hands. "Just roast it up."

"Oh, but I couldn't," she began.

Clay raised his hand. "You have it," he laughed. "It should make a meal for you and the little ones."

"Well. . . thank you." The woman swallowed and tried to smile.

The girl thrust out her purple tongue as far as it would go, eyes bulging, and ran into the house.

The stony road carried Clay downhill toward home. He took the last drag of his cigarette and savoured the way the cold wind stripped the smoke in strands from his open smile.

Yvonne Roberts watched the old man until he reached the bottom of her hill. Only then did she breathe a sigh, and frown at the meat in her hand. She had never wasted good meat, nor cooked tainted food. She held the flesh gently to her nose and breathed in the forbidden perfume. The scents of freshness and of carnage mingled. It smelled like the rabbits her father used to gut for Sunday dinners. She wondered if she really could eat the bird.

When she opened the kitchen door her daughter Emma was standing, hands on hips, astride the table. The girl watched her mother wash the bruised flesh and saw her pat it dry. "We're not going to eat that, Mommy," she said.

"We may." Yvonne avoided her child's eyes.

"Well, it isn't fair. God made the birds and all the wild animals, and he didn't mean us to eat them."

"How do you know?" her mother said softly.

"Because I just do. Why else would Daddy bury the dead birds and say a prayer with me?"

"Well," the mother said carefully, "perhaps Daddy did those things for you, not really for God or the birds."

"My Daddy would have done it. . . to be nice. You never would." Emma flung herself off the table. Her face, pushed up at her mother's, was pale and wet. She ran upstairs.

Yvonne wondered if she would cry too. She had waited for the tears to come since the police knocked on their door with the news of Peter's death. "And would you know, madam, the name of the young woman who died with him? We're having trouble tracing her."

No tears. Nothing came. Only a dry empty wind that seemed to blow through everything. A listlessness. She felt as though she had been locked out of her own home, and she couldn't find her keys.

Yvonne put the bird on a glass dish and into the oven.

Jeffrey was asleep on the couch now. She moved to cover

him. Even the redness of his hair would not make her cry. Later, she thought, Emma would fall asleep in her bed. She would go up and kiss her puffy face goodnight. Twice. Once for Emma and once for Daddy's princess.

Yvonne perched on the breakfast stool and looked out at the woods. Stupid birds. Flying for cover straight into their own reflections. It wouldn't be immoral to eat the bird, since it had killed itself. It wasn't wrong to keep living here, in Peter's house, now that the debts were all paid by his insurance.

"He shouldn't drive so fast on our country roads," old Clay Leister had told her from the pit of her well. "It's suicide."

Good old Clay Leister. An honest man could always be counted on to rip your heart out.

Peter was an Honest Man. Self-servingly honest, ambitious, conscientious and charming. Oh, how Emma worshipped him. Then, she never had to judge him.

Yvonne found Peter's old Wellingtons, pulled them on and went outside. In the dusk, the north wind was coiling ropes of leaves.

She took a shovel around to the side of the house, below Emma's window, and chopped a little pit of clay at the base of the dogwood bush. The feathered head with its gory necklace was hanging there. She scooped it off with the point of the blade and dropped it into the hollow. The legs and tail feathers were hard to find in the scrub, and her cold hands ached. She remembered partridges took partners for life, and imagined the other bird coming upon pieces of its mate. She dragged every scrap of offal from the branches until nothing remained, then buried the hindquarters. The fanned wings drying on the wood steps had begun to look innocuous, artificial. Jeffrey would want to keep them if he were older. They felt soft on her fingers as she laid them over the hole. She spattered them with clods of earth until nothing showed. Then, thinking of wolves, she put a stone on top.

This is what separates us from wild animals, she thought, stones and rituals. She looked down on Clay Leister's roof in the valley. It wasn't a question of honesty, brains or brute strength. Emma was right to want to bury the bird.

She wanted to pray over the little grave, but couldn't think what to pray for. She gave thanks that she had retrieved the scattered pieces, and that she had done something for Emma. One persistent thought betrayed her reverence; would she be able to eat the rest of the bird?

When she came back in, the house was dark and still and smelled like Thanksgiving dinner. Rituals. She laid a linen cloth over the dining room table and put out her mother's crockery, the anniversary cutlery, and a wine glass. From the back of the stereo she drew out a faded record cover, and lay a scratched disc gently on the turntable. The needle kissed the old French songs.

She went into the bedroom to put on a dress. Her shoes were in the hallway cupboard, but when she opened it the scent of Peter's aftershave wafted out. One of his jackets was hanging at the back. She stepped into the darkness, slid her hand into the cool lining, pressed her face against the softness, breathed in the smell of his office, of his books and papers, of him. Swaying softly in the dark, she was caught by the ghastly hollowness of the hanging cloth. The sleeves grew damp where her face pressed against them.

The oven beeped and beeped and beeped.

After it had stopped she went back to the kitchen. The roast meat looked brown and crisp. She set it on the dining table. Then she poured herself a glass of cider, and cut fine thin slices of white meat onto her plate. She sat looking at it.

Emma appeared in the doorway with Jeffrey in her arms. "He woke. Didn't you hear?"

Yvonne smiled. "Come in, come in and sit with me."

"We're starving," said Emma, watching her mother.

"I'll make you some soup."

"I'd like some chicken," said Jeffrey.

Yvonne lifted a small piece of white meat on her fork. "It's partridge," she said.

"That's okay." He took the first bite.

"I'm not afraid to try some," said Emma, looking squarely into her mother's eyes. They each took a slice.

Yvonne rolled the sweet tender meat in her mouth. It was disgracefully delicious.

"I'll get our plates," said Emma.

There was a knock at the door.

It was already dark through the windows, so the children followed close behind their mother. She opened the door only a crack.

Clay Leister thrust his yellow-toothed smile through the gap, and waved a clouded plastic bag in front of them.

"Two more partridge," he beamed. "You might have to pick some shot out of them, but they'll make a decent feed."

What You Know
Patrick McLeod

A MATCH FLARED IN A DARKENED CORNER *of the room, casting jack-o'-lantern shadows across Al's face. It touched the joint and transformed its tip into an orange ember. Seconds later a jet of hash smoke blew out the light.*

He sank back into the couch and settled his gaze on the aquarium that sat on top of the stereo cabinet. In the eerie, blue-lit water, a quintet of piranha tore the fins off a goldfish.

Below the tank, the stereo's light meter flashed the beat as the Stones pounded out 'Honky Tonk Woman.'

Al dragged deeply on the joint and felt his 'stoned grin' creep onto his face. As he reached for the ashtray, a shadow caught his eye. A paranoid rush straightened him.

"Who the hell are you!" he snapped, cupping the joint behind his palm.

A figure stood in the unlit hall, near the kitchen. A man. In a long, dark coat. Darkness disguised further description.

"How'd you get in here?" Al was on his feet. There was only one door into the basement apartment and he'd locked it. Hadn't he?

The intruder raised his right hand. Al squinted to see what it held.

He lived long enough to see the first muzzle flash. The

gun fired six times in perfect rhythm to the heavy thump of Charlie Watts' bass drum.

Once again Death stalke...

"Shit!"

Larry ripped the sheet from the typewriter, scrunched it into a ball and threw it at the wall. The dining room floor was littered with crumpled paper.

"Crap!" he spat as he swept a foot through the pile.

The phone rang. He flicked a glance at the clock. 1:35.

Marie, on her break at the hospital, was calling to say good night.

Larry lit a cigarette. Halfway through the third ring, the phone silenced. He snorted out a puff of smoke. She thought he was in bed or on the can, so she hung up, worried that she'd wake the baby, who was upstairs in his crib and wouldn't wake up if an F-14 landed on the roof.

A tow truck sped past the house, momentarily strobing the room with orange light. Larry circled the table and slid open the screen on the patio door. Cool June air greeted him as he stepped onto the deck. A block away, arc-sodium lights from the CP railyards cast a ghostly hue on a pair of grain elevators that rose from the banks of the Kam River. Framing them from across the water was Mt. McKay, a black blot in the sky, outlined by winking aircraft warning lights.

Larry sighed out a stream of smoke. He liked the night. It suited the writer in him.

His momentary mood upswing faded as his eyes drifted south. A scowl twisted his face. Had the sun been out, he'd have been able to see the plume of steam billowing out of Can-Am Paper's towering orange and white stack. Day after tomorrow and it was back to making the brown stuff into white stuff.

The Stones faded into a DJ's voice that muttered something about the weather (you're never more than twenty minutes away from the weather on 580 CKPR) as he put on Mellencamp.

The mill paid well and the work wasn't hard. The problem was, Larry wanted to be a writer, not spend a quarter of his life poisoning himself to make some corporation rich.

He flicked his cigarette into the grass and went inside. The typewriter taunted him.

Write about what you know.

It was the one consistent piece of advice offered by writers and publishers.

As long as you know something people want to read about, he thought. His thirty years hardly contained the adventures of a best seller. Besides, he loved writing horror stories. The few people who had read his work seemed to like it. A couple of publishers had been encouraging, but noncommittal. He knew he was getting better, but not good enough or fast enough.

Larry plunked his forehead on the typewriter.

"Write about what you know," he whispered. "I know the people, the places." He pressed his head against the return bar. He could create tension, character, plot, but how could he show fear he'd never felt, or describe pain he'd never experienced or seen? How could an innocent man know how a killer feels? How...

A second later, he shook his head to clear the thought. "You're losing it, Field," he said and started to type.

A few minutes later the thought crept back. Larry pushed it away.

Thirty minutes later, just to kill time, he started to make a list.

CIGARETTE CUPPED IN HIS HAND, Larry turned his attention to the rear of a house three doors down an intersecting alley. It was a two and a half storey, pre-war house that hugged a six foot fence on the far side of a double lot.

A half moon drifted below a star-freckled sky. Down near the harbour the humid air was cooled by a breeze that rolled off Lake Superior. A tug hooted as it edged a laker into a pier.

Larry slouched in his half-ton and flicked ashes out the no-draft. Beside him, dangling in his car seat, Kevin snored softly. The Ford was parked at an alley's edge at the back of a parking lot. Seventy feet away, the steady thump of a bass drum permeated the old wooden walls of The Pen, a Simpson Street country and western bar.

Muted light spilled into the lot as a side door burst open. Larry sank deeper into his seat and stared at the rear view mirror. Two denim clad couples filed out. One man muttered something about rednecks that sent the women into a chorus of giggles. Larry's chest tightened as they came closer, voices loud, feet scraping asphalt. Though the windows were up and the doors locked, he quietly eased in the clutch.

Redneck was a gentle term for The Pen's clientele.

The women and one man passed the pick-up, but the second man stopped and turned, T-shirted belly inches from the tailgate. Larry met his eyes in the mirror. His hand moved to start the engine and hightail it, but was stopped by a familiar sound. Exhaling through clenched teeth, he grinned as the man zipped up his pants and joined the others. Seconds later, an engine roared and a car bounced into the alley and disappeared.

Larry butted his cigarette, glanced at Kevin to make sure he was breathing (a paranoid habit he'd had since the day his son came home from the hospital), and looked back at the house.

Like The Pen, the house at 154 MacGiver Street had a reputation.

For five nights during the past month, Larry had watched the house. From the southeast corner of the parking lot he could just make out the back landing through the trees. At erratic intervals, if at all, a young woman would step out onto the porch. She would stretch, lean against the railing, usually light a cigarette. Sometimes she was blonde, other times brunette or redhead. The majority were white, a few black; once an Asian.

Using binoculars, Larry would study the women, their movements, the time they spent outside. He would watch the windows of neighbouring houses and the street at the alley's mouth.

On this particular night, the porch door opened and a young woman stepped out. ''Long time no see,'' he muttered. This one hadn't been out since the first night. Dark hair, trimmed above the ears and long in the back, she wore a fishnet pullover and a leather skirt, slit to the hip. She stayed long enough to smoke half a cigarette, then disappeared inside. Larry jotted a few notes on a pad.

A hooker was the logical choice for his little exercise, a criminal, so the police might not pursue the case with much enthusiasm. Nor would there be a public outcry to do so. Police attention would turn towards a drunken john or enraged pimp.

Larry also considered that a hooker couldn't conceal a weapon under her clothes and, if something went wrong, would be easier to handle than a man.

But, most important, he believed women showed fear

better than men. ''You're a chauvinist pig, Larry Field.'' He glanced at his watch, tucked the notebook in a jacket pocket and started the truck.

''Please don't blow up in my face,'' prayed Larry. Eyes clamped shut, he pulled the trigger.

BOOMFF.

Twenty yards away a geyser of sand exploded up.

A grin crept across his face.

''Larry Field, master gunsmith.'' He pumped in another shell, took a few steps closer to the sand pile and fired again.

''Not exactly silent,'' he muttered, ''but not loud enough to upset anyone.'' He pumped in another shell.

It was Sunday, so the sand pit which was owned by the construction company Larry's brother-in-law worked for was deserted. Still he glanced around after every shot.

The shotgun was a Savage 12-gauge pump he'd gotten six years ago from his Uncle Dick. Dick, a trucker, had picked it up as a bonus when he bought a hot 30.06 in a Texas bar. Marie was the only other person who knew he had it and, since he didn't bird hunt anymore, she'd probably forgotten about it.

Larry hadn't taken long to pick the shotgun as the logical weapon. With a gun, a person could get close enough to see a reaction while avoiding contact.

Yet, guns had drawbacks. Pistols and rifles left traceable bullets. Shotgun pellets weren't traceable, but the gun was bulky and loud. Bulky had been overcome with a hacksaw, and Larry made the silencer on midnights at the mill while Ralph and Frog, his co-workers, tried to pretend they weren't sleeping. In the pipe shop, he scrounged a piece of titanium piping that was a fraction bigger than the shotgun barrel.

After cutting it off and threading it to match a thread on the barrel, he spent hours drilling holes in it, making sure they all angled forward. Then he wrapped it with thin, dense asbestos packing, inserted it into another pipe that was also peppered with holes and soldered them together. Bulky and crude, it performed better than expected.

BOOMFF.

At twenty feet the shot spread was about eight inches.

Fifteen feet max, he thought. Close enough to see the whites of her eyes, far enough to stay clear. He unscrewed the silencer and walked back to the truck. At home he would strip down the gun, oil it, hide it . . . and never again touch it with bare hands.

TIRES HUMMED OVER ASPHALT. Larry thumbed up a gear and zipped past two kids playing frisbee. Two blocks of Marks Street disappeared in a half-dozen breaths.

Ahead, a burst of traffic sped down Arthur Street. Larry banked a sharp right and hugged the curb. Seconds later a gap opened between cars and he shot across all four lanes into Vickers Street.

He'd rarely ridden a bike since he got his driver's licence the November after his sixteenth birthday, but lately he'd been riding whenever he could.

Fast and harder to identify than the truck, the twelve-speed wouldn't be hindered by traffic lights and stop signs. The coming and going of the truck might be remembered by neighbours, but the bike could slip down the back lane unheard.

Larry passed Fort William Gardens, hopped the curb by a ball diamond and squeezed the brakes as he neared the centre-field fence. Forty-five seconds later, he sped off.

Two minutes after that, he passed the MacGiver Street alley, one block up from 154, clicked off the stopwatch and coasted.

Not bad, he congratulated himself.

Slowly, he pedaled down the alley, eyes flicking from side to side. He'd decided to risk exposure to the neighbour-hood in order to see what the house looked like in daylight. In spite of the risk he felt good, high on adrenalin.

He stopped the bike and spent a long time lighting a cigarette. The house was quiet, its nocturnal occupants prob-ably sacked out. It appeared no different than any other house on the street. If anything, it was a little better kept.

Two things about the yard bothered Larry. A three-foot chain link fence ran from the front of the garage to the neighbour's fence. The small gate near the leaning wall of the garage had a rusty looking latch and hinges that would have to be checked out.

The other thing was the trees. There were lots of them, which was in his favour. But while birch and poplar sepa-rated this yard from the next, the ones that huddled around the garage and ran along the hedge at the front yard were maples. Maples started losing their leaves in early Septem-ber. Lost leaves meant lost cover. That could affect his timetable.

Wanting to stay, but knowing he was pushing his luck, he pedaled away.

TEN DAYS LATER, LARRY PEDALED the same route. He rode leisurely to accommodate Jack, his German shepherd, who trotted at his side. To the west the first hues of orange signaled sunset. Coasting up to the ball field behind the Gardens, he leaned the bike against the fence and hopped over. Jack ran around to the gate and was sent scampering after a tennis ball. The field was deserted. There were no homes nearby. The arena loomed out beyond left field. Behind home plate was McKellar Park School. A soccer field stretched out past first, and behind where he stood at centre field was Vickers Street and a lumber yard that closed at six.

Jack came back and was sent off again. Larry looked around and sat down. With a pocket knife, he sawed a foot-wide circle in the grass and pried out a cone-shaped piece of sod. For fifteen minutes, during pauses while Jack fetched, he scooped handfuls of dirt out of the hole and flung it in all directions. When the hole was six inches wide and as deep as his arm, Larry replaced the sod, stood up, and tramped it down.

Stepping back, he smiled at his handiwork.

"If I didn't know it was there, I wouldn't know it was there. Come on, Jack."

Two days later they were back. Jack pouted on his leash. Larry rode slowly and obeyed all traffic laws. By the time they reached Vickers Street, darkness had settled, which left only the occasional streetlight to snag his shadow and fling it across the asphalt. Despite the cool air, sweat filmed his forehead and slipped between his palms and handlebar grips. Again he felt the adrenalin; he liked what he felt.

They reached the ball field, and when he was sure there were no eyes on him, he vaulted the fence. While Jack ran after the ball, Larry found the fence post with the knot in the centre. Two feet in front of it, he grabbed a handful of grass and pulled up the sod plug. After lining the hole with a garbage bag, he took another look around, and unzipped his windbreaker. Velcro scratched at the night air. One strip was glued to the gun's side, the other attached to a belt that ran from shoulder to hip. Larry dropped the gun into the hole and replaced the sod. As he did so, an image emerged from the backwaters of his brain. A book cover. The likeness of a dead harlot. A bestseller... A blurb: ''The best young terror writer to come along in years.'' And, another image, a headline: Suspect Apprehended in Murder of Local Prostitute. Larry shook it off as he hopped the fence and mounted the twelve speed. As he sped off down the street followed by Jack, the image of the bestseller reshaped itself.

THE SECOND MONDAY IN AUGUST was 'Dollar Day' at K-Mart. Larry picked out a pair of size ten TRAX sneakers.

In the twenty minutes he was in the store, he counted at least six other people buying the identical shoe, with the identical tread pattern.

He paid cash, refusing to look the checkout girl in the eye.

THE FOLLOWING THURSDAY, LARRY walked in the door and dropped his lunch box on the floor. Marie sat on the couch, arms crossed, cigarette clamped between two fingers, her lips stretched white by a scowl.

When the toes of Marie's right foot tried to tie themselves into knots, she was severely pissed.

What did she know? Larry squirmed beneath his sleeveless overalls. His throat constricted. What had she found? The gun was gone. His notes were burned. Had someone reported him spying on the whorehouse?

''What's the matter?'' he asked to avoid admitting guilt through silence.

Marie looked up, eyes hard as flint. ''I have to go on

midnights,'' she snapped.

Relief. Followed instantly by a flutter of anticipation.

''When?''

''Wednesday. The day after you go on holidays.''

The fluttering grew to the thundering of a flock of frightened geese.

''COME ON . . . COME ON.''

It was a quarter past midnight. Larry paced the kitchen. Marie had gone to work at eight, Kevin to bed at nine-thirty.

He looked at the phone, willing it to ring. It stared back, the fingerholes in the dial a toothless grin laughing at him. For the fifth time in the past hour, he lit a cigarette.

The wait had been tolerable while the baby was up — nothing can compete with a two year old on a sugar buzz — but now the second hand wound in ever slowing circles. He stood before the phone, fists clenched.

''Ring!''

He couldn't call her, that would be unusual. He'd been too careful to make a mistake now, even if it was his wife. Marie loved him, Larry knew that, but he didn't want to find out how she would react to this. He had to wait, had to be sure she was at work. If she came home to find Kevin alone she'd... well, best not think about it.

It rang.

''Hello.''

''What were you doing, sitting on the phone?''

''Just passing by.'' Larry strained to sound relaxed. ''How's work?''

''It's the middle of the night, we've had three teenagers from a car accident, a heart attack, a drunk who stabbed himself in the leg, and my feet are killing me.''

"That good?"

"Nobody's died yet. Are you writing?"

"Yeah."

"Going to bed soon?"

"In about five minutes."

"Don't forget to close the window in Kevin's room."

"Yes, dear."

"Give him Cream of Wheat for breakfast."

"Yes, dear."

"And don't forget to... "

"Good night, dear."

"Good night," she sighed. Larry knew she was smiling.

He sweated out another thirty minutes to make sure she didn't call back. After checking Kevin and closing his window, he put on the blue windbreaker and pulled on a pair of surgical gloves (Marie kept a box of them in the hall closet for God knows what reason).

At 12:52, he took the phone off the hook, stepped out the back door and started the stopwatch. One hour maximum. Ten minutes there, thirty-minute wait, ten minutes back. The other ten was for unscheduled delays. If opportunity didn't knock in that time frame, there was always tomorrow.

The gate swung open on freshly oiled hinges. The bike scrunched over patches of gravel as he picked up speed — around the corner out onto Frederica Street.

LARRY CHECKED HIS WATCH. Twenty-five minutes and the back door hadn't opened once. He fidgeted, tried to concentrate on the house, anxious about getting caught, anxious to get back to his son. Hating the idea of waiting another night.

He crouched among the young Manitoba maples that

grew by the garage. The setting was perfect. 154 MacGiver was built so close to the next house that it effectively blocked most of the second house's windows. The other neighbour was shielded by the birch and poplars, and the street was hidden not only by the hedge and maples, but by a huge willow that draped the house with its branches.

Out back, in the alley, garages and trees blocked all light except for a few flecks of pinkish-orange that filtered through the leaves from The Pen's parking lot and struck the garage door.

Larry wiggled a small stick between his fingers. The shotgun lay in the grass within arm's reach.

The door opened. He stifled a breath.

A figure appeared, silhouetted against the screen door. Hinges rasped as she pushed it open.

Barely able to control the urge to run, Larry felt his Adam's apple swell, felt his fingers slide around the gun.

She was Asian. Wrapped in a short silk robe, her black hair gleamed in the light from the house.

''Easy, Field,'' he told himself.

Slowly, he rose, hugging the garage's shadow. His knees popped like pistol shots to his adrenalin-charged ears.

Another silhouette materialized at the door. ''Kiki,'' said a voice. ''Come on, we have gentlemen waiting.''

Kiki lingered for a moment before she slipped back inside, returning the porch to darkness.

''Jesus!'' gasped Larry, collapsing against the garage. He sucked in a dozen deep breaths while arming sweat off his face.

On shaky legs, he trotted down the alley toward the bike. It took all his concentration to unscrew the silencer without dropping it. Thirty seconds later, shotgun Velcroed inside his windbreaker, he tried vainly to pedal off the tension.

THE SKY WAS CAMOUFLAGED by low clouds that threatened rain. A low breeze blew cool air off the lake. The occasional glint of a streetlight seeped through the swaying branches of the willow that leaned on the house.

Larry huddled against the garage, the quiet fueling his paranoia. A creaking tree was a passing neighbour who loved the idea of getting to use 911. A bird on a roof was a patrol car turning into the alley.

"You're wasting your time, pal," he told himself, half hoping he was. His enthusiasm had waned considerably since Wednesday. Thursday, he'd waited the whole half hour without seeing a soul. Yesterday, Marie had been too busy at the hospital to call, forcing him to stay home. To-night, it had been almost one before she'd called. Now, the bars were closing, and the hookers would be too busy to come out for fresh air.

Just as well, he thought miserably. This shit is getting out of hand. It's a game, a scenario, war games. You do every-thing as if it were real. Everything but pull the trigger.

That was the plan. Except on Wednesday he'd damn near crossed the line. When his fingers curled around the shotgun and sensed its power... "I wouldn't have done it," he argued with himself. "I'm not crazy." Still, he'd lain awake that night wondering if there was a dark side to him that was capable of coldly snuffing a human life.

The thought produced a nervous shiver.

What if he'd actually done it? Premeditated murder. Twenty-five years! Without parole. And in a concrete battle zone with real criminals. He'd go nuts. And what about Marie and Kevin?

"Stop it!" he scolded himself. "I'm not a murderer. At worst, I'm a peeping Tom with an illegal firearm. Tell the judge the truth about being a quirky writer out soaking up atmosphere."

With resurgent confidence, Larry checked the stopwatch and looked around. All the nearby houses were dark. Even the windows of 154 were heavily curtai...

The door opened. Larry caught sight of her in the brief flood of light before she stepped out. She wore a white lace halter top and a dark wrap-around skirt.

A match flare sent light sparks off a pair of dangling earrings.

Larry's fingers laced themselves around the shotgun.

The match disappeared into the orange glow of a cigarette.

"Easy. It's just a game."

Despite the cool air, Larry's lips tasted salty. *It's not real. Close your eyes, visualize what would happen. The blast hits her in the chest. Her eyes...* She...

The picture wouldn't come.

"Fuck it." He stepped into the open, shotgun in the shadow of his leg.

"Who is there?" French accent.

Great, thought Larry, I'm stalking a cliché.

"Come here," he croaked, glad for the security of darkness.

"Oh, but why don't you come here?" she teased.

Larry sucked in air to control his breathing. "I can't go in there." This was taking too long.

"So you are a shy boy." Spiked heels clicked on the steps. "Or perhaps too easy to recognize?" Larry sensed she was smiling, enjoying this. "Collette likes to play with shy boys.'' She was only twenty feet away. He could make out the tight curls in her shoulder length hair.

''Over here,'' he whispered, stepping toward the back of the garage.

''No, no.'' She held up a finger. ''Inside or out, it is the same price.''

Larry's mouth felt as if he'd eaten a bowl of sand.

''A hundred bucks for five minutes, okay?''

She grinned and silently swung open the small gate, long legs slipping out the slit in her skirt.

''Okay, shyboy, you have a date with Collette.''

She faced him, back to the garage's wooden door, face caught in a small circle of light from the parking lot. ''Pay first, or I go back inside.''

Larry's breath slowed. Fear drained away. His blood iced. The gun came up.

''Oh, God!'' Collette stumbled back against the garage.

''Don't scream,'' spat Larry, finger on the trigger, muzzle leveled at her chest. He soaked up the terror in her eyes, the mask of fear, the nervous twitching of her limbs.

''W... what do you want?''

His finger tightened on the trigger.

''...please... don't hurt me...''

The shotgun woofed.

A fist-sized hole appeared in Collette's chest and pinned her to the garage. Dark flecks sprayed the door. A gurgling choke erupted from her mouth, followed by a river of blood. As the pellets tore into her, the terror in her eyes gave way to pain, disbelief, confusion.

The blast had blown her halter off, and Larry gasped at the hole and the blood that flowed down her flat, white belly. His eyes lingered on her erect nipples as she slid down the door. The wide streak of blood left behind was flaked with bits of bone.

A barking dog snapped him out of his trance.

"Jesus!" he wheezed, bolting, choking for air. "Jesus! Shit!" His head burned. Tears blinded him. His feet ran of their own will.

Another dog took up the call.

Vomit burst out of his nose and mouth, splattering his jacket. He staggered, almost fell. *Christ, dogs! Didn't think of dogs. Every alley has dogs.* Balance regained, he ran the gauntlet of barking hounds, more of them taking up the chorus with each passing house. Larry brushed the bile from his face. *Think... don't panic... go by the numbers.* He got off the gravel and ran down the grass at the alley's edge.

Pump empty shell from the gun. Then the other two.

The sliding action of the pump sounded like rifle shots.

"Shit!" One shell jiggled out of his hand. He skidded to a stop, dropped to his knees and palmed the grass. A porch light flicked on as his hand closed over the ribbed, plastic shell.

Don't look back. Shells in pocket. Unscrew silencer.

The gun was in place under his zipped jacket by the time he reached the bike.

Streets whizzed past. Headlights behind brought panic, then relief when they weren't patrol cars.

It began to rain.

Good. Yeah. People expect bikes to go fast when it rains. Rain covers tracks.

Ball field. Over fence. Pull up sod. Drop in gun and silencer. Replace sod.

Marks Street. Sewer grate. Slow down. Throw in three shells. Two new, one used.

Selkirk Street. Sewer grate. Surgical gloves, inside out, knotted. Bombs away.

The streets were a blur. Hours later, it would be difficult to recall any details of his flight.

Home.

Leave bike in yard. A bicycle in the shed all night wouldn't be wet.

Back door. No noise. No neighbours.

In house. Put phone back on hook. Check Kevin. Still breathing. Check again. Yeah, breathing.

Basement. Strip. Look for bloodstains. None, just puke.

Soak clothes with Spray 'n Wash. Hot water, lots of soap. Wash mud off shoes.

Upstairs. Shower. Scrape under fingernails.

Cigarette.

THE DAY AFTER THE KILLING, the Chronicle-Journal screamed: EXECUTION-STYLE MURDER AT BAWDY HOUSE.

Everyone had an opinion: disgruntled john, blackmailed john, drugs, she was an informant, she owed money, a random slaying. The last of these was repeatedly played down by police to avoid panic (it was barely two years since a psychotic killer had terrified the city by strangling six people before committing suicide).

Larry's fear and anxiety waned after a few days. He'd read somewhere that homicide cases grow cold after the first twenty-four hours, but they never disappeared altogether.

Sure, there was guilt, but it wasn't uncontrollable.

And there were dreams, though most people would have called them nightmares. Larry didn't. For him, they were a reminder that he would never forget Collette's terror or eyes, or the gamut of his emotions in those few short seconds.

Sometimes Marie would waken him and stare at him, and he'd wonder if he'd talked in his sleep.

But nothing was ever said.

"NEVER GOING TO GET ME, BOYS," Larry crowed as he cruised past Robin's Donuts, where an empty police car sat in the lot.

The shotgun and silencer were gone. Dismantled and thrown into the Kam River from three different bridges. The shoes and bike tires were shredded and long buried at the municipal landfill.

No witnesses. No forensics. No loose ends.

Larry had spent a lot of time at his typewriter since that night behind 154 MacGiver.

TWO MONTHS TO THE DAY AFTER he'd got rid of the gun, he returned home after a run with Jack. The mailman had just left the yard. Phone bill, something from Greenpeace, and a white envelope that stopped Larry in the living room. A lump swelled in his throat as he tore it open. He scanned the words, blinked and read it again. As he read the signature for the third time, he became aware of the smile that had stretched his face.

"MARIEEEE!!!!"

Larry Field had just sold his first story.

* * *

"CRAP!!"

Larry stabbed the Delete key and spun around in his chair. Outside the study window, moonlight rippled the river as it slipped past the end of the yard. His reflection glowed orange on the glass as he lit a cigarette. The disc player kicked on the Black Crowes.

Three years.

The stories sold well. His first novel, moderately well.

The house was bigger. So was the mortgage.

The '79 T-bird had become a '92 Riviera.

Marie still worked nights at the hospital so he could write full-time.

That was the best. He was a writer — a real I-make-a-living-doing-this writer.

And yet sometimes it still wasn't enough. The Riviera wasn't a Porsche. There were no movie deals. Marie still worked.

And writing for a living was hard. He had to produce.

And he was getting stale.

Larry crushed his cigarette into an ashtray full of butt stumps and lit another. Leaning back, he closed his eyes and looked for Collette.

There she was, green eyes never more alive than just before they died.

Or were they blue?

He felt the shotgun jerk. Saw the blast knock her back into the garage door... No, she was already against the door.

He could smell the gunpowder, but had he been able to smell the blood? Or her bowels?

Larry opened his eyes and stared at the river.

Time may have fogged the images, but he remembered how he'd felt. That emotional rush. And how his mind fought through it. He wondered if he'd ever feel like that again.

Then, it came.

"No way, Field," he snapped, shocked that he'd even had the thought.

A while later it came back.

He pushed it away.

An hour later, he faced the computer and began to make a list.

Just to kill time.

Lady Day
John Futhey

SHE AWOKE DISCOURAGED, the hands of the clock still some
way from her usual hour of 5:30, Dora May Marriott, *anno
aetatis suae* 60. Promptly at 5:30 she would arise, put on her
1943 dressing gown of the sleazy material and padded shoulders, and a pair of mottled orange Woolworth slippers, move
past the curling beige wallpaper of her frosty bedroom, through
the black hall, past the cubicles where her brothers slept, to
the yet colder bathroom. From there, carefully, down stairs
with worn-out rubber treads, to the kitchen, to the lighting of
the wood stove, to the cooking of the same breakfast she had
cooked in the same quantities, the ingredients bought at the
same place, for the past 30 years. She pulled back the eider-
down which had slipped to the floor during the night and
drew it up over her head. Its cozy enclosure brought a kind of
peace, eventually a strange comfort. Surely if she could feel
discouraged, given this long and repetitive sentence, that was
a kind of triumph, however bleak. This sense of triumph was
itself part of the repetitive nature of her life, she knew, and
was always thin and short-lived. If she stayed in bed, the
monstrous truth would again overcome her, and return her to
a state more desolate than the first. The only way to combat
the enveloping despair of aloneness was to get up, no matter

how much earlier than necessary.

With a determination to oppose what always was, she went this time directly downstairs. After lighting the stove, she sat for a moment at the table with just the vague flame of the fire through the stove lids and the soft light of the tiny globe of the 1940 world, which sat on the television. She was surprised at how dark it was outside. Yesterday had been so bright and spring-like. The light from the kitchen fell through the window on the misshapen rogoza rose bush. It would eventually bloom in a bounty of pink scent; now it looked its ugliest with its shrivelled branches and few wrinkled hips. With renewed despair she saw its body swaying stiffly in the thrust of a north-east wind — a north-easter the twenty-fifth day of March! It was like a denial of parole, another sentence just as the torture seemed to be ending.

She always found it hard to accept a desolate day on the heels of a divine one: it seemed illogical and perverse. Even worse, though, was the coming of desolation upon a day already established in sunshine and colour; the appearance of ragged cloud steamers moving inexorably in and thinning out the sun's growing warmth, then taking it away entirely as the sky turned to steel and bleakness.

Perhaps, she concluded as the kitchen warmed and the rosebush grew pale, it would be best if changes of weather could always occur while one slept, as this one had. Brightness should not fade from the air while one watched. Of course there were those who had to go out at night and people on shift work. They would see these transformations, and it didn't seem fair that such persons should always be required as witnesses. Still, she would prefer such an arrangement: to have it over, done with before she got up! Still thinking it over, she set to work on the porridge that her brothers shunned, but ate. They had not accepted this ''fast'' kind — ''swill,'' they called it. Real porridge sat on the stove all night and was then fit to eat. Dora May saw no difference in taste at all and had at last refused to prepare the double-boiler, all-night variety. Finally, after persistent parody had no mending effect upon their sister, the men had eaten it, sullenly, swallowing it down in lumps so that its taste would not linger and taint the palate.

The brothers arrived in the kitchen, as they always did, just as she began the frying of the eggs. They waited while she served the porridge, all the while keeping an eye on the eggs that must not have yolks broken. As usual, breakfast was silent. Its images were of Dora May passing back and forth from stove to table, and of fingers pressing toast into runny eggs. No one spoke; the men because sleep had wiped out yesterday's subjects, and today's had not yet occurred — no barn had yet been visited, no cattle touched — Dora May, because she enjoyed the silence. The babble of the noon meal was always excruciating, for in the morning's work her brothers found their tongues.

The departure of the pastoral quintet was led by the eldest, the first to shove back his chair and wipe his hands on his pants. (She had foiled their use of the tablecloth for this purpose by switching to a thick plastic cover, which they now scored with knife edges.) With due lapse of time, the other four pushed back their chairs and waited in line to pick up jackets, boots and gloves from their pegs in the back kitchen. Dora (it was her brothers who insisted on Dora May ever since, as schoolboys put in contact once and only once with a French song, they had hit on the hilarious similarity of sound between *dormez-vous* and Dora May-vous) regarded the table litter, the egg congealing on plastic, the scatter rugs (failed attempts at sprucing up the kitchen) despoiled. Time to look out the window, she said to herself, as she raised the shade which her brothers insisted on keeping drawn while they ate.

In the stiff frozen earth stuck the dead grasses and last autumn leaves; tormented corn stalks leaned crazily before the wind, and in the lilac tree, the pinched valentine heart leaves, drained of colour, still resisted pitifully. Down the road walked a solitary figure, and somewhat nearer, two ravens, swarthy northern vultures, alighted and jabbed at something in the frozen ditch. On the sill, geraniums, like Jesse-trees, huge and knotted, weeks away from going outside, gave off their fecund pungency.

Getting dressed seemed a greater effort than doing the dishes. Her brothers hated what they called an "unclean" house. What they meant was anything that ran opposition to their own mess or that interfered with a food-laden table and their immediate satisfaction. She often imagined a reversal of conditions — her brothers confined within the house, perpetually preparing meals for her, drying and washing dishes, mopping floors, scrubbing their own underwear after they had picked it up with an underwear stick (she smiled). She wiped desultorily at the cooling stove with a piece of waxed paper. Since bread was no longer wrapped in waxed paper and she'd had a desperate mess when she'd forgotten and tried to clean the stove with cellophane, she occasionally used the waxed paper on the roll, though never in her brothers' presence. A terrible waste they said. What did they think she should use? The unsliced bread they demanded was no longer wrapped in waxed paper; and having got it, she always cut it too fat or too thin, never just right. She turned on the radio and a voice prophesied a glorious future with the purchase of a lottery ticket.

The stove needed wood. She ought to get dressed. The old house was full of draughts and sighs — fine for brothers who came in to eat, sleep and watch TV in their long underwear, but a trial for someone to live in. Essentially, it was not cleanable. Uneven floors, corners out of kilter, cockeyed windows plugged with wadded Kleenex. Her brothers thought they looked after her very well — the woodbox was always full. She wanted for nothing, because, she thought, I need *everything* that they can't imagine. The piece of wood was large and she looked about for the lifter, making so much noise that she missed the first knock at the door, and was quite startled by the second, so imperious it was.

For a moment she could not think what to do. Her brothers had warned her about Raleigh men and Amway products. They didn't need any, they said. Moreover, there were the "Witnesses" and assorted lots like them creeping around the countryside. She went finally to the back kitchen, climbed the woodpile, and peeped out the holes between roof and wall to see a small man in a fedora carrying what seemed more like a briefcase than a suitcase of wares. He looked tired, not at all full of the pent-up energies and happy zeal she had seen on the faces of the evangelists. This one had a tiny beard. She patted her own untidy top, re-arranged her kimono, stood well behind the door, and opened it a crack. "Yes?" she said, in anything but confidence. The little man seemed surprised and peered around the door tentatively. With him came the cold breath of clouded March. "Miss Marriott? Miss Dora Marriott?" He stepped forward past the door. He was not wearing boots, just shoes, and his trousers were ankle-length, showing his crinkled socks. Dora had never liked pants that revealed socks; they made you look ridiculous, even if you were good looking. Here was this short man with even shorter pants and now, she noticed, something of a paunch pushing past his coat. "Miss Marriott?" he said again. This time she nodded. He broke into a toothless smile. "You don't know me," he said in what now seemed a cultured voice, "but we've written a lot of letters to one another. I'm your pen pal, Vern Rameau, from Quebec City. Glad to meet you, at last. Are you busy? I see you're just up. Couldn't call — couldn't find your telephone number. I'm really glad to see you — strange to meet what has been only a projection of the imagination based on handwriting. You don't look at all as I imagined you."

She was shocked. It had never crossed her mind that a pen pal would turn up here. Indeed, she couldn't remember ever really much wanting to meet any of them; just to write to them and hear from them seemed enough in the face of her brothers' mockery. She stared foolishly at him.

"I see you're surprised, too; bet you thought I'd be tall, dark and handsome, didn't you?" He smiled the toothless smile again. The open door made the stove smoke. That was finally what brought her to her senses enough to ask him to sit down. He wiped his feet carefully and took no notice of the disarray. "Oh, warmth," he said. "This is a very inclement day. I prefer clement days. Even my feet are cold." He saw her looking at the pants. "Meant to have these old-fashioned cuffs removed. Didn't have time." As if it had to be done at once, Dora went to the window and snapped off a piece of yellowed parsley and began picking up dishes from the table.

"Here, let me help," said Vern, and Dora's gratitude was unbounded. Here was the dim figure of letters, in the flesh, wanting to help with the drudgery of the day. "Have you had anything to eat?" she asked; and while he ate, he talked. It was to her a wonderful conversation, in which she partici-

pated tacitly. He told her of Quebec City — of Bonhomme
Carnival, of the Chateau Frontenac and the Plains of Abraham,
of the churches, the bobsled run, and of the splendid view of
the city as one came up river on the *Empress of England*. He
didn't tell her that the *Empress* no longer sailed, but did pause
eventually to say that someone had stolen his money on the
way up and that he would like to borrow just enough to get
back to Quebec City.

She turned cold. Indeed, she was terrified and she saw
again the clutter of the kitchen and the unprepared dinner.
Her brothers wanted a hot dinner — usually she spent the
morning preparing it. Vern said he was sorry he'd asked; he
could probably manage to get home some way or another.

"No, no," she said. "You came all this way to see me. It's
just that I . . ." She hesitated, then remembered a line from a
TV play — "I don't just know whether I have a cheque."

"I have one," said Vern. "Suppose I just fill in twenty
dollars. I'll write in my name and you sign it." The process
astounded her; it seemed so complex, so impossible that so
significant and legal and tremendous a thing as a cheque
should have two people writing on it. It must be illegal. A
dreadful mix-up would ensue, she was sure.

"Wait," she said, controlling the panic of future and
present. She knew her brothers kept cheques and wrote them.
They mystified her, so magical they seemed. Sign them and
you had money. It didn't seem to follow. In the desk in the
parlour she found the cheques and was afraid to touch them.
"I'll be right out," she called. "I'm going to put it in an
envelope for you. You can put it in your briefcase and keep it
safe from stealers." She went dazed up to her room and
stared at the impossible thing.

"Pay to the order of" confounded her. Whatever would

she do. She stood in terror at her table and noticed finally her Grade 8 arithmetic book and remembered with joy pages of cheques, I.O.U.'s and promissory notes, none of which she'd ever got right. Good in literature, utterly ignorant in arithmetic, she'd heard one teacher tell another. With relief she found the pages of cheques and copied laboriously. Two she had to destroy, for she put the same name as the example copy in the "Pay to" line. At last it seemed right: "Pay to Vern Rameau Twenty Dollars." The signature was another matter. Examples gave M.E. Aston, G.O. Fox. A note said that one should always sign with his regular signature. At last she put down Pen Pal Dora, her normal signature when writing to Vern, and felt it right — it certainly looked right. In the space for account number she put 5396, for she saw that number was used on all the example cheques. It must be the number of the account where all the money was that you got with the cheques. As she put the arithmetic book back, she saw something else; a leather volume of Milton presented to her in Grade 8 for reciting "Lord Ullin's Daughter" and the Books of the Old Testament so well. She had never indulged in her reward, though she knew that Milton ought to be admired, for Miss Rumford called him "God's poet" and she'd always liked the feel of the pebbly red leather. One day she'd get around to him, when she had more time and no mocking eyes upon her. At night, in the privacy of bed, tiredness always triumphed despite intention. Miss Rumford had given it to her, Miss Rumford of England who'd lasted just until Christmas at the school and had then scurried home. Dora lasted until June and was then made housekeeper. And in Milton Dora kept the still crisp $5 bill given her so long ago by a visiting uncle she'd not seen before or since. She longed to keep it, so fresh and fine it was, and felt that in parting with it she parted with an asset indefinable, yet cogent. Still, she knew that Vern might need it; she put it beside the cheque in the envelope and sealed it.

She moved quickly downstairs, the pressure of time so terrible. Her brothers wouldn't throw him out, but they'd behave rudely. They were always suspicious, more suspicious the more she was innocent. They made guilt out of innocence.

"Vern," she said, handing him the envelope as he stood touching the geraniums and looking out the window, "thank you for coming. I've enjoyed the visit so — it was wonderful of you to come to see me. It's been a real visitation, as we say here." She hesitated, then kissed him on the cheek; he smiled. They shook hands and he set off through the shed into the mean noon hour. At the gate he turned and waved, then moved off down the road. Dora lashed into cleaning and cooking, deliberately blanking out the morning and concentrating on the meal. No hint of her morning should they ever have. Would three pounds of frozen beans be enough? She thought so — if she didn't eat many herself.

At eleven that night, in their underwear, the brothers watched the news, listening raptly but uncomprehendingly to the closing item of the local, read by a fat sweaty young man with thick glasses — the item *de rigueur*, slightly off beat, but significant. It concerned a short man, without boots, who had tried to cash a cheque at a local bank, around three that afternoon. However, the sharp eye of the teller, a certain Mrs. Kralin from Concession 6, employed there for only three weeks, had spotted the fraud, for the cheque had been signed "Pen Pal Dora," with no surname. When she had tried to question him he had turned red and frightened. The screen then showed a shot of the bank, on a tilt, from an old

postcard, and a watery photo of Mrs. Kralin. The man had
grabbed the cheque and fled the bank. Although he'd managed to take the cheque, he'd left an envelope. In it was found
a $5 bill with a picture of George V. Police surmised that this
had been stolen from a coin collection and anyone knowing
anything of this or anyone recently robbed should contact the
police. The teller had also been very suspicious of the name
"Vern Rameau" and suspected herself that the person en-
dorsing the cheque was not the same as the person named on
the cheque. Forgery was declared; everyone should be on
guard.

"Sounds French to me," said the eldest, without looking
at the others, his face reflecting heavy thought. They nodded
together. "And that's unlikely around here. Lots of I-talians,
no French."

The second brother said tentatively, "Unless that was only
his father's name. The mother could've been English."

"Don't know the name in these parts," declared the eldest. After a silence meant to impress the finality of that
consideration, he added, "This Dora, though, we might know
of. Wonder if it's that Dora Lurey up off the second sideroad?"

They considered this sagely, still watching the TV, as the
fat man's pointer hovered over Canada's climatic surface.

"Or Dora May Marriott," proffered the youngest, with a
sly grin. What a stroke that was! How they laughed and
poked each other in mirth at this outrageous suggestion. The
rest of the weather report was lost as they repeated again and
again the absurdity of *Dora May Marriott*, casting the name
back and forth in a jubilee of hilarity.

Upstairs, Dora slept undisturbed, unaware of the little
branches tapping on the pane as the March sleet slapped them
to and fro. Nor did she hear her brothers laughing. She knew

her own rapture and dreamed of some day going to Quebec City and surprising Vern. The brothers banged up the stairs, laughing, shoving each other into the walls. The house fell silent, except for muffled outbursts of laughter from the bedrooms and the seething of the sleet outside. On the kitchen window-sill, the tomato juice tins gleamed like *argent-vive* and the house was filled with acrid fume of geranium.

Vern rode through the sleet in the front seat of a car with a man and his wife who were returning from Florida. He sat careful and small beside them and thought, "Lord, what I have to go through to get west." He was telling them about his trip: a cross-country tour to visit all of his pen pals, twenty of them, right to the west coast. "Wasn't that a remarkable project?" said the wife to her husband after they'd let Vern off at the crossroads and turned into their drive. "It's so seldom that pen pals ever meet. What an adventure — to set off to meet all those that he corresponds with."

The husband waited to reply until he'd unlocked the door and stepped in out of the sleet. "Well," he said with barely suppressed mirth, "I hope they all like somebody that smells like geraniums."

There was a brittle silence. "So, he smelled like geraniums. I liked him. He will be well received wherever he goes." The statements were acid-etched. She was about to say more to destroy the bewildered expression on her husband's face — he was always bewildered when the reception of his remarks was not what he had pre-determined it would be. As she took off her coat, however, and watched him pouting in with the luggage, then slamming the door, she decided not to cap her remarks with the news of the $20 bill she'd given Vern as he had left the car. That would be their secret.

Last Swim

Marianne Jones

THE TIRES CRUNCHED OVER THE gravel as the blue Toyota fought its way up the winding camp road, slapped by jackpines where the way was narrowest. The arrival of a car had always brought bathing suit-clad children and barking dogs running to the top of the hill, but only the unnatural silence greeted Anja as she pulled up behind the camp. She paused for a moment, as if expecting to feel more than the normal nostalgia. She regretted again not bringing the children, but they were both too involved in their own plans; and Peter had opposed it.

There was no point, he had told her reasonably. It would just upset them, losing something they wouldn't otherwise miss if she didn't make an issue of it. After all, it didn't mean the same thing to them that it did to her.

That, at least, was true. Bryce and Sara had enjoyed visiting here while Hannah was alive, and later, when the camp was Anja's; but it was hardly the same as growing up here every summer, with her aunts and uncles and cousins and dogs and grandparents. She hardly knew how to explain to them the significance of it, other than to say lamely, ''There's where we used to go to swimming lessons,'' and ''This is where we used to hike for picnics.'' She wanted them to appreciate the richness of those memories, to pass them on as a precious legacy, but succeeded only in sounding like a tour guide.

Well, if Peter got his way, it wouldn't matter anymore. Once they were settled in Belleville, Bryce and Sara would have to make their own memories. The camp would just be a soft-focus photograph in Anja's mind, growing paler and softer with time, like the snapshots in her parents' family album.

She walked down the long wooden stairway to the bottom of the hill. The steps were perpetually rickety. Her grandfather used to limp around every summer after his stroke, stubbornly repairing the loose boards with his one good arm, swearing at his own clumsiness. He had built everything: the camp, the dock, the sauna, the boats, before his health began deteriorating. One summer he had taught Anja how to saw a two-by-four, and how to nail down the short boards in the stairs. She had been interested, but her parents had disapproved of girls doing carpentry, and the lessons stopped.

She built a fire in the woodbox behind the steambath and went to fill the boiler with water. She left it to heat while she looked around.

The agent had told them there was an interested couple. There was still some disagreement over the price; the place hadn't been kept up the last few years. She and Peter had taken the kids travelling, and she only managed the occasional weekend here. The dock was swaybacked and shifted like a suspended bridge under a person's weight.

Four crumpled and faded pop cans rusted in the sooty bed of the firepit beside a few charred logs: the remains of someone's party from a year ago. Some of the surrounding bricks were scattered in the grass. The aluminum lawn chairs had been folded and tucked away under the steambath, but the wooden one sat out as always, too heavy to move. The last flakes of paint had peeled away aeons ago.

Anja reached out a finger to touch the weathered chair, still referred to as ''Grandma's chair'' five years after her death. There Hannah — Grandma — spent her summer afternoons, talking to her daughters, her puffy fist curled around a bottle of beer. Snatches of her conversations, in her heavy Finn accent, would float like music to Anja and the other grandchildren playing by the water: rumours and comments about people named Limpi Heinamaki, Matti Oikenen, Jari Ittala.

Hannah did all of the talking, while her daughters nodded and let the flow of words wash over them. Trying to insert a sentence of their own was as futile as trying to stop an express train by stepping in its path. Hannah would close her eyes and roll on, hypnotized by the summer air and the beer, and the sound of her own voice: *Like, she doesn't have no common sense, she's a nice person, but not so intelligent, I said to her, 'Why do you put up with that? The hell with them!' And she knows I'm right, but she goes on and on, yust the same, some people are like that, they yust can't help themselves, it's their condition...*

Pausing only to swig and belch comfortably, she didn't appear to need the polite murmurs of her listeners, only their presence. Sometimes the adults took shifts listening to her. She was inexhaustible then, in her prime.

Anja went to check on the steambath. The thermometer registered a comfortable 70 degrees Celsius, and the water in the boiler was steaming. A few leaves had drifted in from outside, but otherwise everything was orderly: a half-full bottle of Suave shampoo, several cakes of yellow soap, the loofah and long-handled brush hanging on the wall. She went back outside to shove more split birch into the firebox before changing.

The dressing room looked the same as it had for twenty years. It still boasted half a dozen ancient bathing suits in a variety of sizes and colours, hanging from nails in the wall. A few faded plastic baby toys from someone's childhood, the words "Hi girls" penned on the wood beside a knothole, a tattered rag rug on the floor, and a container of Johnson's baby powder on the shelf, for after the sauna. She changed quickly into an old pink bathing suit that was out of fashion but still wearable.

It felt strange to be here alone. Steambaths were not solitary events; they were taken in pairs, or groups with lots of laughing and reminiscing, cold drinks and confidences. She had never in her memory sat in here alone. Peter had disapproved of her coming by herself. She was just prolonging the pain, he said, making it harder on herself.

She threw a dipper of cold water at the rocks and sighed, an exhalation of pleasure at the hiss and the cloud of steam that curled up around her. She listened to the fire throb in the woodbox and leaned back, eyes closed, knees pulled up against her chest. Sweat beaded her face and arms, and her hair formed small damp curls. The smell of birch smoke, hot cedar and Sunlight soap permeated the room. It was a good smell, a smell of childhood, of keeping cool in the old washtub on the floor of the sauna, while her mother and aunts and grandmother filled the top bench, and their chatter rose to the ceiling with the steam.

Her grandmother, with her heavy accent, her puffy hand clutched around a sweating bottle of beer, had been the largest of all those large Finn ladies overflowing the wooden benches. Everything about her was larger than life: her appetites, her temper, her opinions. She dominated and bullied; chased the grandchildren into the lake for a before-breakfast swim every morning. She sent the adults on blueberry-picking expeditions for the pies she would bake in the woodstove. Her fights with her husband were legendary.

Anja lacked her grandmother's fire, her drive to be always on top. She disliked scenes, finding it easier to acquiesce. If Peter decided that she should stay at home or that they should or shouldn't cultivate another couple's friendship, or that they should sell the camp, she might feebly attempt to argue her point of view, but quickly sank under the waves of his over-whelming logic. Except that her own conviction remained there, submerged, like a wreck on the ocean floor, indefensible but real.

"What are you complaining about?" her mother would demand. "You have a good husband who's a good provider. He doesn't drink or chase women."

Good men, by her mother's standards, were defined by the horrendous things they didn't do, but women could never do enough good to be deserving of such men.

A log shifted in the firebox and popped, while the water bubbled in the rusty boiler. The sauna temperature was rising. Anja wrung out a washcloth in the water bucket and put it on her face. She smiled, picturing her grandmother as she used to sit up there, with an old pair of water-soaked underpants on her grey head, to substitute for a washcloth. As a child Anja would stare at them and wonder what stores sold such gigantic gar-ments. Her grandmother was never self-conscious about any-thing, least of all the picture she made in the intimate darkness of the sauna: white mounds of naked flesh flowing like bread dough across the top bench, round pink face partially obscured by her indecent head covering. In her domain she was arbiter of what was correct. She made pronouncements with unchal-lenged authority: Never Let a Man Rule You, The Capitalist System Was to Blame, We Have to Fight For Peace. She subscribed to *Northern Neighbours* and was scornful of the western news media and its coverage of world events. The real truth was to be found in the socialist publications that came in her mail every month.

When Anja was ten her grandmother had brought her to play the piano for a Communist Party talent night. The hall was filled with grey-haired sympathizers and their grandchildren. The meeting was conducted in Finn, which Anja didn't understand. One young boy stood up on the stage and recited a poem in Finn about war, which had all the grandmothers searching for their Kleenex. He was warmly applauded and followed by a woman who made a long and emotional plea for peace.

Then Anja was introduced and stumbled up the aisle toward the piano where she played a Chopin waltz. The bourgeois music did not appear to offend the comrades, who were pleased to welcome young blood to the Cause.

Afterward, Anja's grandmother said, "I will never forget you for what you did for your grandmother tonight." But Anja's brother told her later that her name was now on the RCMP's list of suspicious persons.

During the first years of her marriage, Anja would receive little gifts from her grandmother — tea towels and aprons, folded neatly around communist tracts. When she opened her grandmother's wedding gift of dishes, a pamphlet fell out of the box, explaining that universal peace would happen when the world embraced communism.

Then, as if in retaliation, Peter's great-aunt put them on the mailing list of the Monarchist League of Canada. They received magazines with the Royal Family's picture on the covers, and pens emblazoned with the motto, "Monarchy is the Best Policy." Anja wondered if the RCMP was aware of this new twist, and if it cancelled out past indiscretions.

When Anja had met Peter at university, he was a member of

the Young Liberals Association. He was a supporter of Trudeau, a believer in federalism and bilingualism. She was drawn to his energy, the strength of his commitments.

Later, she realized how suffocating his drive and assurance could be, and his politics. She preferred her inner world to the irrelevance of the real one. Thoughts had always been more important to her than events.

Peter was affectionate and thoughtful, scrupulous about remembering anniversaries and birthdays, but his excitement was reserved for big projects and plans that did not involve his family. Of course, Anja could have immersed herself in his interests, but that would have meant getting babysitters in the evenings, and anyway, she felt out of place among all those energetic, outwardly-focused people who were not given much to reflection; they seemed always to know the answers without hearing the questions. She preferred to spend her evenings playing with her children, smelling their sweetness and reading them stories. Peter's friends thought her dull.

THE TEMPERATURE GAUGE WAS UP to 80 degrees Celsius, and Anja was feeling uncomfortable. She climbed down and stepped outside, where the breeze off the lake made her shiver. Quickly, before she lost her nerve, she ran the length of the trembling dock and dove into the cold water, coming up quickly to gasp big breaths of cool air. She struck out on her back, blinking up at the comic-book sky. From out on the water, for some reason, the shoreline had always seemed to threaten her. The sense of menace increased as she swam further out toward the centre of the lake. It was the sense of being in foreign territory, away from familiar rocks and trees. Always, she had swum out as far as she dared, until panic drove her back in hard, churning strokes.

But not this time. She swam out steadily, fighting her unease, determined to cross the lake. Not that she was in any real danger. The lake was too small and heavily-populated, and she was too strong a swimmer to have any qualms about drowning. But as she glided past Tapio's dock toward Nevala's bright red steambath, her mother's cautioning voice blended with her swimming teacher's, nagging her to turn back. *Never swim alone. Wait a half hour after a meal. You're too young to go across the lake.*

As she passed the bay and approached the sandbar at Wainio's, she felt prickles of apprehension. She tried to distract herself by wondering again why Hannah had left the camp to her. Anja had been as surprised as the rest of the family when they found out. She was not aware of any inordinately loving bond between them; her grandmother was not the affectionate type — a commander has to be wary of familiarity with the troops. Perhaps, with the rest of the family now scattered across the continent, Hannah simply wanted the camp to stay with the only relatives left in Thunder Bay. There would be less likelihood of it being sold.

But circumstances had outfoxed the old girl. Peter's firm was transferring him to Belleville. He saw little sense in keeping up a dilapidated cottage a thousand miles away for sentimental reasons. Besides, lake property was in high demand. They could make a substantial down payment on a house in Belleville with what the camp would bring.

Anja could not disagree with such reasoning; but the finality of such a decision worried her. Could she amputate her past, with no allowance for second thoughts?

She knew what her mother would do. She would shed her tears quietly in private, and then bravely dab them away and put on a cheerful face. She would not consider this remarkable or courageous; just her everyday duty, like making the bed or replacing a button on her husband's shirt.

There was an appealing simplicity to that way of life. One never had to make decisions. When things went badly, women could always blame their men. "I didn't really think we should," they would murmur confidentially, "but, you know, Harry insisted..." Their voices would trail off while the other women nodded sympathetically. They all knew what men were like.

Saying no to a husband was as indelicate as a girl handling carpentry tools.

Hannah would have had no patience with such submissive gentility. Anja remembered her pounding her fist like a general, her voice rising in excitement as she decried the brainwashing of women into giving in to the tyranny of men, until her husband, in search of peace and quiet, slipped outside, looking for something to fix as the rest of the family exchanged furtive smiles.

Anja shuddered as some weeds brushed her ankle. She was more than halfway across, and it wasn't getting any easier. She used the camps and saunas on the shore to maintain her bearings, but avoided focusing on them. They were a reminder of how far she was from the safety of her own shore. She forged ahead, breathing lightly and aiming steadily for the white boathouse on the far side. Her heart was beating rapidly, not from exertion, but from dread.

A motorboat started up from one of the camps around the point. She treaded water until it passed, then floated on her back to catch the waves, a habit from her childhood. She listened to the tinny whine of the motorboat under water, a sound that always reminded her of a large mosquito.

Smoke was puffing from the chimney of the blue steambath closest to her, with its matching cottage. All the camps on this lake came as matched sets: small saunas on the shoreline, larger cottages behind, always painted the same colour. In the early days when the Finns were buying up the camp property, the saunas were the first things to go up. The families would live in them until the cottages were built. It was a question of priorities.

Someone emerged from the blue sauna and waved at Anja. She waved back briefly and swam to the dock next to the white boathouse. She hung on the dock for a moment to catch her breath. She would come no closer than the end of the dock before turning around, feeling too much of a trespasser already.

Anja had been eleven before her mother had relented and allowed her to swim across one way. Her mother was at her side the whole time, in the rowboat. At the far shore Anja had begged to swim back, but, at her mother's insistence, had climbed sulkily into the boat and wrapped herself in a thick towel.

Her mother would disapprove even now if she saw Anja on the return journey with no accompanying boat. The thought made her feel bold and cheerful as she pushed through the silky folds of water that simultaneously resisted and yielded to the forward motion of her body. She churned ahead, feeling steadily stronger as she marked off camps on the passing shore: Heinamaki's, Himanen's, then Wainio's with the long white sandbar, Nevala's, Tapio's.

Approaching her own welcoming bay, with the birch stand almost obscuring the sauna, she felt a burst of exhilaration and began to race. Finally she was at the end of the swaybacked dock, out of breath, then touching bottom again. As she stood, momentarily dizzy, she saw Peter standing on the shore. He handed her a towel.

''You went across the lake?''

She nodded, out of breath.

"By yourself?"

"Sure," she said, rubbing her hair with the towel and smiling. She was still enjoying the feeling of having gotten away with something. "What brings you out here? I thought you weren't coming."

"I have some good news," he said. "I thought we might go out to celebrate."

She looked up at his boyish grin.

"That couple that was looking at the camp — they came up to our price. The agent just phoned me half an hour ago. We could drop in at the realtor's and sign on our way to the restaurant."

She looked at him without speaking. His head was framed by the poplar tree at the foot of the stairs. The same breeze that stirred his hair made the poplar leaves flutter like a frenetic garland. She felt a deep compassion for him. He had never known childhood summers at camp.

"Are you still feeling bad about selling the place?" he said. "It's the only sensible solution, honey. You know that." He looked suddenly deflated and apologetic. "Okay," he said, "maybe I shouldn't have rushed out here like this."

She smiled kindly. "I've decided not to sell it."

For a moment he was speechless. Then irritated. "What do you mean? We've been all over this."

She sat down on Hannah's chair and wrapped the towel around her. "I want Bryce and Sara to be able to wake up out here in the summer and play by the water and in the woods. I'd like them to have memories like I have, of steambaths and skinny dipping and campfires at night. I want them to feel connected to something." She spoke gently, lovingly, because she was so rich in memories that he had never had.

"You're not being rational, Anja. The place is falling apart.

My holidays are not that long, and I don't intend to spend them fixing this camp.''

"We'll work something out. My brother could come here with Gina and the kids. We could summer here together, and he could help me fix it up."

"You don't know anything about carpentry."

She smiled. "Maybe it's time I learned."

Peter left for town, Anja stayed to tidy up. A brisk late-afternoon wind had come up, whipping the water into manic waves. She remembered a morning when she was nine and woke to find herself alone in the camp. She had dressed quickly and run barefoot down the hill. Her mother was sitting on the end of the dock, her knees folded up under her chin, gazing across the lake, still white with mist. Vapour curled from the mug of coffee beside her. Anja ran along the dock, making it tremble under her feet, as her mother turned and smiled. She sat down and dangled a toe in the water.

They sat together for a long time, staring at the lake and the misty shoreline. Soon the morning mists would burn off as the sun grew hotter, but the lake would remain a sheet of clear glass, reflecting everything perfectly, without a tremor. It seemed as though it would stay that way forever.

The Kid

Anne Kent Jollymore

BEING THIRTEEN AND UPROOTED was awful enough without wondering who she was becoming, and if she wanted to be that person. Since arriving in Canada, Katy Lynn had found herself becoming many different people. Some she liked, some she loathed. The faces she liked she adopted by staring at pictures of them, or simply by willing the transformation. The ugly ones she could not control. And she knew only one thing for certain: Katy Lynn was ugly and she hated being herself.

The only good thing about her new life was American TV, especially the Wild West shows, especially the handsome outlaws. Her favourite was Billy the Kid. He was so beautiful, so wild and free. When she willed it, his face became hers, his body too; then she *was* The Kid.

Katy dreamed. The Kid rode alone across the desert on his mare, hearing nothing but the hawks, bugs and the occasional rustle in the dry thatch. Without warning, his horse reared her forelegs high in the air, nearly tossing him. But The Kid was too good a rider, and a great shot. He fired, hitting the coiled rattler square in the head. Dismounting, he stroked his mare's muzzle to calm her. Letting her graze, he lay back dreamily against a boulder. The world was a fine place today; The Kid was contented and suddenly dozy.

"Hey, kid! Wake up!" The boy next to her in the auditorium elbowed Katy. "Everybody's leaving. What's the matter? You high on something? Got any for me?" he asked.

"Sorry," she mumbled and struggled to get up. Her legs and feet prickled, and she reached to rub her right knee. "I was just... thinking."

"You from England?" the boy asked. "It's your accent. Been over here long?"

"A month." Katy hung her head. Turning abruptly, she followed the last few students from the room.

The school day ended none too soon. Katy fumbled the combination twice before her locker opened. Zipping her cardigan over her blouse she thought, Tomorrow it's jeans and a sweat top.

She ran home and slammed her bedroom door. Stripping off her blouse and skirt, she dropped them to the floor. Then, remembering what her Mum would say, she kicked them into the closet. Katy caressed the stuffed horse on her bookshelf. She adored horses. She had never ridden, but...

The Kid's mare thrust her soft nose into his face. "Yeah, Girl," he said, getting to his feet. "Time to be movin' on." The Kid felt his stomach rumble. "Got to get to Phantom Gulch for some grub," he thought aloud. The sun was sinking and he spurred his mare, riding at a fast clip. In the darkening distance, he spotted a light. A campfire. He rode closer. In a grove of trees he found it — with three rough and dirty men squatting around the flames, picking meat from stew with their fingers. They passed a jug from mouth to mouth. Suddenly one of the men jumped to his feet, pointing a rifle at The Kid.

"Hey," said The Kid, raising his hands above his head.

"Saw your fire. That's all."

"Whatcha want, Mister?" grumbled the leader, rifle ready.

"Just to ride on in one piece," he answered.

"Then git movin'."

The kid lowered his arms to grasp the reins. The gunman fired, but missed. The Kid shot back, watching two men slump, and aimed at the third. The shot was off-centre, and the man groped for his dropped pistol. The Kid fired again, piercing the man's heart. He slid from his horse and dragged the bodies clear of the campfire. Wiping bloodied hands on his pants, he squatted before the fire, wolfing down stew as fast as he could swallow.

"Katherine, love." Her mother shook her by the shoulder. "My, but your attention is hard to get. It's suppertime and look at you! Not even dressed." Her brow furrowed. What have you been doing in here all afternoon?"

"Nothing, Mum. Just... thinking."

"Well, you slip something on and come to the table." She paused. "Thinking of home?"

"Yes, sort of. And a new friend."

"A friend! Thank goodness. It's high time." She smiled and rumpled Katy's short hair. "Get dressed and eat now. Then you have school work to do."

"Yes, Mum." Katy's mother closed the door; her daughter shook her head violently to rid herself of her mother's face. Katy grabbed her desk chair and sat on it backwards, legs straddling the seat. With a tight grip on the reins, The Kid whispered, "Giddiup, Girl. These bodies'll soon be found. Let's get the hell outa here."

THE KID CLIP-CLOPPED ALONG the mountain passes, whistling. As he passed an outcropping of rocks and stunted trees, they jumped him, three men with pistols and knives ready. The Kid grabbed for his guns, but the big man with a broken tooth crashed the barrel of his Colt .44 onto The Kid's head. The Kid struggled through the nausea, trying to remain conscious as he was gagged, bound hand and foot, and thrown gut down across a horse. His own mare had bolted.

Mr. O'Connor stopped his rounds beside Katy, holding out his hand. "Your poem, Miss Jessop, please."

Katy hesitated, then thrust the paper into her English teacher's hand. She hid her face in her crossed arms. Mr. O'Connor read:

> *Death it brings*
> *stolen from the half-living*
> *running, running*
> *from the Dark Angel*
> *they cannot see.*
> *Red death, yellow death —*
> *He pours from prescription bottles*
> *down thirsty throats.*

"Katherine. You were supposed to compose a sonnet. This — poem. The sentiments concern me."

"I'm sorry, sir. Really. There's nothing to be concerned about. May I have it back?"

The teacher handed the foolscap to Katy. "The sonnet. It's homework."

Katy slipped into The Kid's mind and body, drew his pistol and shot Mr. O'Connor in the back. As the man fell, blood gushing from the wound, The Kid muttered to himself, "Never shot a man in the back before. Only a coward... but he deserved it, nosy, ugly, lyin' bastard."

The bell rang. Katy jumped from her seat and hurried to

the door. Before she could leave the classroom, Mr. O'Connor signalled to her, and Katy squirmed her way to his desk.

"Katherine, I've been watching you, and I've spoken to your other teachers. We know something is troubling you. We think you should speak with the guidance counsellor, or let one of us speak with your parents."

"NO!" Katy screamed. "All that's wrong is you and my parents, and this bloody school and... " she sobbed. "Just leave me be!"

She ran from the room. Elbowing her way through the hallway, she tripped down two stairs, caught herself and stormed out of the school. Rifling her handbag she found the bottle of Valium she had taken from her mother's bathroom, and choked drily on a handful of pills. Throwing the empty bottle on the steps, she stumbled off the school grounds.

The Kid felt sick. Soon the lawmen would catch him again. His head swam and the pain in his gut nearly made him vomit. "Bad meat," he thought. His mind wandered back to the shooting. "Coward. Only a coward would do a thing like that. A preacher's what I need. Confess. Get a pardon for my sins."

A church loomed suddenly before him. Staggering up the steps and down the aisle, The Kid fell to his knees at the altar.

"How do I pray?" he asked himself. "I never really talked to God before." A priest appeared before him.

"Miss? Miss?" he asked.

The Kid was puzzled. Why did the preacher call him "Miss?"

"I'm dying," he whispered. "I'm gonna die! Help me!"

The priest knelt in front of Katy Lynn. "What, child?"

"Dying... dying, Father." The Kid groaned and fell to the dirt.

He awoke in a hospital bed. Strange, cold metal discs were taped to his chest; a tube fed into his arm. His gut ached horribly and his throat burned.

"Katy Lynn?" a nurse in pink spoke softly.

"Who?" The Kid croaked.

"Do you know where you are?" the nurse asked. The Kid shook his head.

"Your mother's here, dear." The Kid looked away. He had no mother.

"Mrs. Jessop," the doctor said, "does Katy hear voices or see things that aren't there?"

Mrs. Jessop hesitated and said, "She hasn't been herself since our move here. She talks about a friend, but doesn't visit one. She talks to herself, too."

"I believe she needs intensive therapy, in hospital," said the doctor. "There's a good facility just west of Toronto where I think she can get what she needs."

"Is she... insane?" Katy's mother whispered.

"They're talking about me!" The Kid thought, astonished. "They're... they're gonna lock me in an asylum. Oh, God." The Kid jumped on his mare, the pain of a knife in his forearm, and rode away as fast as he could.

KATY LYNN'S FATHER OPENED the car door. "Katy, love, get out. We're at McDonalds." She groaned. Why did they have to do this to her now?

"Katherine, we have three hours of driving ahead of us. We all need food and a pit stop. Come along."

Katy opened her mouth to speak, but no sound came out. Her body had grown to fill the car, and she knew she could never squeeze out the narrow door.

Her father took her by the hand, pulling her from the car.

A spotted plush horse fell from her lap to the oily pavement.

"Da-ad," she croaked in protest, reaching for the horse. Her father threw the toy onto the back seat.

"Come now!"

Grabbing The Kid's arms, the Deputy dragged him toward the town jail. All eyes turned in his direction. Activity ceased as the jailhouse door opened and the Sheriff stepped out.

"Two Big Macs, and a McChicken sandwich for my daughter. We'll share a large fries," said Katy's father. He paid the cashier, and her parents guided her to an empty booth.

Katy Lynn looked around. The restaurant was filled with giggling couples and groups of teenagers. *Ugly children*, Katy thought. *They open and close their mouths all day and half the night and all that comes out is noise that hurts my head.*

The restaurant became a kaleidoscopic blur and her mind turned itself loose. The Kid began to grow. Soon he would fill the room, crushing all the trash in his way, breaking down the walls. They might have her body, but never her mind!

"Katy Lynn, eat your food," her mother scolded. "We can't stop here all day."

The Deputy opened the cell door and shoved in a tray of foul-smelling snakemeat. The Kid sniffed it, stomach wrenching, then kicked the tray against the bars.

"Whatsa matter, Kid? Don' like yer grub? S'all ya get."

Katy's parents guided her to the car.

"Three more hours, love, and we'll be at the hospital."

Katy didn't reply. Clutching her toy horse, her eyes blank, she grew roots into the car seat. She did not hear the whine of passing cars, or her parents' hushed voices. Her head throbbed, and she longed for sleep.

Katy's father drove through the maze of roads within the hospital grounds, past the sign that read ''Forest Lawn Sanitarium.'' Signs led him to the administration building, a converted Victorian-style house. Parking the car in the shade of old elm trees, he eased himself out of the car. He looked at Katy for a long moment.

''Wake up, honey, we're here.''

The Deputies dragged The Kid from the wagon and up the steps of the building. He waited, still bound, while his escorts talked to people called Doctor and Social Worker. The Judge — Doctor — spoke to The Kid, but he kept a stony silence. The Kid hadn't missed the enormous elms growing on the grounds. Perfect hanging trees.

The Social Worker led Katy and her parents to a cottage set back from the road. Once again The Kid glanced up at the strong trees.

''Is this where they stone prisoners, then lynch them?''

The three adults turned. ''Katy Lynn.'' The social worker's voice sounded hard and cruel. ''We're not here to hurt you, we're here to help you. And you're not a prisoner, you're a patient.'' The woman paused. ''Katy, do you know where you are?''

Katy was led past a nurses' station to a small, green, private room. Mum and a nurse examined everything in her cases, putting clothes in a closet and bureau drawers. Mum took her by the shoulders, staring into her face, then kissed her goodbye. Brushing Mum's tears off his face, The Kid sat on the bed. It was too hard, but he lay down, closed his eyes and slept.

Day followed day, week followed week, while The Kid

ate, bathed and slept. There were visits from the doctor. The Kid sat mute through it all, dreaming of his free days. He desperately wished for his mare, but magic as she was, she never came to him.

"Stay free, Old Girl. Don't let Them catch you. Wait for me... only me," he said aloud.

The doctor came up behind him. "It's good to hear your voice, Katy Lynn. Care to talk to me?" she asked.

"No! And I'm not Katy Lynn. I'm The Kid!" He stopped, surprised by his own words.

"Well, Kid. Would you like to tell me about yourself?"

"There's nothing to tell."

"Oh, I think there is a lot to tell about yourself. For example, who are you? And why The Kid instead of Katy?"

Deep inside The Kid's mind a memory fluttered: another country, another self, a loneliness.

"I... don't know. I just became," Katy Lynn answered. "I can't talk about it."

"Try."

Katy thought hard, her finger twirling a tendril of hair near her face. "It was the only way to... to get away. To not be me anymore," she said.

"And?"

"I can't think. I don't know."

"That's okay, Katy Lynn. We'll talk again."

AUGUST ARRIVED WITH A TOUCH OF autumn air. Katy spoke in therapy sessions, and made friends with one of the other patients. At night she lay in bed, trying to conjure The Kid, but he wouldn't come.

One day the doctor told her, "Katy. You've been here for five months. You've come a long way in therapy. Now I think it's time for you to return home and to school.''

"But I can't!" Katy cried.

"Why not?"

"Because I'm no one. Not Katy, not The Kid — no one.''

"I thought when you gave up The Kid you became Katy Lynn again.''

"I only pretended because I wanted... "

"To go home?"

"Yes."

"Well, now you have your chance.''

As she left the room the doctor wished her luck.

THE DAY HER PARENTS CAME FOR HER, Katy sat packed and ready on a bare mattress. She longed for home, yet her fear paralysed her. Her father carried the cases to the car, and Katy looked up at the old elms.

"Well, Kid, you didn't get hanged after all.''

Her mother was startled, but Katy squeezed her hand and smiled. "Let's go home, Mum.''

In the back seat, Katy closed her eyes, letting the drone of the tires lull her. A soft nose nuzzled her face, and she raised her hand to stroke it. "Thanks for coming, Old Girl,'' The Kid said softly. "I've really missed you. We're beautiful together. Once we reach the desert, then we'll be free.''

Window Dressing
Bonnie Blake

ANITA RUBBED HER BROW AND turned toward the bed. She stopped, startled. The curtains were open with a clear view into the neighbour's garden. Mr. Cerroni, in his red plaid shirt and green work pants, was pulling weeds in the cooling evening. She watched for a few seconds. Intent on his chores, he probably hadn't noticed her undressing after work.

Poor old guy. Ever since his wife died, all he does is work in that damn vegetable patch. He might as well not even have relatives, for all the company they give him. At least when he's gardening, he's not slugging back the homemade wine.

As she adjusted the curtains, Mr. Cerroni glanced up.

Did he see me move? If he can see me now, he must have seen me with the lights on.

She peeked through the window while the white-haired man continued down his rows.

This is stupid. If he saw me, he saw me. Give the old guy a thrill.

She smoothed her white uniform on the hanger. There were two black smudges on the left hip, but she could wear it another day. *If one more jerk rams me with a cart, I'll make him eat it.* She pried off her shoes, pausing to rub at a scuff.

She propped up her pillows and half lay, half sat on the bed. In her large bedroom, the gleam of mahogany was dulled by a gradual accretion of dust. Bare carpets, scarred by indentations of absent furniture, lay throughout the rest of the three-bedroom bungalow. The kitchen suite was intact, but the dining room empty. The living room held a white wicker rocker, its canes split like barbed wire, and an old shoe box of cassettes, useless without the tape deck. The spare room was bare.

Often she felt like this house, a collection of atoms through which cold drafts could pass unhindered by any solid monuments to the past. She had sold her personal things, too — the sewing machine, her Dresden dolls, even her jewellery.

Still, whatever, she wouldn't sell the house. There had been too many late nights alone, painting, wallpapering, laying carpets. Two years on the mortgage when she had caught him on the couch with the little bitch from the Marina. The couch was the first furniture she had let him take.

She lay there considering the fresh, crunchy vegetables in the garden next door. She imagined the minerals and vitamins surging through her body. In her own small plot, dandelions, crabgrass, thistles, and vetch were on the verge of smothering what was edible, a far cry from her expectations. She felt beaten by their persistence. She glanced at the clock — 9:20 p.m. Tomorrow she would tackle the weed-pit. Right now she should make something to eat, but. . .

She woke with her wrinkled slip twisted under her back. The digital clock read 11:06 p.m. Her stomach growled. She tugged on her slippers, one toe peeking out the end, wrapped her house coat over her slip and shuffled into the kitchen. In the first cupboard she found three cans of soup, in the next four packages of Kraft Dinner and an opened onion soup mix with the tinfoil rolled down. The bang of the cupboard doors echoed out through the dining room. In the third cupboard, she found a tin of sardines, a can of spaghetti sauce and a package of Chinese noodles.

She munched the last apple while eating the macaroni and cheese from the pot. She washed the dishes and brought the mail to the bedroom.

She peeled off her pantyhose, stitched the hole in the toe, and liberally covered it with nail polish. It was her last pair.

There's not enough money for the hydro bill, she thought, and I can't buy groceries.

It wasn't as though she'd always had regular mealtimes. Her mother cooked when she thought of it. By the time she was five, Anita knew enough to feed herself when she was hungry, when there was food available.

She remembered helping her mother pack and unpack, evicted from apartment after apartment for delinquent rent. Her mother was always distracted, often unreachable. Twice Anita had stayed in foster homes while her mother pulled her life together. Her foster parents had done a better job of providing food and shelter, but little in the way of nurturing. Her mother had overdosed on prescription drugs when Anita was fifteen.

She would never live like that. This house was hers. She was glad she had no family to hassle her into selling. She could make it on her own.

She fell asleep still hungry and woke ravenous. After a breakfast of Scotch broth, she dressed for the garden attack in her bleach-stained, mauve jogging pants, a frayed white shirt, old winter gloves and rain boots. The grass was heavy with dew.

She yanked a thistle as tall as her knee from the lettuce

row and flung it across the lawn. In the short northern growing season, vegetables needed diligent coaxing. The native weeds thrived even on frost and drought. Mr. Cerroni stood by his bean poles, watching her. *The hell with him and his Eden.* She tugged at a clump of chickweed. *Damn his greenhouse.* The plant released dirt in a shower. She threw it across the garden. *As soon as the house is paid for, I plant grass.*

"How's the lettuce?" called Mr. Cerroni over the fence.

Anita jumped at the sudden voice. "Buried," she said.

"You got a difficult life," he said in his heavy Italian accent. "Work all day. Run a house alone."

Anita studied his weather-browned face. He smiled.

"It doesn't leave much time to garden," she said. "I'm lucky if I get the grass cut."

"Well... now there's just me at home, I grow more than I eat. My lettuce, she's going to overshoot. You *take* some!"

"Sure!"

The old man disappeared for a few minutes while Anita continued her assault on the intruders.

"Couple of salads," said the neighbour, setting a paper bag on top of the fence.

"Thanks, Mr. Cerroni."

As soon as her neighbour had left, Anita reached into the bag, pulled some lettuce from the top, rinsed it under the hose, and ate it while she worked. When the weeds had been stuffed into a large black garbage bag, she mowed the lawn. It was midafternoon before she retrieved the paper bag from the back fence. It felt too heavy for lettuce, and when she opened it, she discovered young carrots, radishes, parsley, and sweet red strawberries.

TWO WEEKS LATER, ON A FRIDAY, a co-worker treated her to a couple of vodkas after work. When she got home, she felt carefree and lazy. Half undressed by the bedroom window, she looked over her shoulder through the glass. Sure enough, Mr. Cerroni was working in his garden. He bent down hurriedly at her glance.

Anita laughed and continued to change. She stuffed her clothes in the hamper, and glanced at Mr. Cerroni, standing in the middle of his onions, staring straight at her. She snorted and snapped out the light.

The next morning, Anita found a large grocery bag on her doorstep. Radishes, lettuce, onions, carrots, raspberries, young cabbage, and beans. She filled her refrigerator.

Over the next couple of weeks, whenever Anita's vegetable crisper was close to empty, she watched for Mr. Cerroni to appear in his garden. She would leave the curtains open as she changed for bed, and the next morning a brown bag of vegetables would appear on her porch.

One steamy summer day, they were both outside weeding. Anita was nibbling on a young carrot when she felt him watching. She stood up and met his gaze.

"I like the grey one best," he said quietly and he bent back to the rows of tomatoes.

Grey one? My God, he means my grey silk teddy! He's telling me what to wear to bed!

She spit out the carrot and, leaving weeds tossed about the lawn, fled indoors. She downed two large glasses of cold water at the sink. That night she closed the curtains tightly before undressing.

After the vegetables were consumed, Anita scrubbed the refrigerator clean. When she ate the last of the packaged Kraft Dinner, she saved some of the cheese powder for the remaining spaghetti noodles. At work, she popped stray grapes into her mouth, retrieving them from the bottom of carts and counters. She developed a talent for palming candies whenever she walked to the washroom.

Salads danced through her dreams, crisp lettuce, crunchy cucumbers, hot radishes. She swore she smelled bacon frying in the mornings. Mr. Cerroni's cherry tomatoes ripened, bright with invitation.

One evening, when she limped in from a double shift, lightheaded with hunger and fatigue, a large brown bag sat on the doorstep. It was filled with a variety of perfect garden delights. As she pulled them from the bag, she pressed each vegetable against her face, inhaling deeply. She danced around the kitchen, clumps of dirt filtering through her fingers. Intoxicating surprises were wrapped in a separate plastic bag — a bottle of Caesar salad dressing and a box of chocolate-covered almonds!

As the salad dressing ran down her chin, Anita wiped it on the back of her arm. It glistened on her skin, stiffening the hairs. She devoured the entire box of candy, melting the chocolate on her tongue, sucking the nuts bare, then crunching each one to bits. Her body shivered with satisfaction. She hadn't felt this full in a long time.

Behind the closed curtains, Anita hesitated. She pinched the blue fabric between her thumb and finger, forming a peephole. Mr. Cerroni's ripening corn swayed in the golden sunshine. He was sitting in a lawn chair, glass in hand, bottle of red wine beside him. He was alone. He seemed smaller than she remembered. Her full stomach gurgled. She took a deep breath and ripped open the curtains. A curious half-smile transformed her face as she smoothed out the grey teddy.

Blueberries

Leandro Frigeri

SHE STOOD ON THE ERODED slope. All around her grew the blueberry bushes, their fruit shriveled and seedy under the scoured blue of an August sky. But sometimes, shaded by a birch or alder, the bushes grew green, laden with dusky-blue spheres. Those were the berries she would seek, the ones that would shorten the long hours of stooping but would still please their mother.

The dust suspended in the still morning air choked her. She watched as the poplars swallowed up the half-ton, a red drop in a sea of green. She could still hear the clatter of its tailgate breaking the silence. Then nothing.

They would pick blueberries until the night's coolness descended, then eat supper and make camp. It was a ritual they had repeated many times since that summer their mother had changed.

A mosquito tormenting her ankles reminded her she should start picking before the midday heat subsided and the insect plagues advanced. Two crows passed overhead, their wing-tips whistling in the air. Their grandmother, Gocom, said lost spirits made that sound.

Tommy was thirsty. Rebekah searched inside a burlap bag, drew out a clear plastic Coke bottle full of water, unscrewed the cap and gave it to her brother. He sucked noisily at the bottle, his face tear-stained, his hands grubby. Sarah stood under a pincherry bush that hung heavy with red, translucent cherries. They glistened in the sun like fresh drops of blood.

"Sarah, take this pail and pick over by that birch. Ma said we better fill this tub or she's gonna get mad. Tommy, stop your cryin' and follow me." Tommy stopped. Sarah took the pail. She wove her way over stumps and hollows gouged into the rocky earth by the logging machines to the single birch.

The tiny berries fell into their containers, tap, tap, tapping like a sapsucker drilling for birch sap. Sometimes, Gocom told them, sapsuckers would peck so many holes in the birch they would kill it. Tommy had already forgotten the blueberries and was trying to catch a grasshopper with his pail.

Rebekah knelt down by a shaded hollow sheltered from the searing heat. Her blue-stained fingers raked the berries into her basket. She was careful not to catch too many leaves as she sifted the low bushes in a steady motion.

WHEN HER MOTHER HAD DUMPED the doll into the rusty-red oil drum at the back of the house, she had cried. The only other time she remembered crying was the day they had taken her uncle away. That was when Gocom had told her that, towards evening, if you walked to where the river made a twist under the cedars beside the log jam, you could see it. But only if you were really careful. It had the body of a fish and the head of a man and brought evil. Gocom told her it was the reason the people died or got sick in the town. Sammy Small burned to death in the old shed at the end of the bush road the kids called Dead Man's Road. Uncle Abraham was taken away to a hospital where they tied him up in a white shirt. Old Man Peltier died drinking. Seven gone, Gocom had said. But Rebekah could only think of three.

A BRANCH TURNED INTO A garter snake as she stretched for a large cluster of berries. Rebekah sat down on a jackpine stump, picked up a stick and, leaning, looked over to where Sarah was picking. Her sister's white dress looked like a dirty piece of paper as she stooped by the birch. The stick felt hard in her hands.

REBEKAH'S FATHER CAME BACK with a walking stick that day her mother got sick. Her father had gone with Sarah to the river to catch a jackfish for supper. Sometime later when they hadn't returned, their mother went out after them. Their father returned alone just before it was time to eat.

"Where's Ma and Sarah, when they coming home?" Her father's red, checkered bush shirt smelled of sweat and cedar. His hot breath reminded her of the old men that came late for the Catholic mass in Jamie Morriseau's church.

"None'a yer bizness. She'll come when she's good and ready. Now take this pike and clean it for supper. Tommy, git some wood for the woodstove. I'm hungry." Her father sat down by the scarred pine table in the kitchen. With his left arm he swept the dirty dishes to the floor.

Their mother came back after supper, in the darkness. The spring peepers had already started their singing. She just lay down on her bed and cried. Sarah had come back before her mother and had been beaten with a willow branch. Their father's new walking stick leaned crooked by the firewood. After everybody was asleep, Tommy started crying too. Rebekah shook him and asked him what was wrong.

"I seen something in the woods. It was long and twisty. It was hiding under the bank. I seen its eyes in the water — like fish eggs, only bigg'r, lookin' at me."

"Yer just imaginin'. Ain't nothing there to bother you. Stop playing with them snakes in the gravel pit, like I tol' you before and you'll be okay. Go back t'sleep." Rebekah held Tommy until he slept.

SARAH STOOD UP AND STOPPED picking. She started walking toward her sister, her white face empty, her eyes shiny. Rebekah looked up at Sarah. "Why ain't you pickin' no more?"

"I tol' Tommy."

"Tol him what?"

"I told him my dream that day Ma came home late and cried."

THE NEXT MORNING THEIR father had gone to get Gocom. She entered the cabin and went straight to their mother's bed without a word. Tommy pulled at Gocom's skirt and held his hand out for the usual gum and licorice she would bring from the store. This time Gocom ignored him and told the children to let her be and to go out and play. Gocom shook her head as she said this. Their mother was still turned over on her side and groaning. Their father looked down at the floor and took his walking stick out in the yard. Freshly washed sheets hung from the line that afternoon. The house smelled of Javex and ammonia. Even their dog never moved from the porch as Gocom left. She carried something wrapped in an old blanket and stopped behind the house by the oil drum and dropped it in. Gocom's eyes never left their father as she hobbled down the road. Her cane made twisty streaks in the soft gravel.

That night their father burned the trash in the red barrel. His clothes smelled of kerosene. The fire got hotter. The smoke smelled of sweet grass and the sap from black poplar in the spring. Once they had caught three leopard frogs. They stuck them with a sharp stick, then wrapped them in the poplar leaves and scorched them in a fire made with cedar branches. They were ashamed Gocom might discover what they had done. She told them not to kill the animals in the forest — only if they had to survive. Later they had burned the evidence and watched as wisps of smoke curled from the pyre.

THE DOLL WAS A GIFT FROM Uncle Abraham before he went to the hospital. He gave it her name, Becky, short for Rebekah, because he told her it looked like her, only it was white like Sarah, not dark like her and the others. Except for its black hair. Sarah cried because she didn't get one, so Rebekah named it Sarah-Becky. That was one week after Gocom's visit. Two weeks after that, her mother came home and said she was going to church now, and they all had better, too. She had joined up with a Baptist Church in town. They told her to give up things she didn't need. The first thing she did was to take the doll and drop it in the oil drum. No matter how much Rebekah and Sarah cried, they couldn't touch it. The next day their mother cleaned the house and burned the trash in the barrel until it glowed red in the twilight. They hadn't seen their father for more than a week.

THE SUN WAS GETTING HOTTER. Rebekah yelled to Tommy to stop. Together the three threaded their way through the bone-white rocks and swampy pockets to the lake. They had filled almost half of the steel laundry tub. Now they could swim, before picking for a few more hours and then making supper. The lake was bordered with a yellow sand beach. Parts of it were free from reeds and leeches. Tommy played in the shallow water and caught pinheads with his blueberry pail. Sarah swam with her white dress still on. She looked like a perch floating with its belly up. Rebekah took her dress off even though the teachers at the school told them it was wrong to show their bodies to others. Her dark skin merged with the dark bottom of the lake. Only her shiny black hair bobbing up and down gave her away. She looked like a beaver rippling through the golden water.

"Why'd you skip school today? They're going to find out and then Pa's going to take it out on you." But Sarah said nothing to her sister. She only looked down at her bare feet. Then she turned her back to Rebekah. She scratched the first letter of her name with her toe in the cool sand by the river's edge.

"You ever seen it?"

Rebekah could just make out the outline of her sister's form against the dark shadows of the cedars. "Seen what?"

"You know — that snake thing by the river."

"No, but Gocom said the river goes north to a big bay and most times it lives up there. It only comes back when the snow geese come back. Then it hides by the dark pools in the river. That's why we never seen it."

"I seen it. It's got big scales like the whitefish Pa catches to smoke and a head like a man. Sometimes it just lies there in the fast water by the logs and looks at me. The willow branches make checkered shapes all over it. Once it swam towards me. Then a squirrel in a tamarack got mad at me and

I started running. I seen it again last night when I was sleeping.''

''You never seen it. You was just dreamin' — just like Tommy. Ain't no one seen it 'cept maybe Gocom back when she was just a girl up north 'n once when Gomshom died from the sickness.''

''I seen it.'' Sarah moved away and sat under the big birch by a black patch of ground where Sammy's cabin once stood.

IT WAS GETTING DARK AND the mosquitoes were waking up to the coolness and their hunger. Together, they had picked another half tub-full. Their backs hurt and their legs were scratched by raspberry thorns. Tiny beads of blood clung to their legs like dew. They set up their tent by a black spruce near the beach. Over a fire of twigs and cutover pieces they cooked their bannock and chunks of bacon. The white dough, twisted around the alder sticks, darkened and puffed up. The fat dripped and sizzled in the hot flames. Mosquitoes and no-see-ums hovered just beyond the flames. Tommy fell asleep without eating. Later, they dragged him to the tent and, hugging to keep warm, they too fell asleep.

''PA'S NOT COMING BACK NO MORE and we can't affor' to live here like before. The Baptist preacher said he'd take Sarah 'til the summer while we gets some money. Tommy can stay with the Sisters at the school in the city. I needs you to help me do the cooking and cleaning for Old Man Vander. Said we could stay in his tourist cabin, the one he ain't fixed yet. We gots to take what we kin. Come summer we kin get t'gether agin and pick berries, then maybe pinecones to sell.''

THE NEXT MORNING WAS COLD. Instead of dew, there were ice crystals on the bushes. Rebekah took some bannock with her and began picking. Their mother would be back soon to pick them up and the tub wasn't full yet. She left Tommy and Sarah asleep in the tent.

By a pocket near a cedar swamp the ground was damp. There she found blueberry bushes with berries big as grapes. Her uncle brought them some once from the store in Valora. That was the day he walked down the CN tracks for more than 30 miles. She walked through clumps of labrador tea, sweet and spicy in the sharp air. The smell reminded her of the incense the priests burned that time Jamie took them to the Catholic church. Jamie had told them they were celebrating a day the priest called Ashwendsdegh. She knelt down and picked. She hardly noticed that some of the blueberry bushes had already turned blood-red. She picked steadily, her fingers numbed by the cold. Three crows flew low overhead. Their wings sounded like willow branches whipping the air. Whoosh. . . whoosh. . . whoosh. Her movements accompanied the sound like a dance. Soon the tamaracks would turn gold and then bare. Still she picked. The big berries, glazed with frost, seemed to glow like the eyes of a yellow pickerel in the early light — luminescent in the shadows.

I'll Sing You A Song
Dorothy Colby

THE PARKING LOT WAS EMPTY when Peter and I pulled in at Trinity Lutheran Nursing home in Round Rock, just outside Austin, Texas.

No conversation, no laughter, only the murmur of televisions as we walked down the hall. The smells of food and antiseptic and cleaners almost masked the human odours that permeate nursing homes.

My stomach contracted when I saw Mother parked in her wheelchair with a group near the nursing station. A few residents looked up at us but most continued to stare into space. Three or four puffed cigarettes while the nurse on duty monitored them.

Mother's chair was against the wall. On her left was a woman whose head lolled on her chest. On her right, a man shouted, ''Hey, girlie!'' She was as oblivious to his call as she was when we stood in front of her.

''Hello, Mother.'' I leaned over, rested my hands on the arms of her wheelchair, and looked directly into her eyes. I kissed her forehead. ''It's me, Mother. It's Dorothy.''

She raised her chin, tilted her head back and studied me through the bottom of her glasses. The whites of her eyes were creamy and her pupils were magnified. Her eyes looked uncommonly blue behind the thick lenses. The lack of expression disturbed me as she scanned back and forth searching my face.

"Do I look like Dorothy?"

"No."

"What does Dorothy look like?"

"Not like you."

She didn't recognize me now that gray had touched my blonde hair and crow's feet fanned from my eyes. Which Dorothy *did* she remember, if any? The child with Dutch bobbed hair? Or the bobby soxer, in skirt and sweater with a pony tail? Or the young mother in jeans trying to rein in three little boys?

"Women should never wear jeans," she'd tell me. "They aren't feminine. They show every curve."

"I know," I'd reply.

I really hadn't expected her to know me. She hadn't known me last year. Three years ago, at ninety-four, when she fell and cracked her hip she couldn't remember the fall even while she was still in pain. She didn't know where she lived. She couldn't remember she had been moved to Texas to be near my sister. I shouldn't have been disturbed, but I was. She was still Mother.

For the past three years, in October, Peter and I have visited my mother, my sister Joan and her family. We drive. We spend three days in limbo on the highways between Thunder Bay, Ontario, and Austin, Texas.

When our sons were young and all five of us were trapped in the car the boys would fight: "Mom, Jim touched me," or "Craig is sitting on *my* side," or from Scott, the youngest, "Why do I always have to sit in the middle?" Pete and I would clash. He'd say, "What the hell's the matter

with you? Can't you learn to read a map?'' I'd say, ''If you'd
discuss our route before it was time to turn I'd be able to
navigate.''

But now, there are only two of us and it's pleasant.
Sometimes we chat or read *Time* or doze. We use our old
maps and triptiks, on which by-passes of cities are marked,
and we have noted where to stop to eat, or for the night, and
where not to stop.

Two years ago we bought a Chevy Blazer. It has air
conditioning, cruise control and tape deck. Cruise is set five
miles above the speed limit, and every two or three hours we
switch drivers. Our tapes fill a Reebok box and the in-car
rule is not to repeat a tape until we play each one once. Peter
likes Hank Williams, Jr. and Willie Nelson. I like Barbra
Streisand and Nat King Cole, songs with melodies. I hum
and sing along. We both like ''light classics.'' We borrow
Ray Charles and ''The Best of Andrew Lloyd Webber'' from
our son.

Our home is in Thunder Bay, Ontario. The road between
Thunder Bay and Duluth, Minnesota, is the prettiest part of
the trip. The highway plays peek-a-boo with Lake Superior,
at times hugging the cliffs that rise above the water where
seagulls swoop and soar. Other times it cuts through trembling poplars, white birch and evergreens. For four hours on
this particular trip Eddie Arnold croons, Barbra Streisand
aches and Mozart soothes.

I-35, which begins in Duluth, is our route to Austin.
Andrew Lloyd Webber, Willie Nelson and Johann Strauss
take us to St. Paul. We stay with friends, David and Muriel,
and talk and laugh and remember until our eyelids droop.

When I was growing up in Michigan we always stayed
with relatives or friends when we travelled. I hated listening

to the adults talk about the past. I wanted to stay in a hotel, like the ones I'd seen in movies — a room with a tiled bath, on an upper floor where I could use an elevator and look out over the city.

In those days, Mother liked car trips. She could never hide her excitement when we were going "up home." "Up home" was Pulcifer, a tiny community in northeastern Wisconsin that can't be found on many maps. Grandma lived up the hill from the general store, gas station, post office, cheese factory and two taverns.

There were nine children in mother's family and she, Cora, was seventh. When she and Dad married they moved to Michigan.

We were the only family members who didn't live in Wisconsin, so when Mother and her family travelled to Grandma's the family gathered.

The women chattered in the kitchen while they prepared food and the men lounged on chairs in the back yard and smoked. Now and then, two or three would wander off to the woodshed. Later, I learned, Uncle Al kept a bottle in the woodpile. We children chased through the apple orchard, climbed trees and threw green apples at each other. I loved belonging to these aunts, uncles, first cousins, second cousins and cousins once removed.

Uncle Jake sang, "You are my sunshine... " to Joan and me. He called us Sunshine One and Sunshine Two. "Are you big enough to touch the fence?" he asked. An electric barbed wire fence penned in the neighbour's cows. "Yes!" Our hands darted out and back. We screamed and jumped and Uncle Jake laughed.

Grandma's front parlour and upstairs bedrooms smelled like our basement. The bedroom wallpaper had water spots.

When it rained, water ping'd on the tin roof and, when it was sunny, dust moats floated above the bed. In the morning, her kitchen smelled of wood from the stove and coffee and oatmeal. Moustache cups and red carnival glass were displayed behind glass doors high in the cupboard.

Two years ago, my cousin Willard told me, "We all cried when your mother got married and moved to Michigan. We didn't want her to leave."

She was thirty-seven at the time. Until then, she had lived with her parents and was a prize-winning saleswoman for Fuller Brushes. She drove a Model-T Ford that she'd had painted lavender. She had spending money and took her parents, sisters and their families on little jaunts, rare outings for rural families during the Depression. She, too, cried when she left her family.

My dad bought a black Hudson when I was seven. He polished his car and shoes each Saturday, and did the same before we drove to Wisconsin. For the trip, he wore a long-sleeved white shirt, sleeves rolled to the elbow. Even though Mother liked to "take the wheel" as she said, she didn't often drive on trips. Dad drove with both hands on the steering wheel, except when he was smoking Chesterfield cigarettes.

Mother chose our clothes and packed the suitcases. We wore dresses even though we begged to wear shorts. Our Sunday hats, four of them, lay on the shelf above the back seat. Joan and I sat beneath them, with jackets or sweaters and magazines and newspapers between us. One reason Mother resisted flying in later years was that she couldn't limit her packing to one or two suitcases.

It was three hundred miles from Battle Creek, Michigan, to our first stop in Milwaukee, my dad's mother's. We started out singing and sang until we reached the orchards by Lake Michigan. "She'll be coming 'round the mountain when she comes," "Anchors away, my boys," "Daisy, Daisy," "Mairzy doats and doezy doats," and on and on. By the time we saw the steel mills in Gary, Indiana, we were bored. We argued in Chicago. Mother turned and pulled the corners of her mouth into a frozen smile and said, "Now, girls." On Lake Shore Drive beside Lake Michigan we watched people play on the beach. But despite our pleas for a swim, we never stopped, just kept pushing to Milwaukee.

ON THE SECOND MORNING OF our trip to Texas we drive through the farm lands of Minnesota and Iowa: flat, predictable, stretching to the horizon. Ray Charles, k.d. lang and Schubert.

Missouri and Kansas are Jesse James country and, sure enough, the landscape looks like a western movie set where outlaws could have disappeared with bags of gold. Patsy Cline, Wagner and the Ink Spots.

On two previous trips we've spent the night in Emporium, Kansas, a cattle town that smells like an abattoir. And, from other visits, we know its motels do, too; it's in the carpets and drapes and sheets and, by the time you leave, in your clothes. This time we don't stop, and as we roll on to Wichita we break our tape rule and replay Andrew Lloyd Webber's "Memories" and "Phantom."

Oklahoma is brown range, scrub brush, oil wells, gullies, places where rustlers could hide. Tom Jones, Chet Atkins and a selection of Viennese operettas in German.

And on into Texas, where Fort Worth presents an endless series of waits and entanglements, one-lane traffic and paving equipment. Pete fumes and I fret until Tandy Towers and the downtown skyline are in our rear view mirror. Mother never wanted to live in Texas.

"HELLO, CORA. IT'S PETER." My husband leans over so she can see him.

"Peter?"

"Yes, it's Peter. My husband. Peter Colby. You know him," I say.

He touches her hand, and she grasps it with both of hers. I can see she is puzzled.

"Say 'Peter,' " I coax. "Say 'Peter.' "

"Peter." Her voice is flat and she rubs his hand with her fingers. She rubs hard, as if she could absorb by touch what escapes her eyes and ears.

I want to say, "Think! Remember! You know us!" Instead I repeat, "Say 'Peter Colby.' "

"Peter Colby." She draws out the syllables, continuing to rub his hand. "Peter Colby." Her voice changes, her eyes widen and she smiles. "Is that you, Peter?" My eyes fill with tears.

Mother may not have recognized me but I know, too, that she would not have recognized herself. She hasn't looked in a mirror for years or even decided what she would wear. She would be shocked to see herself — a shrunken old woman, tied in a wheelchair, wearing a housecoat, ankle socks and a red plastic headband.

Mother was the runt of her family and ours. Barely five feet tall she maximized those sixty inches. She stood erect, with her head tilted slightly back and her chin up and out. When I was a child she swept her gray hair off her face into a French twist. A few wisps would escape and she would brush them back as she worked. I wanted her to wear her hair down, like my friends' mothers did, in a page boy or front pompadour with the back loose. "Women with gray hair wear it off their neck," she would say. She was married at thirty-seven on her parents' fiftieth wedding anniversary. But the solemn woman in the wedding picture looks as if she were approaching thirty, not forty. A leghorn straw hat with the front brim turned up covers her short flapper bob. Her cream satin dress, with cap sleeves, reaches her shins in front and tapers to her ankles in back.

She wore dresses: in the kitchen, the garden, washing clothes and listening to the radio. My friends' mothers wore dresses sometimes, too, but more often these younger women wore pleated skirts, crisp blouses and wool sweaters, even slacks. "I can't wear blouses and sweaters. My waist is too short," she said. Of course her waist was short; she was short. What she meant was she was round with a full bust.

After she was seventy she changed her appearance, rejecting her old hair style and rigid dress code. She got a wash-and-towel-dry perm, and fell in love with pant suits and pantyhose: she had matching pants and jackets, and patterned and plain blouses. Dresses were saved for weddings, graduations, the symphony and special church occasions.

We can't pinpoint when Mother became forgetful. If she misplaced her purse or a book she would say, "I've always been forgetful." We believed her.

However, we can pinpoint when we knew it was more than bad memory. At ninety-two she forgot my birthday in September. She had remembered Joan's in February, but missed the grandchildren in April and July. On my birthday, Joan called.

"Did Mother send a card?"

"No."

"Did she call?"

"No."

Even before Mother fell, Joan realized she could no longer stay in the seniors complex, where she lived alone. The complex provided meals and minimal supervision for baths and medication. But, for Mother, dressing became a problem; sometimes she wore two dresses. Frequently, she couldn't find her apartment. After her fall, she spent two weeks in hospital and, from there, went directly to the nursing home. I flew to Texas.

In the beginning, she would study her room or the cafeteria or the hall where people gathered and ask, "What is this place?"

We never said, "Trinity Lutheran Nursing Home." Our family never answers difficult questions honestly or directly. We said, "This is a place where you'll get well — where you'll learn to walk again." We couldn't bring ourselves to tell her she was living in an institution, confined to a wheelchair, probably for the rest of her life.

"Do I know these people?" she'd ask, referring to those around her.

"You'll make friends." Another non-answer.

She continued to watch and question, and we continued to be evasive. The day she said, "I think I saw Clara," we knew we hadn't deceived her. Clara was her only sister to live in a nursing home. In Wittenberg, Wisconsin. She died there.

ON THIS, OUR THIRD VISIT TO TEXAS, the days are sunny and warm. When we go to see Mother at the home we put my dad's straw gardening hat on her and sit under a Virginia live oak. The hat makes me think of Dad concentrating while he steered a bobbing Rototiller between rows of peas, beans and corn.

We try to include Mother in the conversation.

"Do you see the squirrels?" we ask. They chatter and run from the oaks to the pecan trees, gathering nuts.

"No."

"Listen! Did you hear the mockingbird?" Sometimes she says yes.

If she begins a sentence, she can't finish it. Her mind plays tag with an idea and she is always "it." She chases words, but they sidestep, dodge and evade her. To fill silences she mutters, "un hun... hun hun." Most frequently she asks, "Have you seen Mother?"

I find it difficult to accept who Mother has become. But finally a moment comes when I feel encouraged. She leans toward me and says in a confidential voice, "My family is visiting me." I know we have made some contact.

One morning Peter and I come at the end of chapel. We find Mother in her wheelchair surrounded by other residents. She wears a pale pink sweater and housecoat; the colour gives a glow to her skin. Her hair has been washed and looks like a white halo around her face. I watch as she leans forward to touch the woman in front of her. She can't reach her. She tries again, oblivious to her surroundings.

Later, while we sit outside, the chorus of the final hymn keeps repeating itself in my mind, like a needle stuck in the groove of a record.

Joan has told me sometimes she will respond to hymns if she is encouraged. "Do you remember this?" I ask, and in my off-key voice I begin, "Blessed Jesus, blessed Jesus. You have bought us, we are yours."

"I don't think so."

"I know a song you'll remember." I begin the first song she taught me. "Jesus loves me, this I know." She doesn't seem to be listening, so I stop. "You can sing this. Come on, Mother. Jesus loves me this I know." I hesitate.

"For the Bible tells me so," she responds in monotone.

"Little ones to him belong." I wait but she doesn't continue. "Your turn. You can sing it." I repeat, "Little ones... "

"to him belong."

Eventually we finish the song. Her voice is expressionless and she never smiles. But my non-singing husband smiles at us. For a moment we're silent while I think of other songs we had sung on trips "up home."

"I know one." I am excited. "Daisy, Daisy, give me your answer do." I sing with conviction because her childhood friend's name was Daisy. "Let's sing! Daisy, Daisy... "

I sing one line and sometimes she follows with the next in a thin passionless voice. We don't sing together but respond to each other. We try "Jingle Bells," "Happy Birthday," "Take Me Out to the Ball Game," whatever pops into my head.

When a melody trickles through the maze in her mind, she says a phrase immediately. Other times she hesitates before responding; sometimes she is silent. That morning she never once asks, "Have you seen Mother?"

I am elated when we take her in for lunch. Peter pushes the chair and I march beside her, pumping my arms back and forth, singing, "Hi ho! Hi ho! It's off to work we go." I can't remember the rest of the words so I sing, "Ta dum, ta dum, ta dum, ta dum, hi ho! Hi ho!" I march beside her, around her, in front and in back, singing in my best marching voice.

When we reach the door, she stops me with a familiar smile, the one I have always called her frozen smile. The one she used to bestow in public. The one that said, "Now, girls!"

I lean over and hug her.

I had known that I wanted to reach her, to give her comfort and reassurance. But, until that moment, I hadn't realized how much I needed the reassurance that she could return to me.

Wind Driven
David Laderoute

ELLIOT SHIFTED HIS GRIP ON the axe and waited for the cloud of vapour from his breath to clear. The trail of footprints was still visible, in spite of the drifted snow. Still, he had no way of knowing how much of a lead Frank might have. A trapper or guide might have been able to tell, but Elliot was neither. He shrugged. It didn't really matter; he knew he would eventually overtake Frank. And when he did, Frank would deserve everything he had coming to him.

He took a few seconds to brush away the ice that had accumulated on his moustache, and prepared to set off again.

THE FIRST DAY

> *There's a little black spot on the sun today.*
> *It's the same old thing as yesterday.*
> *There's a black hat caught in a high tree-top.*
> *There's a flagpole rag and the wind won't stop...*

"Jee-sus, not this shit again!" barked Frank. "Haven't we heard enough'a this?"

Elliot glared. "Excuse me, Frank, but you're interrupting my enjoyment of The Police. And in case you've forgotten,

it's my turn to play some tunes.'' He turned away again. ''I'll
remember this the next time you put on your head-banging
heavy metal crap,'' he muttered. But he was really only half-
listening to Sting's trademark croon; the rest of his attention
was fixed on the sky. Only two hours until dark, and it was
still an unrelenting grey.

I guess I'm always hoping that you'll end this reign
But it's my destiny to be the King of Pain...

Frank pounded the last nail into the big wooden box that
held the magnetometers. Elliot winced. He hated packing the
sensitive instruments that way, but then it wasn't up to him; it
was his job to use them to find minerals, and shut up. He was
damn glad this latest of surveys was over. Or almost over, he
reminded himself; their generator had packed it in the previous day, preventing them from recharging the instruments'
batteries and finishing the last bit of the survey. Too bad.

Now if only they could get off this goddamn frozen lake,
and back home.

Frank tossed the hammer into a battered red tool box, and
joined Elliot beside the pile of gear they'd already packed
up. ''We gonna take down the other tent?'' he asked, one
hand rummaging inside his parka.

Elliot slowly turned his back to Frank, and scanned the
clouds to the east. Maybe they'd dispatch a flight out of
Nakina. But the sky in that direction was just as grey as the
rest — maybe more so.

''Hey, Mister Bossman, I said are we gonna take down
the tent?'' Frank dug out a rumpled pack of cigarettes, took
one, struck a match, and lit it inside cupped hands.

''Doesn't look good, does it?'' shrugged Elliot. He wrinkled his nose and held his breath until Frank's smoke had

cleared. ''We'd better leave it up,'' he said solemnly.

One of the two prospector's tents they'd brought, their former kitchen and storage tent, was a grey-white bundle of insulated canvas folded up in the snow. Most of their other stuff was packed, too. The idea had been to leave the sleeping tent up until they knew for sure that the plane was coming to retrieve them — that is, until they actually heard or saw it. Only then would they strike it.

But now it was only two hours until dark, and the weather was foul. To top things off, the radio transceiver was dead.

Elliot glanced at the sky one last time, and said, ''Go light the stove.''

''Roger wilco, Mister Bossman,'' Frank replied, throwing a mock salute as he trudged off.

Elliot pulled off his toque and scratched his greasy scalp. ''And drag out what's left of the food,'' he called.

''Roger wilco.''

Something like a brief gust of icy wind swept through Elliot, and he turned and stared at Frank's retreating back.

> *There's a little black spot on the sun today.*
> *It's the same old thing as yesterday...*

THE SECOND DAY

ELLIOT HUNCHED HIS SHOULDERS against a wind-whipped gust of snow and tried to avoid pissing on his leg. The occasional snow flurries that had started just after dark had merged through the night into a steady barrage of white... and now, at dawn, a full-fledged blizzard. Just fucking great, thought Elliot.

He finished as quickly as he could and hurried back into

the tent, pulling the heavy flaps together behind him.

"Don't zip it — I gotta go, too."

Elliot stared at Frank who was still curled up in his sleeping bag, face cradled on one arm.

"So get up and go."

"Ooh, hey, somebody got up on the wrong side of the sleeping bag." Frank shifted, but made no attempt to rise. "Weather don't sound too good."

"Sherlock-fucking-Holmes." Elliot zipped the flaps closed, kicked off his Sorels, and padded over to his cot.

"What's the plan, Mister Bossman?" Frank scooped up a pack of cigarettes from the floor beside his cot.

"Whadaya mean, 'what's the plan'?"

Frank levered himself onto one elbow and struck a match. "Like, what's the plan? I mean, we're almost out of stove oil, food, and all that other kind of luxury stuff."

Elliot grabbed his diary from inside his packed duffel bag, opened it and pulled a pen from the little pocket inside the front cover.

"It's spelled s-n-o-w."

"Very fucking funny."

Frank waved out the match and sat up. "Well?" he asked, scratching his chest.

Elliot looked up. "Well what?"

"You still haven't told me the plan."

"What are you talking about?"

Frank gave a quick irritated sigh. "What the fuck are we gonna do, Mister Bossman?"

Elliot opened his mouth to answer, and suddenly the inner wind was back, swirling through him in icy gusts. But unlike the day before, it didn't immediately blow away, it kept building

"Hey"
kept gathering strength
"Elliot"
until it was a thundering gale
"what's wrong?"
that drowned out the blizzard outside
"WHAT'S WRONG IS I'M FUCKING STUCK OUT HERE WITH YOU ON THIS GODDAMN LAKE, THAT'S WHAT'S WRONG!"
And the wind was gone.

Elliot found himself halfway across the tent, Frank staring up at him, wide-eyed. He didn't even remember standing up.

A long moment passed, filled only by the soft chuckle of the wind in the flue of the Bradley oil stove. Then Frank said, softly, "Hey, Elliot, chill out, okay?"

Elliot was staring at his palms; his fists had been clenched so tightly that his fingernails had left painful half-moon indentations in them. And he was so empty inside...

"Elliot?"

He lifted his eyes.

"Uh... you okay, bud? Look, I... "

"But... "

Elliot turned away and sat back down on his cot.

Frank stared a moment longer, then swung his legs out of the sleeping bag. "Look, Elliot, I didn't mean... "

"I know."

Frank opened his mouth again, but whatever he had intended to say remained inside. He closed it, then stood and pulled on a pair of pants and a checked doeskin shirt. He stuffed his bare feet into his boots and clumped outside.

Elliot glanced up as he left, then looked around the tent. His diary was sitting open on the floor behind the Bradley stove; he tried, and failed, to remember throwing it. What he

did remember was eighth grade. Another boy — Bobby...
Krantz, Bobby Krantz, that was his name — had been the
bane of Elliot's existence that year. Elliot had never really
understood why; maybe he had been an easy target, a slight,
non-athletic boy at an age when appearance and physical
skill were everything. Or maybe Bobby had just been an
asshole. Whatever the reason, Elliot had been Bobby's victim of choice, someone to be threatened and humiliated at
every opportunity. Elliot had borne it as well as he could,
knowing that June and the end of school would be the end of
the torment — Bobby lived in a different part of town, which
meant the boys would be going to different high schools
come September.

But they never made it to June. Elliot couldn't even
remember the details. He knew only that it had happened
after school one sunny afternoon in May as he unlocked his
bike from the metal racks outside the school. He'd just
unwrapped the heavy chain from around the ten-speed's
frame, when Bobby had said or done whatever it was that he
had said or done. And then that wind had come.

Elliot's next memory was of Bobby lying curled up in the
playground dirt, hands clamped over his face. A wet sound
full of blood and broken teeth bubbled out from between his
fingers, and there was blood on his hands, his shirt, in his
hair — and on the chain that still dangled from Elliot's hand.
Kids clustered around in horrified fascination, and there was
shouting, and somebody said, ''He's killed him,'' and then a
teacher that Elliot hardly knew took away the chain and led
him back inside the school...

Bobby Krantz. Elliot shook his head.

He stood and retrieved his diary, taking care not to brush
against the hot stove.

He'd never seen Bobby Krantz again.

The man who had talked to Elliot about it afterwards had insisted that he should feel bad about what he had done, about Bobby's jaw being wired shut, the reconstructive dental work, all that pain.

And Elliot had tried. He really had. But in the end he'd felt nothing, nothing at all.

With a loud thumping, Frank kicked the snow off his boots and came back into the tent, frost on his beard, hands stuck under his armpits. "It's one lousy fucking day out there," he said with an exaggerated grin.

No, there was really nothing to write about today, Elliot realized, and put the diary away.

THEY STOOD SIDE BY SIDE on the ice with their backs to the wind and stared into the western sky. Wispy grey clouds whipped along beneath a higher, darker overcast.

"We should walk out," Frank said finally.

Elliot pressed his lips together, and, in a monotone, repeated the words: "We should walk out."

"Yeah. Out to the winter road. Two days at most."

"What if the plane comes?"

"We leave a note."

"We're not walking."

Frank stepped back and looked at Elliot. "There's only enough oil for tonight, maybe tomorrow. We're gonna... "

"We're not walking, Frank. And THAT IS FUCKING THAT!"

ELLIOT ADJUSTED THE HEADPHONES AND burrowed deeper into the sleeping bag. There was just the faintest of trembles in Sting's voice. It occurred to him that the batteries were going. The music blocked out the sound of Frank snoring.

There's a red fox torn by the huntsman's pack,
It's my soul up there,
There's a black-winged gull with a broken back,
It's my soul up there...

Elliot drifted off to sleep.

THE THIRD DAY

THE SOUND WAS UNMISTAKABLE — a big radial engine, the kind mounted in a DeHavilland Beaver or, more likely, an Otter. The bass throb had been growing steadily for several minutes. Even allowing for the sound-enhancing effect of the cold air, it wasn't far off.

There was only one problem. The sky remained an uncompromising grey.

"Must be clear right above that overcast," Frank said, eyes fixed on the sky. "All we need is a break big enough for him to get down through... "

Elliot nodded. "He must know something we don't — like maybe there's clear air coming in and — " He stopped, as Frank stiffened and pointed to the south. "Ask and ye shall receive, Mister Bossman!"

Elliot followed Frank's finger. Sure enough, just visible over the skeletal poplars that lined the west end of the lake was a ragged patch of blue. As he watched, it cleared the network of upraised branches, and drifted slowly towards the zenith. Another break was close behind. Elliot let out a whoop. Even as he did so, the rumble of the unseen plane's engine dropped in pitch as the pilot throttled back. "Okay, Frank, let's get — Frank? What's wrong?"

Frank was still staring at the approaching patches of blue, but his shoulders had slumped. "Sucker hole," was all he said.

"No way, that's no sucker hole."

Frank shook his head, but Elliot ignored him. Any second now, the plane should break through the overcast.

But it continued circling, now overhead, now off to the south. And the break continued drifting across the sky.

"Come on," muttered Elliot.

Now the break was almost overhead. Blue sky shone through; a poplar-covered ridge to the northeast flared with sudden gold as the unseen sun swept across it.

"Come on... come on, come down... come on..." Elliot's voice was a monotone.

The sound of the plane's engine changed again, rising and getting louder as the pilot advanced the throttle. At the same time, it began to move southward.

"What the fuck is he doing?"

"He's going home," said Frank.

"But..."

The break had drifted off to the northeast. For a moment, as it passed across the rising sun, it washed them in a dazzling light. They were forced to shade their eyes against the unaccustomed glare from sky and snow. Then it was gone as the cloud cover rolled back in, charcoal grey and heavy with the threat of snow.

"Maybe a break between storm fronts," offered Frank.

But Elliot said nothing. He stared to the south, until the sound of the plane was swallowed by the rising wind.

EVEN THROTTLED RIGHT DOWN, the Bradley stove was beginning to gutter. Sucking air, Elliot thought with a frown. But he shrugged as he picked up the metal basin of hot water that sat on top of it. It didn't really matter.

He placed the basin on the rickety table of balsam logs and plywood, threw his towel over one shoulder and adjusted the position of the Coleman lantern. With careful deliberation, he squirted some shaving cream from the aerosol can into his hand and, using the little mirror inside the lid of his Silva compass, began to spread it on his face.

He had just picked up his straight razor, a relic that had belonged to his father, when Frank stomped back into the tent. A draft swirled in with him, bringing a few snowflakes with it and raising goosebumps on Elliot's bare back. His shoulders tensed, but he said nothing.

"At least we got lots of this left," Frank began, holding up a roll of toilet paper. Then he stopped, staring. "What the hell are you doing?"

"What does it look like?" Elliot opened the razor, eyed the keen blade and nodded to himself, satisfied.

"Okay, you're shaving. But why?"

"Because I don't want to look like an animal when we get into town tomorrow."

"Oh." Frank nodded, but his eyebrows were drawn together in puzzlement. "We're going to town tomorrow?"

"Yes." He placed the razor edge carefully against his cheek, and made the first stroke.

Frank watched for a few seconds, then pulled off his boots. "Okay," he said finally, brushing snow off one sock, "I'll bite. How?"

"Plane, of course." Elliot made another stroke.

Frank lowered his foot and shifted uncomfortably. "Uh, hate to rain on your parade, Elliot, but the weather — "

" — is going to be fine by morning." Stroke.

Frank tugged off his parka, picked up his cigarettes and snorted in disgust. "Well, I hope you're right. I'm down to my last two smokes." He stared at the pack, shrugged and pulled one out. "Might have to walk out, just to get some more... " His voice trailed away as Elliot turned, razor poised beside his face. That inner wind, which had been a breeze wafting through him since the incident with the plane that morning, had suddenly whipped up in frigid gusts. "That issue is settled, Frank. We're not walking anywhere."

"I only — "

"I SAID, we're getting out of here tomorrow, and we're not going to walk, because the weather's going to be fine because you're going to shut up so you DON'T FUCK IT UP LIKE YOU DID TODAY WITH THAT PLANE DO YOU UNDERSTAND?" The razor shook as Elliot spoke, causing white naphtha light to flicker off its blade.

Frank backed up a step, but he stopped, nearly tripped, as the backs of his knees collided with the edge of his cot. By the time he'd recovered, Elliot had turned away.

And made another stroke.

THE LAST DAY

ELLIOT KNEW IT AS SOON AS he awoke. The wind told him, in a voice that sounded like Sting's.

He rolled over, taking in Frank's empty cot and the cold Bradley stove — the fuel had run out during the night.

Getting colder, the wind said, and Elliot nodded agreement.

When he'd dressed — an unhurried process, despite the cold — he stepped outside and was struck by two things:

One, Frank's trail was clearly visible, receding down the lake to the southeast. And, two, the reason it was getting colder was that the storm had finally passed, and the hard arctic air that invariably follows was closing in. Elliot glanced up at the ragged fringe of cloud that was the storm's trailing edge, then at the metallic blue sky beyond. The sun wasn't visible, but a golden glow flaring above the trees marked its imminent rise. "Told you, Frank," Elliot said. "You should have listened to me, shouldn't have disobeyed me... " And then the wind rose, drowning all other sounds. Elliot picked up the axe.

He sang as he walked, and other voices sang with him — unknown voices, emanating from somewhere between his temples. And Sting's voice, too, of course.

> *With the world turning circles, running*
> *'round my brain,*
> *I guess I'm always hoping that you'll end this rain,*
> *But it's my destiny to be the King of Pain...*

The miles passed, a steady parade of tree and rock and frozen lake, all covered by snow that glittered diamond-bright beneath the frigid sun. Once, Elliot stopped, thinking he heard a drone overhead, but the wind rose suddenly, drowning it out.

The sun reached and passed the zenith, and began to slide.

Elliot dug into his parka and shoved a frozen wad of raisins into his mouth. He stopped at the edge of a small stream draw. Strangely, a torrent of water was rushing through it. The snow and ice along its banks had been washed away, exposing rocks and frozen peat and spindly alder roots. And then he saw the reason, nearly out of sight up the draw. A pile of logs and branches had been tossed down from a collapsed beaver dam, probably by the shifting weight of ice on the lake above and beyond. The snowshoe trail angled up through the alders and tamarack on the far slope toward the lake.

Taking the axe in his hand for balance, Elliot crossed the stream, which proved easier than it had first appeared; the water level had obviously dropped significantly since the dam had broken. He headed up the slope on the far side.

And then he was at the top, on the edge of the lake. Shading his eyes against the glare of the sun, he gazed across it — and stiffened as something moved.

Hey, Elliot, the voices said, look who's over there...

Perhaps two hundred yards away, Frank was working his way along the edge of the lake. He was limping. Not surprising, Elliot thought, as he spit the wad of raisins into the snow. All this time, he's been breaking trail through deep powder.

The voices crowed, and Elliot gripped the axe and advanced.

For a long while, Frank didn't notice him. He seemed to be studying the surface of the lake — stopping, looking, starting again — as if trying to decide whether to cross. Suddenly, he turned, as though Elliot had called out (maybe it was the voices; could Frank hear them, too?).

And then Frank was running, shouting something, but Elliot couldn't make it out over the wind. It didn't matter anyway; there was no way he could get away.

An explosive crack, like a rifle shot, pierced even the howl of the wind.

Frank spun around and bounded desperately toward the

shore, thirty or forty feet away. Another crack, and the ice around him sagged and began to turn grey. He looked down, horrified, as water swirled up around his feet.

The beaver dam — that was it, Elliot realized. When it had broken, it had caused the water level in the lake to drop, which in turn had allowed the ice to sink and crack. And the weight of the new snow had made matters worse.

There was a drawn-out crackle as the ice beneath Frank failed altogether, and he splashed through, into the lake. At the last second he grabbed a bobbing chunk of ice, but in the frigid water, he had moments at best before his strength would fail.

The voices rose gleefully in Elliot's head.

King of Pain...

He relaxed his grip on the axe,

I'll always be...

stepped back toward the shore,

the King of PAIN...

and waited for the end.

It wouldn't be long.

It was really too bad, but Frank should have listened.

"ELLIOT... PLEASE!"

Frank's cries rose briefly through the wind and voices.

NO... PAIN!

"ELLIOT... PLEASE... HELP ME... "

NOOOO... PAINNNNN! the voices shrieked, and the wind became a hurricane.

"OH GOD... PLEASE... ELLIOT PLEASE!" The words rang in his head, the same words as Bobby Krantz's.

"PLEASE!"

He should have felt bad about what he did to Bobby, the man had said. No matter how mean Bobby had been, he hadn't deserved what Elliot had done.

"ELLIOT!"

Bobby hadn't deserved it, and maybe Frank didn't deserve this.

"PLEASE!"

The voices howled *PAIN,* and the wind reached a crescendo.

And then Elliot made his decision. Raising the axe, he charged across the snow.

"ELLIOT, NOOOO..."

But Elliot didn't falter; reaching the edge of the broken ice, he launched himself forward and swung the axe.

Frank's eyes went wide with horror as the blade descended... and struck the ice inches from his hand.

The voices and the wind rose in a last frustrated wail, and were gone.

"GRAB IT!" Elliot shouted as he splashed down, spread-eagled, on the sagging ice. "GRAB THE FUCKING AXE!"

Frank's fingers slipped across the ice, away from the axe.

"GRAB IT!" Elliot shouted. The water sloshing around him felt like liquid fire; Frank, he was sure, must be half dead. And Elliot thought he felt the ice beneath him sinking.

"GRAB THE FUCKING AXE NOW FRANK OR THAT'S IT! YOU'RE GONE!"

Their eyes met and locked, and Frank reached out his hand.

EVERY FIBRE OF HIS BEING CRIED out to Elliot to stop, lie down and just sleep in the soft snow. But he knew to do so would mean swift death for him and for Frank. The exertion of pulling Frank out of the water and across the broken ice to shore had given him a brief semblance of warmth. Soon it would be gone. Elliot forced himself to his feet and lifted the axe.

Frank raised his eyes to it. Elliot drew a ragged breath. ''Wood,'' he said calmly, ''... for fire.''

Frank nodded.

Elliot looked at him lying helpless in the snow, then turned and walked off toward the trees.

Starting Over
Hazel Fulford

THE DAILY CRY OF THE AMBULANCE died as Lily closed the gate behind her. She could hear the chanting in the pool:

We must, we must, we must improve our bust
For fear, for fear, it all goes to the rear.

The Water Babies were five minutes into their routine. She'd have to wade through row after row of them to find a spot at the back where the deeper water made her fight to keep her balance.

Birds twittered and trilled in the orange trees; white petals sifted to the ground. Old women in the pool stretched and jogged and flung their arms about with the vigour of forty-year-olds. Diamonds blazed on fingers twisted like the branches of ancient trees. A whiff of orange blossom drifted past the gray heads.

At the instructor's whistle all splashing ceased and forty heads turned to the woman in the centre of the group. She had a face like melting wax, coarse tufts of bleached hair, and the lung power of a drill sergeant. "Time out!" she bellowed. "Who's got a story today? Hold on, Sally has a new bathing suit! Some class, honey. Are you looking for a man?'' Everyone stared at the body still trim in black Spandex, at exposed skin just starting to wither. Sally ripped off her name-tag and pitched it over neighbouring heads. She climbed three broad steps to the pool deck and stalked as haughtily as she could to the shower room. After a brief silence the shouted orders and the splashing resumed. It was not unusual for someone new to have trouble fitting in. Lily herself had barely mouthed the chants the first year.

She left the group five minutes early and clopped in rubber slippers to the hot tub. She sighed as she eased herself into the steaming water and the heat began to comfort her knees. Dolores sat in front of one of the jets; foam boiled and eddied around her crooked spine. ''How do you like that bitch?'' she said. ''If Sally can't take a little kidding she don't belong with this gang. And where have *you* been, Lily?''

''Down with flu. Does Sybil have it now? I see there's a new instructor.''

''Sybil's gone. Heart attack. Kids came and took her back to Winnipeg. Hey, you got your tickets for The Silver Belles? It's this Friday, you know.''

''Heavens, I forgot,'' Lily said, recalling last year's singers in feathered costumes, wavering on the high notes but game to the very end. ''I'll get the tickets today.'' Dolores had a sister in the Belles. Someone was always cracking the whip.

After her shower Lily left the top button of her shorts undone and fastened a safety pin under the zipper tab. Under a sign that begged, LADIES PLEASE DON'T DYE IN THE SINK, she examined the limp gray hair dripping around her face. Swimming every day was hard on a perm. She tied a hat under her chin and oiled herself for the walk home to B

Street. White patches gleamed on her bare brown arms. Her eyes shone blue in a face deeply tanned in spite of the Factor 15 sunscreen.

Lily strode briskly down the shimmering sidewalk past familiar bowers designed to distract the eye from bulbous gas cylinders and rusty axles. Seven ceramic dwarfs marched perpetually in one tiny yard; a huge Mexican vase dominated another; Snoopy dogs made from plastic gallon jugs guarded little plots of cacti. Messages lettered on paving stones — WELCOME 2R HOME — no longer made Lily smile. She breathed again the pungent sweetness of orange blossoms and thought of tea and a peanut butter sandwich. There was no time to waste. If she waited for Hank, all the suncots back at the pool would be taken. He'd be home around noon, sunburned and sweating, his golf shirt wrinkled and stained. He'd gulp a beer, then collapse on the couch under the whirring fan. In the long narrow trailer sealed against the heat, blinds drawn, he'd sleep like the dead.

They had borrowed the trailer seven years ago from Hank's brother, and had used it for six weeks during Hank's last holiday before retirement. He said Arizona would be the first of a series of Sunshine States they would try out. She was willing to try a new place each year for a while. But she'd heard that the coastal areas of Spain and Portugal catered to retirees, and she dreamed of white cottages and new apartment buildings with wrought iron balconies splashed with scarlet petals. She could see them on one of those balconies, under a striped umbrella. They would watch the fishing boats come in, late in the afternoon. They would see the last great palace of the Moors in Granada. They would mingle with gypsies and toreadors and flamenco dancers. Lily had read and re-read Michener's *Iberia* until pages fluttered free each time she opened the book.

When they returned to Arizona after Hank retired he had already bought his brother's trailer and installed it on a permanent site. "We'll fix it up," he said. "Make a profit on it next year and move on. Try Texas, Florida, maybe even Mexico." When he was through with it, it would sell in a minute, he told her, going so far as to promise her a two-bedroom place when they found the perfect spot. "Starting over, kiddo," he said. "Let's take our time and do it right."

The trailer was a playhouse that winter. Lily bought blue dishes to match the print on the curtains and found quilted cushions to bring out the desert tones in the chesterfield. She acquired only things that were easily portable; she would keep the same colour scheme in the next place. The furniture would be sold with the trailer. In the meantime Hank was reading *Iberia*, and though he usually fell asleep after a few pages she felt sure that Michener would eventually spark his interest.

The third year, the concrete patio was poured, and during the fourth winter Hank invested two thousand dollars in a metal awning to shade the outdoor sitting area. "This place would fetch a good price now," Lily said. She'd spoken those very words the year before.

"Oh, I don't know," Hank said. "Why traipse all over the country when we have everything we need right here? Count your blessings, Lily. People are freezing their butts off back home. Paradise Park is perfect for us."

Perfect: Sky-high palms with thick trunks lined the streets and converged on the main gate like a phalanx of elephants. It was a circus where the acts never changed. She should have learned to drive; there was no escape without wheels.

WHEN THE INVITATION HAD COME at the end of February during that fourth year, she could hardly believe it. They hadn't seen Tony and Maria for twenty years, not since they had moved to Toronto, although they still exchanged Christmas cards. And now, here it was, a summons to their youngest child's wedding, the son of their middle age, born when Maria was thirty-eight.

Now Anthony was to marry a Thunder Bay girl in the same church where Hank and Lily had stood up for Tony and Maria. St. Andrews. Not far from PACI, the high school where they all had met.

Tony Braziano and Hank White had been the cutest boys in Form I. And Lily had had them wrapped around her little finger. Lily herself had never been sure which boy she liked best. Hank was a full three inches taller; Tony was nose to nose with Lily. When he fixed his dark eyes on hers, she felt like a kitten in thrall to a panther.

In Form IV Lily confided to Maria that she had decided not to go out alone with Tony. "He's all hands," she told her. "And pretty darned hard to resist."

"So why resist?" said Maria.

"WOULDN'T YOU LIKE TO BE LILY WHITE?" Hank asked as they strolled around the school grounds the night of their graduation dance. *Lily White.* She suppressed her giggles; for him this was a solemn moment.

"Mom and Dad would have a fit," she said. "They want me to take nurse's training before I settle down."

"I want you to wear my grandmother's engagement ring," Hank said. Lily had seen it, a ruby the size of a wild strawberry encircled by brilliant-cut diamonds. Even as she envisioned it, she could see Tony in black dress pants, his gleaming Italian shoes jutting from narrow cuffs.

While she mulled over her future, Lily was hired as a clerk in Hank's uncle's clothing store where Hank was edging his way up to manager. He continued to talk about marriage; Lily wavered.

When she was nineteen, Tony married a pregnant Maria. The following year Lily put on twelve yards of whitest satin and, with her best smile in place, drifted to the head of the aisle where Hank waited, as solid and dependable as a brick wall.

On the whole it had worked out well. Hank had been a good father. It wasn't his fault that Diane had ''gone off the deep end,'' as he called it, in her teens. Secretly, Lily had envied Diane, had wished that she were young again. Diane was having a ball — incense, Beatles, boyfriends. One morning before they left for the store Hank caught Lily dressed in Diane's bellbottoms and beaded vest, gazing at herself in the mirror. ''For God's sake, Lily, grow up!'' he rumbled, looming over her like a great gray mountain.

By the time Diane finished university, Lily had been made a buyer for the store. She was just discovering the scope of her talent when her husband announced his plan to retire early. ''Well, if that's what you want,'' she said. ''But I am *never* going to live in a tin box in one of those death camps where old people creep around on tricycles.''

''Of course not,'' Hank said. ''We can do better than that. Maybe a condo near a good golf course.''

''With a big swimming pool,'' said Lily, who didn't golf.

THE SAME WEEK THAT THE METAL awning went up, Lily had felt a surge of desperation. When the wedding invitation arrived a few days later, she could hardly wait for Hank to get home.

"Look!" she cried. "You won't believe it! Can we go home two weeks early? The wedding is Easter week. I'll have to buy a new dress..."

"Whoa!" Hank said. He crossed the kitchen, took a beer out of the fridge and looked skeptically at the invitation. "We haven't seen Tony and Maria in years!" He re-examined the invitation as if it were tainted. "I don't want to go," he said flatly. "There'll still be snow on the ground."

Lily's face grew hot. She twisted the rings on her left hand as she always did at such moments. Her wedding band was plain gold; her engagement ring a conventional solitaire. She could hear Hank's earnest voice: *I want you to have a ring that we've bought together. Our daughter will have it someday, and our granddaughter.* There was no granddaughter. And Diane wore a single silver and turquoise band that she and her common-law husband had picked up in Mexico. These days, they ran a music store and lived in stonewashed jeans and fringed jackets.

"Don't nag," Hank said the next morning when Lily tried to talk to him about the wedding. For some reason it seemed urgent to her that they see Tony and Maria, that they go back to their beginnings, gain a new perspective. Maybe they could pull out of this rut, sell the trailer, do something different. Lily was bursting with the feeling that they still had a lot of living to do.

"I couldn't get away anyway," he said. "I have a golf tournament that week."

"They're our oldest friends," said Lily. "I want to go."

TWO WEEKS LATER, AT FIVE A.M., Lily tiptoed from the trailer and left Paradise Park alone. She'd stashed her suitcase, the day before, in a corner of the utility shed under a pile of laundry. When the airport limo cruised into B Street she was already on the sidewalk. As far as she was concerned, Hank could close up the trailer and drive home alone. He could sell the damn thing, blue dishes and all, and give her Arizona clothes to charity. She might never come back.

When panic struck, five miles above Kansas, she ordered wine. The wedding was a week off. How would she explain turning up in Thunder Bay without Hank? What would she do for a whole week? She could stay a couple of days in Toronto, go to the Royal Alex, maybe call Maria and Tony in Mississauga. Lily refused a snack and tossed back another glass of Chianti. As her third glass took its effect she wondered if Maria had ever known she was Tony's second choice?

She checked into the Royal York (Hank would be livid) and took a cab to the Eaton Centre. The cunningly draped rose crepe was three hundred dollars, but it made her look almost slender. At the beauty salon she demanded an immediate appointment. ''I want to return to my natural colour,'' she said. ''A golden brown.''

The stylist drew swatches of false hair from a drawer and held a soft honey blonde against Lily's cheek. ''My advice is to go a shade or two lighter,'' she said. ''It'll take off ten years.'' Sure, what the hell, thought Lily.

Back at the hotel she eyed the phone book. She knew the name of Tony's company. But she needed a pick-me-up. She lifted the receiver and asked for room service. ''A half litre of your best dry white wine, please.'' Should she order a sandwich? No, Tony would take her to lunch. A late lunch, she thought — it was nearly three o'clock.

She sipped her wine and studied her reflection in the bathroom mirror. The new hair colour reminded her of a doll she'd had long ago, a Shirley Temple doll. She drew a circle on each cheek with raspberry blusher. Nothing in her suitcase seemed stylish enough for Toronto and the fair curls. She put on the rose crepe gown. A bit dressy for street wear, but the mid-calf length was okay. Too bad she hadn't bought a new coat. Her gray all-weather would have to do. It was raining now anyway. She pulled it on and dialed Tony's number.

"May I tell him who's calling?" said the secretary.

"No," she said, "I want to surprise him. I'm an old friend."

"Very well, come down, I'll let him know."

In her haste to leave the taxi, Lily forgot to pay the driver. She stood in the downpour and fished in her purse for cash. In the elevator's mirrored walls she saw that the coat was three inches too short for the rose dress. The new hairdo clung to her skull, soaked out of shape. She pushed at it with both hands; it would curl up as it dried. Men never noticed details, she told herself. Besides, Tony would see nothing but her eyes, the bright blue eyes of a teenager.

She stumbled in the doorway of the outer office. The new high heels. She teetered to an overstuffed chair. "I'm the mysterious lady friend!" she called, waggling her fingers at the secretary. The girl raised her eyebrows, nodded and returned to her computer.

When Lily had waited fifteen minutes, she rested her head on the back of the chair, doing further mischief to her coiffure. Suddenly, she was peering at a giant who stood over her speaking in a faraway echo. "Mr. Braziano will see you now," the secretary repeated, tapping her on the shoulder.

And Lily found herself in the corner office where Tony,

standing behind his mahogany desk with the phone in his hand, stared at her in blank astonishment. He was as trim as ever, the only change a silver streak in his black mop. He turned toward the window and murmured into the receiver, "Honey, I'll be there. No problem. I have the tickets in my shirt pocket, right next to my heart. See you tonight."

He cradled the phone and looked at Lily enquiringly. "Yes?" he said. "How can I help you?"

"Tony!" she cried. "Don't you know me? Lily! Lily White!"

"*Goodness,*" he said. "How stupid of me. Sit down." He nodded toward a chair. "How have you been? When did you get to the city?"

"This morning," she said. She wondered if she sounded as muddled as she felt. "I thought I might stop over a few days, see a show, do some shopping. Nothing but straw hats and bathing suits in the shops down south. I might give Maria a call."

"Maria's already in Thunder Bay," he said.

Lily looked at him — *who had he been talking to on the phone?*

She could feel her focus beginning to waver. Tony kept talking... how's Hank, when do you expect him, how's the south treating you? "He's in Arizona," she said slowly, and it occurred to her that she didn't even know Tony now. What was she doing here in this strange office with this strange man? "He doesn't know I'm... "

"Are you all right?" she heard him say.

"Tony," she said too loudly, "I have to go." She stood up, staggered, clutched the back of the chair, kicked off the high heels and walked in stocking feet to the door. The sodden hem of her dress clung to her legs below the short coat. Her head was high; the dye job frizzed out around her ears. As she reached the outer office, she heard Tony mumble into the phone, "Call Hank White in Arizona."

BY NOON THE NEXT DAY, LILY was back at the trailer park. The rose dress, rolled into a tight ball, was at the bottom of a Toronto trash can. The note she'd left Hank was still on the fridge, surrounded by newspaper clips and shopping lists. At dinner that night she tried to explain but Hank cut her off. "Let's forget it," he said, looking at her over the top of his glasses. There was a touch of re-appraisal in his glance. *Was the old girl cracking up?*

THE FOLLOWING JANUARY, she said to Hank, "Can't we drive into Mexico for a few days?" This time he humoured her. They crossed the border at Nogales in good spirits, but in Hermosillo the car broke down. When they both got sick, even Lily was ready to go home to Paradise Park.

NOW THAT THE PATIO WAS CARPETED and they had a new utility shed with their own washer and dryer, they stayed put. Lily returned to Thunder Bay every year with a tan that was the envy of her neighbourhood. This would be the last year she'd dare to lie for hours in the sun. She would tempt fate for one more season, in spite of coming face to face with the man from C Street who had a piece missing from his nose.

Lily finished her sandwich, closed the venetian blinds and hurried back to the pool deck. By twelve o'clock, half naked and freshly anointed, she lay still under the powerful rays. Maybe Hank would take her to the dance tonight. They hadn't danced in years although they both enjoyed the live band and the old tunes. "Sentimental Journey," "Stardust,"

"Dance with a Dolly."

She needed a new blouse. If not a blouse, perhaps a belt for her blue dress, some glittery beads or a little white cardigan like the one she'd lost when she left it drying on the patio table. She'd seen a woman wearing one just like it, but that didn't prove anything; most of them shopped at the plaza nearby where sales were frequent and prices good. Lily didn't like shopping there. Children screamed in the stores, and teenagers with spiked hair stared through her as though the space she occupied were empty.

No, she'd look elsewhere for something to wear tonight. Perhaps she'd find a Liz Claibourne shirt or a Jantzen sweater, like the clothes scattered on the benches when the teams came here for the shuffleboard tournaments. People came from all over the state for the playoffs. Some of them were very smartly dressed. Yes, Lily thought, I really need something new.

If only the girl behind the glass at the main office would look up, *just once*. She always said, "Lost-and-found-first-door-on-the-left-hope-you-find-it," her bright head bent over something or other. At first, Lily had chosen only two or three things of good quality from the largest carton while her eyes shifted every few seconds to the head of the young secretary just visible over the half wall. These days she took her time and emptied all the boxes, littering the floor with socks and sunglasses, half-knitted sweaters, board games, peaked caps labelled "Old Fart's Wife," and, once, a huge plastic bag of popcorn. Sometimes she returned things that didn't fit or were not quite the right colour. After all, Lost and Found went to charity at the end of the season. And no matter how much mess she made, Lily always took time to ram everything back into the boxes, then pushed and panted until the containers stood in their rightful corner of the room.

As for Hank, on the rare occasions when he noticed what she wore, she'd say, ''For heaven's sake, dear, you were with me when I bought it.''

Yes, she'd stop on her way home today. The shopping bag was folded and zipped into its separate compartment in her swim tote. Tomorrow, perhaps, she'd join the craft class. She would give her Snoopy dog a purple tongue and ears, just to be different. Black was so boring, Lily thought as she dozed off under the broiling sun. In the distance a siren howled. The screech intensified as the ambulance charged the main gate and sped down B Street. Lily did not stir.

A Canadian Story: 1955
Elizabeth Kouhi

THE FINNISH PART OF BAY STREET starts at the steambath and continues for two blocks westward. While not strictly within these bounds, the two beer parlours are immediately to the east and thus well within hailing distance. There is on the east side, too, a shoemaker shop and a small watch repair place that belong west of the steambath if you wanted to tidy up the area ethnically.

On one side of the steambath is an insurance agent with a name full of vowels and on the other a travel agency whose posters urge passers-by to spend *Juhannus* or Christmas in Finland depending on the time of year. Next up the street is a men's clothing store that hardly differs from those elsewhere in the city except for the occasional display of work shirts, heavy boots and overalls. The small restaurant next door, with salt fish and *viili piima* signs, draws most of its clientele from the beer parlours down the street. The wall in front of the restaurant and the neighbouring pool room has a nice wide ledge that makes for good leaning, half sitting. In the spring on warm sunny days, after pulpwood camp layoffs, the men leave their little rented rooms and perch on these ledges like so many oversized sparrows.

This area west of the steambath is not altogether tidy ethnically. On the opposite side of the street sprawl an Anglo-Saxon fish market, a Chinese laundry, and an Italian shoemaker. The drug store at the corner boasts a good Scot Mac in its name. However, any Finlander can get along in these establishments as the laundry man and the shoemaker speak a few words of Finnish and the clerks in the drug store and the fish shop have been picked for their linguistic abilities.

Kitty-corner from the drug store is a coffee bar and a novelty and magazine shop, run, it seems, mostly for the passers-by, the clerks and bookkeepers in the vicinity and for second and third generation Canadians who no longer patronize the *Suomalainenkirjakauppa* next door, where the newer immigrant can get Helsinki and Vaasa newspapers.

There are more shops up the street — a small watch repair shop, an appliance store; a bakeshop with its loaves of rye, long, or round with a hole, or round without a hole. At baking time, sweet fragrances float across the street where the benches by the Labour Hall provide another popular congregating place for the lumberjacks. This is, of course, the first Hall and it has a Co-op restaurant in its basement. There is another Hall next door and these two buildings are of great significance, especially to earlier, more politically conscious generations. On the far side of the Halls a chain saw sign flashes with its reds and greens chasing each other around an ellipse.

It was a day in May and the sun was warm. Where one was sheltered from the cool breeze off the lake, it was quite comfortable in shirt sleeves. The bench against the taxi stand wall was well protected and this particular day three men sat on it, hunched over with their elbows on their knees, their shoulders and long backs making a strong series of curves against the weather-beaten wall. Jussi, the oldest of the three, in a blue-striped Sunday shirt, with suspenders straining his shoulders, was reading a newspaper. He was a stocky man, heavy but not fat, and his silvery white hair shone in the sunlight against the brown of his neck and face. Something in the left hand column suddenly took his interest. A puzzled look came over his face and his small eyes crinkled even smaller as he examined the spot in the newspaper.

Lauri, the man in the middle, was younger and taller, dressed in a sport shirt and slacks. He was fairish in a sandy way and would soon be bald. He merely sat, his hands folded, looking at the cars and trucks going by and at the flashing chain saw sign.

Matti, the third man, sat up and rolled a cigarette. He had just finished smoking one, but with the same motion used to throw away the butt, he reached into his pocket for makings. Years ago, Matti had been a picture of the lumberjack usually found only in novels: tall, broad-shouldered and blond with his large northern blue eyes set wide apart and a grin that sent girls of all ages into giggles. In age Matti was somewhere between the other two, and only remnants of his good looks were still visible. A few days in town had put a stoop back into his shoulders, which were much thinner now, a greyness into his cheeks, and had bleached his eyes to a watery paleness. He wore a rumpled suit with one wing of a limp white collar sticking out and his bright blue tie awry to the opposite side.

Jussi leaned in front of Lauri to show the paper to Matti and pointed to an item in it.

"Matti, is that you? The same name but I don't know what village you come from."

Lauri peered into the paper and read: "Matti Peltonen —

sister Alma Peltonen desires to contact, last heard from in Port Arthur.''

Matti threw away half a cigarette and reached into his pocket for makings. He stared at the paper and spit out all the Finnish names for the devil. Jussi pulled the paper back and said, ''Seems to me I've heard you say something about a sister but for sure you're not the sort who disappeared into the Americas.'' Jussi was gentle and kindly, and when they first met many years ago, Matti had taken to this older man with the soft, musical Karelian accent, even though he had many times since scorned Jussi's concern for him and made fun of his pronunciation.

''But I don't know of any other Matti Peltonen.'' He looked at Matti. ''What do you say?'' he persisted.

''Maybe your sister has money and wants to give you some,'' Lauri interjected. ''I've heard that you're a real *talonpoika*, not a poor farmer's seventh son like most of us on Bay Street. I sure wouldn't stay here if I had a home in the Old Country.''

''What the devil do you care what I do, what are you doing worrying about it for? Some dame looking for some guy through the newspapers and right away you think it's for me. The papers are full of those notices.'' Matti bit angrily at the end of his cigarette and made a move to get up.

''Now, now, don't get mad,'' Jussi placated. ''I've known you for years, been at dozens of bush camps with you, so you needn't get huffy with old friends. But if that *is* your sister I sure think you should write to her right away. Why spend winters in the bush if you have a home in the Old Country? You aren't getting younger, you know.''

Matti sat back and focused his eyes on the burning cigarette. He made a jerky movement with his hands and feet, sat up again and looked at the other two. "Devil take you, didn't you know I came here only for five years, and I bet that's all either of you meant to stay. I came to peel off some American gold with my wooden knife, shovel it into my packsack and then head back over the puddle. I bet that's what all those guys meant to do." He spread his hands towards the Labour Hall steps where men were leaning against walls or standing around in groups.

"You didn't do too badly for yourself for a working man," Jussi reminded him. "Especially in those early days. You were a smart stepper then, all the girls watched as you walked down the street." Matti smiled and his eyes caught the ankles of a young girl passing by.

"Hmmnnn, *jaa*... hmnnn." He stared at her until she turned the corner past the chain saw place and the grocery store.

"What did you say, Jussi? Ahh, yes, in the old days...*jaa*, I had the world by the tail then. Even the girls of other tongues danced with me then. That's how I learned my English... they taught me to say 'ai loove you.' " Matti chuckled and rubbed himself against the bench.

"I don't mean just on the dance floor," Jussi said. "For a working man you made pretty good money those days. Not exactly slicing off gold, but you made four cords a day."

Matti's mood changed quickly at Jussi's words. "*Jaa*... four cords: That's rich! Now any skinny-legged brat can do ten cords with a chain saw. It's like any other job now, might as well be digging ditches. It no longer makes you feel good to go into a good spruce stand." Matti stood up, tried to pull back his shoulders which hardly obeyed. His hand trembled as he lifted it into a fist, and he swayed slightly.

"You were the best saw filer in the whole area, maybe all

of Canada. Nobody could get a bucksaw so sharp. Cutting didn't even seem like work to you.''

"Sometimes among the spruce trees I'd stand, my breath coming white in the frost, the snow squeaking under my boots. I'd just look around at the green spruce and feel the muscles in my arms bulging. Like Wainomoinen in the forests of Suomi.''

A gust of wind whirled dust at Matti's feet and a bunch of noisy young men, recent immigrants judging by their trenchcoats, descended the steps into the Co-op restaurant. The chain saw sign continued on its merry way.

Lauri took the newspaper from Jussi and stood up. "What about that notice from your sister, you going to write?''

"Didn't say it was me, did I?''

"Let's go and see Antti at the mission,'' said Jussi. "He'll write a real diplomat's letter for you. It'd be easier than writing yourself. Think of your sister, doesn't know if you're dead or alive.''

"Oh, she'd know if I were dead. They'd have shipped my gold watch back to her. In my papers I have the address carefully written.'' Matti took the watch out of his pocket and looked at it, holding it in his hand toward the sun. "A solid gold watch. The old man gave it to me when I turned eighteen, about the same time he gave me my own horse.''

Lauri looked first at Matti and then at the watch.

"What's the matter? Haven't you seen it before?'' Matti half jeered.

"Thought it was an ordinary this-country watch, the kind we all got. But that's the kind only the rich have. You must have been stark raving crazy to come here.''

"Told you, didn't I?'' Matti put the watch back into his pocket. "Came here for five years to chip off that gold, was going to show them all a thing or three. Wasn't going to take orders all my life." He lifted his head. "*Jaa*, I had the old thing by the tail in those early years. By God, I learned to file the saw and nobody, but nobody was going to beat me... me the best man with the bucksaw." His face brightened as he went on. "Just the right flick of the wrist to make those shiny teeth sharp and keen until they cut into the spruce like knife into butter. Do you remember, Jussi?" Matti was grinning now. He leaned over and rubbed his elbows on his knees. "Do you remember that winter at Park's camps when that Frenchman came and boasted all over the place that he was the real, original pulp cutter. He was going to show us Finlanders a thing or two. The guy was damned good. It was a fierce winter. But I always had an edge over him. I couldn't even take an easy day once in a while. To let him beat me would have been a national shame."

Jussi laughed. "I remember how he soon stopped boasting and never even came into our camp for cards anymore. Bet you had a good-sized cheque that spring."

"That's the closest I've gotten to going back. That spring I thought I'd hear the cuckoo again."

"Why didn't you go?" Lauri asked.

"Ha! Came into town and had a good time."

"Not on the whole cheque!"

"Drunk for a week, nothing left when I woke up. I heard the cuckoo alright. Had to head right back into the summer peelwood camps. But those still were the days, those Saturday nights, to walk into the dance hall and have those girls look at me, could've had any of them, even from those born in this country. And not just the girls, their Mammas liked me too, me a good worker. I should really have married one of them. *Jaa... jaa.*" His eyes narrowed as he reminisced.

"Girls in those days were young and soft and tender and warm to my hands. I had the gift of tongues. I sure had. Could talk the prettiest into the woods. But now!" A look of distaste came over his face. "Now the only damn whores I can get are either so fat they're like a mountain of flesh or so skinny their bones dig into you and usually smelly to boot. And it's all a matter of money. I bet Onni down the street has better luck just because he's a businessman now. He has money. His big belly won't matter even to the younger ones. Onni and I used to get along well in the old days when he was still a lumberjack... oh, hoh, we had some good times together. Now the bastard crosses the street when he sees me coming."

"That's just it," Lauri butted in. "Money! Your sister has money, more than likely enough to do you both for the rest of your lives. Let me tell you, I sure wouldn't sit on this wooden bench on Bay Street if I had a home in the Old Country."

"You'd never guess it but in the Old Country I was a white-haired Mamma's boy," said Matti. She cried when I left. But I guess that's nothing. All the Mammas of all the Bay Street lumberjacks must have cried when their sons left home. And the girls! From the village I could have had my pick... me with my own horse and gold watch." He suddenly turned to Lauri. "When did you decide you weren't going back?"

"Never had to. Nothing to go back for, no home, no relations. Used to have nightmares about going back. There I'd be in the home village in rags or stark naked. Always wanted to crawl under the closest rock but my feet would be like lead and couldn't move and there would be coming those rich kids who used to torment me. I'd be soaking wet when I woke up.''

''Every immigrant has dreamed that one,'' said Matti. ''I looked at myself in the mirror one day after a week or two with the bottle and said to that man in the mirror, 'Suomi will never see you again.' Jussi, I guess you never even wanted to go back.''

Jussi sat with his arms up on the back of the bench and the newspaper over his knees. ''It's different with me,'' he said. ''I'm an old man. A few bullcook jobs and I'll be on pension. And besides, Liisa sleeps up there by the river.'' The soft Karelian inflection became more apparent as he spoke.

''When we came, Liisa and I near fifty years ago, we too were going back someday when we made enough money. We were going to buy that *tupa* near a lake, like the old song says, with a cow, a horse and some fowl and of course our own sauna where we would *kylpee* on Saturdays. But wars came, depressions came, one thing and another and instead we became citizens, bought a house on McIntyre *katu*. And now of course my parish, my village, everything is gone. For me it would be a strange country to go back to.''

The three men sat still, each in his own thoughts. A breeze lifted the corner of the newspaper on Jussi's lap and played with a torn envelope at his feet. The sun still shone brightly on their side of the street, but the buildings on the other were casting a long afternoon shadow. The chain saw sign flickered in its orbit.

''We were very young when we came,'' Jussi said, almost as if to himself. ''Children really, and brave when I think of it now. The first winter we both were sick with the fever. It was a funny thing, everybody had it in those days when they first came. One kind lady let us stay in a room in her house until we were well... she was a good woman, I have never forgotten her. And now when I think of Karelia it is always *Juhannus* singing and gaiety, oars splashing in a glittering lake, white birches shining on the shore, *piirakkas* smelling in the *Tupa* and the *Juhannus* bonfire crackling on the big rock. We never slept during that mid-summer night, it really wasn't night, of course, just a long twilight." As Jussi talked he slipped more and more into the Karelian rhythms. More and more j's took the place of hard sounds.

"I remember the nightingale, and the other song birds and of course the cuckoo. No, I don't think I could stand the beauty of those summer nights anymore." The old man's face quivered and he wiped his eyes with the back of his hand.

The shadow from the other side reached half way across the street.

"It's getting chilly. Should have worn my jacket," said Lauri.

Jussi turned to Matti. "But it is different with you, you have a home there, your sister needs you. How many more years will you have for cutting pulp even without the bottle?"

Matti threw away his cigarette and ground the butt under his heel, then straightened the knot of his tie and tidied the collar of his shirt. He reached into his pocket for his tobacco. "I wish you'd shut up about that damn notice. Pardon me, Jussi, even though you are an old man you don't know everything. The way you talk you'd think I was an old man."

"Yes, yes," said Jussi, "but you yourself just complained that the power of the bucksaw has gone and women are too fat or too skinny. And no matter how I try I can't imagine the pulpcutter Matti Peltonen as a bullcook, and that's what you'd have to do by and by. You have many years to go to get into the manor or even for the pension. Or worse still, you'll end up sitting on the edge of the sidewalk in thirty below, frozen solid like that poor fool last winter.''

''Ah, but there's another way out when things get to that point,'' said Matti, ''and many a man from Bay Street has found it. I always admire the boys who go out into the bush with their pieces of rope. That's what I'd do too. I would be a gentlemanni and not mess up my landlady's house. It isn't as messy as a bullet, but it's still not nice to do it inside.''

Lauri turned pale, mostly because the same thought had entered his head as he considered the future. But it was shocking to hear it voiced so openly. ''But it was different with me,'' he said. ''I hardly had shoes to wear at eighteen. A horse and a gold watch were like the moon.''

Jussi stood up, folded the newspaper and put it into his pocket.

''I'm talking to you like a father. Now let's go to Antti at the mission and send some kind of a message to your sister. It doesn't mean you have to go back.'' Jussi spoke with authority, convinced this was the right thing to do.

Matti stared at the older man standing there, short and stocky and somehow solid. Perhaps, too, he was sobered by his own threats — anyway his mood changed.

''Well'' — he took a step with Jussi towards the sidewalk — ''maybe, maybe, wait a bit, just a little. Do you know who I saw yesterday? Remember Mikko? He used to cut pulp and a darn good cutter he was. Saw him in the beer parlour, was in there with his oldest son, a mechanic in town. His wife was there too, ugly as sin. They live out Intola way, mostly farming now. With a few beers in him he boasted about his son's boy in high school and his girl's big farm — she's married to a man of another tongue.'' Matti joined Jussi on the sidewalk.

''I'll come with you,'' Lauri said. ''Maybe Antti's got my income tax ready.''

The three men stood for minutes on the sidewalk, then started slowly towards the mission.

The mission was an old house in the block around the corner from the grocery. It had served in turn as a store, a restaurant and now a mission reading room.

Just as the three men began to cross the street towards the building, Antti, a small slight man in a dark suit, came out of the door, locked it and hurried up the street away from them. Jussi made a move forward as if to call but gave up. All three turned silently and began to walk in the opposite direction.

''We'll go tomorrow,'' Lauri said.

This White Wail, This Loud Blur
Claude Liman

EVERY TIME I STARTED MY poem about ski jumping, it turned into prose, and always at the worst possible moment. I was usually able to climb with poetry to the top of the trestle, capturing in my ascent the terrifying sound of the other jumpers as they sped down and past me, as they turned into flight. I got the sound of their speed and the clumsy racking noise as my heavy jumping skis scissored about my ears.

I was able to keep the poetry right up until the moment of my own launching out from the top of the jump. I could never get beyond this last poised moment without turning into prose:

Everything is ready.
It is time to push off.

Everything would be ready. My skis were attached to my feet and no longer felt clumsy. I slid them back and forth in the worn, icy grooves of the starting platform. Holding onto the rail up there, I could push my eight-and-a-half-foot skis forward until the whole front, right up to the boot almost, was in the air, sticking off the end of the platform. Below my ski tips, at about a 45-degree angle, the in-run track fell

away, fell away, down into another world where miniature
spectators turned their faces up the hill and a tiny man with a
red flag on the end of a long pole tested the air. The winds
would always be constant at the top of the trestle — there
was never a single moment of stillness up there that I can
remember. The whole structure groaned and swayed. Left to
ourselves, we jumpers would never have known when to
push off. We needed the little man down there to test the
currents of that other world and tell us when to come.

> *His flag is down:*
> *The other world waits.*
> *It is time to push off.*

But, as I said, I could never get beyond this point with
poetry. I could never speed down the icy in-run with it and
take it into the air with me. Always at the pivotal moment,
just as I was about to push off into the one-way track that led
inevitably to flight, it would become prose. I would become
once again the mindless skier who was so serious about
jumping, about its purely physical sensations. The instincts
would begin to take over once again, the instincts which had
carried me through so many jumps but which could never
take me into poetry.

I never even got down the in-run. I would love to be able
to say that the poetry flew away as the wind rushed into my
ears with the steep descent into another world. That would at
least be poetic, a fair exchange of wind for words. But it
simply would not be true, for I always lost the poem in that
last poised moment in the starting gate, before speed ever
began:

You have to get grooved,
Skis pointing down in the steep, icy track,
Tips pushing out for the steep, downward air,
Aching to hinge, to plunge over the edge.

It is time to push off.

This was my limit. I could never carry the poem with me as I gripped the starting rail tightly with both hands and slid back and forth in the slick starting track. The hands would tighten and relax, tighten and relax, as I pulled myself forward and pushed myself back to find the rhythm I wanted. Then, once the rhythm felt right, and when I was all the way back at the end of the starting platform, I would look down once more to the people with their small faces turned up to me and the tiny man with his limp flag off to the side of the takeoff, and I would say "Now!" and pull quickly with my hands.

Only this time I would let go, shooting down over the edge of the platform with a slap as my skis enter the track. Then hands find their way down into a prayer position in front of the low-crouching knees. Sitting low and back coming down the steep part of the trestle, I hear a queer high wail starting to build in my ears. As the in-run flattens toward the lip of the jump, I make myself rock forward, preparing to accept the invisible support which will start when the trestle gives out.

This is the hardest part, to move forward for air that comes like a whistling vacuum. Here is a transition between earth and air, here is where the trestle seems to rise for the final boost into flight. Then instincts take over. There is a grunt as the knees spring open and out with the passing of the last fractional second of trestle under the skis. Then there is wind in the face and the ski tips are coming up with the pressure of the unseen air.

This force under the skis is a friend — you trust him, you lean into him, pressing from the ankles and hips and waist and neck to let him take you forever. There is the single consciousness of a white blur beneath, a visual translation of the loud wailing cry that sings in the ear of speed and of height and of distance. This white wail, this loud blur, presses forever down the hill, trusting that the air will hold. Eyes and ears will not return until the ground comes back.

The return to earth is as instinctive as the takeoff into air. It is another of the transitions that come quite naturally to man. As you feel solid ground under the skis, a large solidness slips in beneath you, pulling you down.

Only I knew that if I ever wrote my poem about ski jumping, I would end it in the air, in poetry. I would never bring myself back to earth once I was launched in a perfect flight. The problem is to get started, to take poetry into the air with me, to get off the ground with it. I can never get that far. I always stall on earth, in prose.

Going Places
Mary Frost

KATHLEEN LAY ON THE SUNLOUNGER. Ten a.m.; already the day's heat buzzed like a drowsy insect. July, and within ten miles of Stratford, they had an orchard campground to themselves, apart from one tent at the far boundary. Incredible luck. If it hadn't been for Rory, they'd never have found it.

"Happy?" Something shaded Kathleen's face. She opened her eyes to find Rory leaning over her from behind the head of the lounger, his mouth and chin above her eyes. She squinted at this inverted vision of him. "Happy?" he repeated.

"Lazy," she answered. "Same thing." She wiggled deeper into the spring-tensioned canvas. "I'm not awake yet."

They'd had breakfast together at eight, the kids still asleep in the trailer. They'd walked a mile along the roadside path, while it was still cool enough to be pleasant. They'd watched other people setting off to work, one of the great joys of being on holiday.

"Come on. Let's go see places."

"I've seen all I want to see. I'm going to lie here and listen to the apples swelling."

"I don't want to go on my own."

In the end, he went alone.

Kathleen closed her eyes as she heard Rory drive off, and let her arms flop out to each side. Her fingers scratched the scalp of the field, burrowing in its green hair. She hadn't felt this good for over a year. She thought of Kilderrin; of the orchard she had planted — though she'd not been there to see it grow to any sort of maturity; of the March morning in the garden, not much more than a year ago, when she'd been planting the first earlies of potatoes.

The soil that morning was on the soft side for digging — heavy from the rain of an Irish spring. She had heard the back door bang. Rory must be up. Saturday morning; he could sleep in if he wanted to. He had bunched the bed-clothes up over his face when she lifted the curtain aside to gauge the day's fitness for garden work. She'd let the curtain swing back. Let him sleep. He'd been moping all week. Something was bothering him. Meanwhile, she had vegetables to plant. The pale sprouted tentacles of the seed potatoes seemed fragile, alien, hungry for earth.

Rory came up behind her as she worked. She glanced round to grin an acknowledgement of his presence, but kept working.

"Kath," he said. "Leave that for a minute, and come and have a cup of tea."

"I've just started this." Kathleen went on digging. "I'll take a break in an hour or so."

"I've made some tea. I want to talk to you."

"What's so urgent it can't wait an hour?" She planted the shovel and wiped a fringe of hair back off her forehead, leaving a smear of mud there.

"I want to get this dug by lunchtime; and those things planted."

"Don't bother with them," said Rory bluntly. He took a

deep breath. "We're going to Canada," he said. "We have an immigration interview next week. I've been offered a job in Thunder Bay, Ontario. I've agreed to start in July."

WHEN SHE DIDN'T LEAVE HIM THEN, Kathleen said later, she'd never leave him. They'd done their share of moving. For ten years after they married, they'd moved every couple of years — it would look good on his C.V.; it was a career move; better opportunities, better pay. She'd reared two suitcase kids, had moved house four days after Patricia was born, and not a relative around to give her a hand. But after ten years, they'd come back home to a job in Kilderrin, a good income, a bright, modern house with over an acre of ground and mature trees by the stone wall. Rory joined the golf club. Kathleen joined the parents' association at the school and the badminton club. The children went to the village school. Soon they were on visiting terms with half the parish.

"It sounds too good to last," Kathleen's mother had said. She never quite trusted Rory. Too ambitious for her taste; a go-getter. But that was the kind of thing they knew she'd say. She had a suspicious streak at the best of times.

Kathleen worked on the garden. Within two years, she had put in a small orchard: twenty-four dwarf apple trees, six cultivars, four of each. She put in gooseberries and black currants, rhubarb, and a flowering plum. She planted roses, lavender, fire thorn, winter jasmine, broom, hydrangeas, astilbe, daffodils, tulips, forsythia — it seemed as if there weren't enough plants to satisfy her. By April of the third year, she thought she might be pregnant. By May, she was sure. The garden slipped to low priority. On November 25th, in the year that Patricia was nine and John was eleven, Billy was born. On Christmas Day, they put his daybed by the

Christmas tree during dinner.

"He's an angel," said Kathleen, because there wasn't a squeak out of him all through the meal.

"He's our Irishman," said Rory proudly — as if he might have been an Eskimo but for some good planning. The other two had been born in England.

And now, not five years later, they were to pack up and go back on the road. Kathleen became a woman of few words.

Rory tried to talk to her. Providing for the family was his responsibility. This place had nothing more to offer him. The kids would have no prospects here. He'd read the writing on the wall — figures mostly — and the family had to go. She wasn't making it easier for any of them.

"I'll go if I must go," was all she'd say.

"We'll sell the house and furniture, and start fresh over there," said Rory. "You can buy whatever you want."

THEY SOLD THE HOUSE TO AN ARTIST whose husband worked with Digital. The artist liked the house; she adored the garden.

Kathleen set aside a room, and stockpiled the things she refused to part with. The Connolly's blue dinner service. Elsa's tea-set. The silver tea service. The cutlery. The silver candlesticks. The Irish linen, the crystal, the photographs, boxes of books. The Christmas decorations.

Patricia put in posters, her Teddy bears, schoolbooks, diaries, her astronomical telescope and her old dolls' house.

John put in his records and his ham radio. Yes, he knew he couldn't use it in Canada, but this was what he wanted to bring.

Billy lugged in the red-and-white Christmas elephant, and

the rabbit that had no ears. He brought Bosco, the puppet from his favourite TV show; and Racketty-coon, the improbably orange raccoon who lived a double life as a pajama-case, and dripped styrofoam beads all over the house.

"They're coming," said Kathleen tightly, daring Rory to argue.

Rory added Vinci, a three-foot statue of Leonardo da Vinci from his grandparents' home; and two Grecian-type bronze ladies waving their arms in the air. These had stood on the mantelpiece of his parents' drawing room.

When he found that, because of handling charges, a small load cost much the same as a full load, Rory gave in. "Bring it all," he said, despairing. "Bring a few bags of food-scraps and vegetable parings while you're at it. Tide us over until we gather more."

They set out for Canada with a load of old things such as anyone there would dispose of in a yard-sale, or haul away to the dump.

THUNDER BAY WAS BELOW THEM: a sea, a table-mountain, and, almost immediately, level ground in the lee of the mountain. Dizzy from eighteen hours travelling, they were driven in from the airport. Their impressions blurred: a hoop of highway; tall conifers and darkness on the left, and lights and one-storey houses on the right; an occasional patch of neon where a radial road from the city crossed the highway. They were to move into a company house but they had booked into a hotel for the first week. They needed to assemble some basic furniture to tide them over until their own stuff arrived. After day four, Rory was at work, a national electronic engineering firm, doing consultancy work. His job would involve travelling mainly in Northwestern Ontario. While Kathleen shopped or dealt with school placement, Rory relayed information about his travels: population figures, distances.

It's an archipelago, Kathleen decided without once leaving town. Inhabited islands in an oceanic and uncharted forest. She wrote home that Thunder Bay was an island surrounded by trees. Her mother wrote back to ask what she had done with Lake Superior. Had it dried up, perhaps?

In September, Billy started school across the road.

"Hey, Bill. C'm 'ere a minute." Maurice McRae called him on his second Monday coming from school. The McRaes were next-door neighbours, very amiable. Their own children were grown.

Billy trudged ahead and up the path. He stood at the foot of the steps, looking up at Maurice who grinned down at him from the porch.

"Ya gotta have one of these." Maurice dropped a yellow-and-black baseball cap onto Billy's head. A matching cap in a larger size adorned his own. "If you're gonna be a Thunder Bay boy, you gotta have a cap."

Billy removed the cap and eyed it doubtfully.

"I'm from Ireland," he said.

"That's right. Ireland and Thunder Bay." With a nod of his head, Maurice endorsed the pairing, making it sound the most natural combination possible.

"Ireland and Thunder Bay," Billy echoed, and swinging the hat by its peak, he hooked it onto his head, and tugged it snug on his forehead. "Thanks, Maurice," he beamed.

From her look-out on the home porch, Kathleen corrected Billy's over-familiarity and added her own thanks.

"WHO WERE THE FIRST PEOPLE to live in Canada?" Billy looked up from plastering a slice of bread with peanut butter.

"Mrs. Niemi wants to know, tomorrow."

"The Indians," Kathleen pursed her mouth in disapproval. So that was what passed for homework over here. He needed nightly practice in number and letter formation; some exercises in simple addition.

"You got it wrong," he accused her, when he came home next day. "You shouldn't call them Indians. They're not Indians. Indians live in India. How would you like to be named by someone else's stupid mistake?"

"What should I call them then?"

His expression faltered, dissolved into one of baffled embarrassment. "You ought to call them... " He drew a big breath, and went on: "She said to call them 'Naked Canadians,' " he muttered.

Kathleen hooted her glee.

Billy stalked out of the kitchen.

"Hey, Billy. That's funny," she called after him.

"What's funny?" he answered, turning stiffly toward her, half-way down the hall. "And don't call me Billy. My name is Bill."

WINTER CAME EARLY AND STAYED late. Outdoors, they bundled in more clothes and thicker clothes than they had ever worn. Indoors, they gasped for fresh air, resenting the cooked atmosphere of the centrally heated house; knowing they needed it. In the early winter, Kathleen opened all the windows for ten minutes every morning to air the house. By January, she couldn't even do that; they were all frozen shut.

It warmed a little; they were buried in snow. They bought a snow shovel, a snow scoop, a sleigh shovel. Most of the snow-digging was done by Kathleen.

"At least it gets you out of the house," Rory encouraged

her, as he brushed by to the car on his way to work.

The snowball caught him nicely in the back of the neck, and lodged in his collar.

EVENTUALLY, IT THAWED: a season of mud and water. Then a brief explosion of blossom.

"We're having a Sunshine tea," said Billy. "All the mothers will be there. Wear a big hat, like a straw hat; and wear gloves."

Apparently anything else was optional.

At Zellers, Kathleen bought a navy straw hat the size of a cartwheel, and added a flowery scarf for colour and good measure. White gloves she already had. She set out, ready for a cut-price Ascot.

They had tea in the gymnasium, at a scattering of small tables, each one set for four. Hers was the only hat in the room. Affecting an air of nonchalance, she removed it and shoved it aside on a chair. Someone might sit on it. Let them. She shared a table with an elderly Finnish gentleman, somebody's grandfather, stone deaf; an Italian mother who spoke almost no English; and a sultry Jamaican girl who glowered at them and said she wanted to go home. Kathleen could not have felt more alien on the moon.

"Do you like your table mat?"

The enquiry came from elbow level, an intense child carrying a styrofoam plate full of tiny cakelets, mainly Rice Krispies in glue. A pale face, spectacles, a worried little mouth; thin fair hair scraped into a ponytail and bound with paired pink glass baubles, "I made your mat. Isn't it good?"

"It's wonderful." A rectangle of drawing paper marked Kathleen's place; it was elaborately scribbled over with flowers, hearts and yellow suns. A sudden inspiration moved

Kathleen to add: "I was wondering — since it *is* so *very* nice — if I could take it home with me?"

"No, you can't," said the face. "I'm taking it home to Mom." She plonked the goodies in the middle of the table and turned away.

"Don't spill your tea on it," she called back, from two tables off.

ON FRIDAY AFTERNOONS IN LATE May, the supermarkets and the roads were crowded with people preparing to go off to the camps or with people in transit to them.

"Guess what we just bought!" Rory and Kathleen were smug as they tramped downstairs to where Patricia and John were sprawled in the basement watching TV with friends. Too full of their news to wait for an answer, they went on, almost in unison: "We've bought a caravan."

"A *what?*" Dave screwed up his face, as if facial muscles had a leading role to play in communicating with folks who spoke such odd English. "Isn't a caravan a thing you'd have in the Sahara Desert. Y'know — camels and things?"

John rose and began to rotate his hips in a parody of belly-dancing. He emitted ululating sounds, and his fingers rose and fell over the stops of an invisible pipe. Patricia, Linda and Cinnemon whooped to their feet. They improvised yashmaks from hands and scarves, and joined the floor show, providing competing sound-tracks. Dave posed on the sofa, feet apart, fists on his hips, uttering rhythmic bellowing sounds at irregular intervals.

Rory and Kathleen retreated from the ambient bedlam.

"They don't call them caravans here, do they?" Rory asked.

THEY WENT CAMPING TO SIBLEY Provincial Park, driving down the highway with exaggerated caution, adjusting to the task of towing the trailer. They found a wooded campsite by Lake Mary Louise. Established, they drove through the park to the shore of Lake Superior, to Silver Islet where the remains of a silver mine had provided the foundation of a holiday area. Grey wooden mine houses, sheltering under a rocky cliff, faced the lake across a narrow road, more country lane than road. A summer community owned the houses now; some of the owners were descendants of mine workers. A large barn-like structure with dusty windows turned out to be the former general store. Kathleen peered through the grimy glass; the old counters were still there, but it seemed otherwise abandoned. She shied away from imagining what the lives of those early immigrants must have been, their isolation, the hardships they must have endured.

They went to Quetico Park, armed with a wildflower guide and the *Audubon Field Guide to North American Trees*. They picked up a stack of the park's own pamphlets, walked the nature trails. Here was some of the oldest exposed rock in the world, and plants so rare and fragile, there were raised wooden walkways above them, and signs directing visitors to keep to the trail.

If Ireland was history, Kathleen thought, Northwestern Ontario was geography. She stared in fascination at smooth rock shining grey in the morning light. She had slipped out early while the others were still sleeping, to come alone along the trail again, and concentrate. She kicked her sandal off and reached out over a patch of rock. Deliberately, she lowered her foot until her toes touched the stone. She willed herself into harmony with this place. Up and down the boardwalk she stomped, humming a chant, trying to touch some ancient magic, older than the Druids' Ireland; older than God, or nearly.

"What exactly do you think you're doing?" Rory was just behind her, leaning against a tree, his arms folded. Further back, Patricia and John chortled over the spectacle of Mother doing Minnehaha in the dawn. Billy watched in wonder.

Eventually even Kathleen joined in the giggling.

"Get on with it. Ye haven't a soul between ye!"

"Were you really singing to the rock?" Bill asked her later, safely out of hearing of the others.

"*With* the rock, love," she answered. "I didn't even know the tune until the rock taught me."

IN JULY, AFTER A FULL YEAR IN the job, Rory took three weeks off. They hitched up the trailer to visit Southern Ontario. In retrospect, they wondered whether they hadn't got funny looks when they said they were going trailering to Toronto.

Kitchener, Killarney, Stratford, Peterborough, York: some of the choice spots of Europe had counterparts down south. Kathleen saw and hated them. Hated Toronto more than all the rest. Six-lane highways shoulder to shoulder, with other highways arching over them. A sizzling flood of coloured metal. The air over the city quivered in shock. Perspiring in the front of the Jeep, she eyed it all with awed repugnance. This was closer to hell than any of the medieval painters dared to come, with their canvases of sinful humanity tormented by demons. At least the demons were half-way human. The old masters had imagined nothing as monstrous as this.

They drove east of the city, stayed in a park upwind of a nuclear station. The lake-water along the shore seethed with carp — a great, ugly mudfish designed by God to be rendered in iron and set up in public to prop up lamp-standards with its tail. The carp slithered over each other in the shallow water, sometimes three deep. Rory and the kids waded in to see them. They got out when they realized no one else was wading there. For the next hour, they expected their feet to break out in rashes, the flesh to flake away from the bone.

They scuttled back towards Barrie, glad to be north of Toronto again. They booked into a Happy Tom Campground, when they could find no provincial park to shelter them.

That night, the Happy Toms had an on-site wiener roast. The management provided the campfire and a zinc bath full of boiling water and wieners. A side table offered buns and trimmings. The Happy Toms came in force with their lawn chairs and their stereos, all tuned to the same station. Late into the night, the place pulsed with sound. Kathleen closed the trailer windows; they stifled in the heat. Rory opened the windows; they were blasted with rock music. Sometime between two and three a.m. they slid into unconsciousness.

Next morning, they gave up on big city camping, and voted to head for home. That was when Rory came up with his plan to go back through Sarnia and Port Huron, turning northward from there. He had a route already marked on the map, and the name of a good campground, privately owned, near Saint Mary's. They should give the south a chance to redeem itself. He landed them that evening in a meadow dotted with apple trees, a dozen miles from Stratford — the best stop since they'd come through Sault Ste. Marie. They had the place almost to themselves. A pool to swim in. Theatre in the evenings. Their holiday plans were saved.

THEY ROOSTED IN THEIR ORCHARD paradise for almost a week. While Kathleen, John, Patricia and Bill slept in, lounged about the campsite, swam, played frisbee, or sipped iced tea in the shade, Rory went exploring: Kitchener-Waterloo, Cambridge, Woodstock, London. In the afternoons, they all went into Stratford, browsed around the stores, walked by the river. In the evenings, they went to the theatre.

Refreshed enough by Sunday to face the road, they lit out for Thunder Bay. They drove all day and part of the night to get back in one run.

"Pull in. Come on; I want to get a look at the place from here." Kathleen, who had been half dozing in the passenger seat, was wide awake and giving orders. Rory groaned.

"It's after two," protested Rory. "We're almost home." But he slowed the Jeep and trailer and drew across the highway into the Terry Fox Lookout, parking close to the monument. In the moonlight, the statue of the curly-headed boy with the artificial leg and the determined jaw was lonelier and more heroic than by day.

While the children slept looped around and over each other in the back of the Jeep, Kathleen and Rory looked ahead and down to where Thunder Bay lay like a heap of swept-up stars beside the lake. Around it, the forest curved, mysterious and protective.

Fifteen minutes later, they had reached their own front door.

"WHY LONDON, FOR GOD'S SAKE? Why are you dragging us off to Toronto?"

"It's a promotion. And it's not Toronto."

"It is Toronto. Every place down there is Toronto. Toronto is a great boil, a carbuncle draining the whole area of its autonomy, of its vitality. Everywhere is X miles from Toronto."

"It's not Toronto."

"It's not Thunder Bay."

"No, it's not Thunder Bay."

Silence. Rory ventured: "You'll like it when you've been there for a bit."

"Yes," she answered bitterly, "I will."

"YOU COULD STAY," BILL confronted her mutinously. He'd been back at school for two weeks. "If you stayed, I could stay. Trish and John want to stay."

Kathleen was in the laundry room, hauling a tangle of hot towels out of the dryer. "You don't really mean that, Bill. You wouldn't want to stay if Dad went, anymore than I would."

"Yes, I would. You're only saying that because you won't stand up to Dad."

"Watch it!" He wasn't yet seven, for Pete's sake; where did he get this stuff? Her thoughts flew to John and Patricia, much given recently to muttering in corners, glowering at her. Their vocalized protests consisted largely of frequent and enthusiastic discussion of their forthcoming university days: their rooms in residence; their apartments, perhaps. John hoped to get into engineering at Lakehead next year; Patricia had a further year, possibly two, before she could move out. Their plans for going compounded Bill's distress.

Kathleen began to fold towels into the blue laundry basket. It was true enough what Bill had said: she had no stomach for a row with Rory. No point. If it came to a choice between Thunder Bay and Rory, she'd choose Rory. He knew that, too.

"I'm going to hate London," Bill vowed, hugging his resentment like a stuffed toy.

"I'm not."

"You're only doing that to be in with Dad."

"No, I'm not. I'm doing it for myself. I owe it to me to be as happy as I can be, wherever I am. And you owe the same to yourself."

"It's alright for you." Bill's lower lip wobbled; he steadied it into a scowl. "You don't have to leave all your friends." If he cried, he'd never forgive her. "It's easy for you."

She picked up the clothes basket and rested it on her hip. "I'll do whatever small things I can do to help, but we're going. That's decided."

As she climbed the stairs, she felt his eyes burning laser-holes in her back.

THEY WERE TO MOVE RIGHT AFTER Christmas. Kathleen wondered whether Rory had planned that, too: in January, her resistance to leaving Thunder Bay would be at its lowest. For the children, it was right in the middle of the school year. They were trying to arrange for John to stay on.

One Wednesday morning in mid-October, Kathleen packed herself a picnic and set out for a last trip to Silver Islet. The children had refused to accompany her. They preferred school, their ultimate rejection. Rory was not invited. He could stay home and balance his cheque book. She turned off the road at Pass Lake, and drove along the headland through Sibley Park.

The road was clear of traffic. Two foxes crossed ahead of her. A porcupine waddled from the roadside into the shelter of the undergrowth — W.C. Fields at his most lugubrious. Chipmunks and squirrels scurried among the fallen leaves. The forest absorbed their flickers of movement into its massive calm.

She parked near the store, its dried wood and dusty

windows, lizard-like, soaking up the sun. It could be so many things yet: a store again; a lakeshore restaurant; a guesthouse. Closed up, dilapidated, a nostalgic shell, its grey bulk dominated the foreshore. As she stepped out and slammed the car door, the store offered itself as metaphor. She rejected it.

She thought of Rory. How the store's profitless existence irritated him whenever he stopped here. She thought of the hours he spent at the computer, summarizing their assets, their gains, their losses. He had them all inventoried on spreadsheets, updated weekly. But she had an accounting of her own to make. It was stocktaking time. She set out to walk the shore road.

On her right, the lake, blue and vital. On her left, the old mine houses, solid buildings with verandas or screened porches in front, and their backs to the rock cliff that had sheltered them from the north. Around the houses, gardens had been dug into the scree; things were planted in tubs and pots. Halfway along the road, a mountain ash grew on the shore side, in a dirt lay-by edged with stone. She had seen this tree intermittently from spring to fall. The blood-spatters of its berries and the gold of its thinning leaves were brilliant against the blue of sky and water. She stopped to fix its image in her mind.

This area was the place she had resisted coming to less than two years ago. Fickle was a word that came to her. Malleable: her affinity to water rather than rock. The stern strength of the cliff-face fascinated her, but it oppressed her too. She had come closer to loving it than she would have imagined possible. Rock shore and lake: herself and Rory. If she were to bring him back a photograph, would he recognize their portrait?

"I know this is rough on you," Rory had said, a few

evenings before. It was after supper, and she had carried her coffee cup and an orange through to the sitting room. ''I know that every time we move, you feel like you lose a bit of yourself.''

''No, I don't.'' A sudden insight opened for Kathleen. ''Every time we move, I gain a bit of myself. Every time we move, I get to rely on myself just a little bit more.'' She glanced up to see a disconcerted frown pass like a shadow over Rory's face.

''You must be pretty self-reliant by now, then.''

''I'm getting there.'' She did not look up when, after a few minutes of shuffling about, Rory rose and wandered away.

Now she bent down and picked up a shard of rock, one of many in the debris of the roadside. She closed her palm around it, tightening her fist until the rock corners bit into her flesh. She relaxed her hand and slipped the stone into her pocket. She gathered three more stones, selecting them carefully, one for each of the kids. She scrambled down to the water's edge and dipped both hands into the frigid water of the lake. She held them there, allowing the cold to soak into them, feeling its pain in her wrists. She lifted two handfuls of water, and watched as it dribbled from her grasp. She shook off the last drops and wiped her palms down the sides of her corduroy skirt.

''I'm from Thunder Bay,'' she called to a soaring raven. ''Ireland and Thunder Bay.''

It was late when she returned to the Jeep. The air was chill. Above the horizon, a glowing cloudbank cushioned a fireball sun. In a spray of sand and gravel, Kathleen reversed onto the pavement, and started for home. Long shadows of the high pines barred her way.

Peach Preserves
Rosalind Maki

GLADIE KNOTT HAD SPENT THE better part of her fifty-six years waiting for the right man. In the meantime, almost by accident, she had made a life for herself. She taught school; she invested in savings bonds; she was a bridesmaid five times; she bought a two-bedroom bungalow, with carport; her hair turned grey; she gained fifty pounds. When the right man did not appear, Gladie knew why: Men were not interested in homely women. And Gladie was a homely woman. Her head sprang direct from her shoulders; her eyes were small and close-set; her lips were thin, her jaw a sack of flesh. Her coarse hair refused to take a perm. Cut short, it clasped her skull like a helmet.

Gladie did not expect anyone's sympathy. Her life suited her fine. It had grown as familiar and comfortable as an old woollen sweater. Take today. By eight o'clock, having risen, dressed, eaten breakfast and washed up the dishes, she was driving her new blue Topaz down Highway 20 and singing loudly to the *Fiddler on the Roof* soundtrack that played on her stereo. At Glorious Groves Farms she picked up her standard yearly order — ten baskets of clingstone peaches, eight for canning, two for eating. Soon she was turning onto the Sixth Concession road, heading for the home place, where her married sister Helen lived. Gladie had been making this trip every August for twenty years.

When she pulled into Helen's yard and parked under the maple tree, the digital clock read nine a.m. She smiled to herself. Right on time.

Gladie waved at Helen's husband Ted as he strolled across the yard toward the machinery shed, all that was left of the original farm buildings. He tipped his hat to her and nodded. Always such a gentleman Ted was, and handsome; he still reminded her of Gary Cooper.

Gladie was climbing out of the car when Helen appeared at the door of the summer kitchen and ran lightly down the steps on her sandaled feet. She wore a candy-striped blouse with matching pink shorts — coordinating, that's what Helen would say.

"Hi, Gladie," she called gaily, settling her blonde hair with a fine-boned hand.

Fifty-three and perky as a cheerleader. Gladie half-expected her to whip out the old blue-and-gold pompoms.

As she opened the trunk, Gladie's mood unraveled like so much snagged yarn.

Helen had everything ready in the summer kitchen, a screened lean-to built years ago by their father onto the side of the house. The washed jars were set on the work table, covered by a clean towel; the blanching water boiled, and the syrup simmered on the back of the old Moffat range.

Gladie dumped half a dozen peaches into the blanching pot. After a minute, she cold-dipped them, then began the tedious work of skinning and pitting. "Did Judy get her promotion?" Gladie asked. Helen's daughter, Judy, was a social worker with the provincial government.

"Someone from the Hamilton office got it. A man. She's

put in a grievance. She's ready to quit. I wish you'd talk to her, settle her down. She respects you, she says you're tough.''

Gladie smiled wryly. ''I've always thought you were the tough one.'' She plucked another peach from the cold water, put a shallow slit in it and watched, fascinated, as the skin shrank from the wound. She stripped the peel into the scrap bowl, then drove the knife into the flesh and girdled the stone. *Exocarp, mesocarp, endocarp.* She pulled the halves apart and using the tip of the knife, flicked the dull brown stone onto the rest of the leavings.

Helen packed the peach halves into jars, poured in the syrup, and screwed on the lids.

''A peach is a drupe, did you know that, Helen?''

''No, no, I didn't. Just blanch what's left in that basket. That should be enough for this batch.''

''Funny word, isn't it, drupe? And those little bumps on a raspberry, those are druplets.''

''Miss Bishop died last month, did I tell you?'' Helen asked.

''Miss Bishop from Sunday School? I thought she died years ago.''

''She was ninety. Lived in a nursing home in St. Kitt's. Mattie McDonald — her family and the Bishops were neighbours at Vineland — she was telling me at church that she'd gone up to the funeral, and there was hardly a soul there. Poor old thing.''

''Ninety. Then she would have been — what? — about forty when she ran the Sunday School. And she seemed so old.''

''A little brown hen. Remember how she always shoved her hankie down the front of her dress. I hated that.''

"Terrible to think of outliving everyone you know. Well, that's the end of this batch."

"By the way, we should go out to the cemetery," Helen said. "Check on our petunias. They're probably wilting in this heat."

Their parents had been dead twenty years. Their mother had gone first, dying in her sleep one Easter Sunday. Gladie was still living at the farm then. She stayed on to keep house for their father. And why wouldn't she? She was single. Nothing better to do. Within days, she had started making plans. When school broke off for the summer, she would drive Daddy up to Ottawa to visit his cousins. But he didn't last until summer. At his funeral their aunts talked about him as though he were some silly character in a romantic novel. "He just pined away, poor dear," they sniffed, their white heads nodding like Hong Kong wind-ups. Still, hadn't he always said he didn't know what he'd do if Mother went first?

Afterwards, Helen and Gladie had divided the farm into four lots, and sold three, leaving the home place for Helen and Ted. Gladie moved into town, into a little brick bungalow, where she wrote out her daily lesson plans, tended her roses and her white Persian cat Max.

"How about next week?" Gladie asked.

Helen settled the jars into the sterilizer and turned up the heat. "Judy's kids are coming over. Their sitter's going to North Bay."

"They can come with us."

"Maybe Ted'll watch Ben."

Gladie started on another basket of fruit. As she slipped the peaches into the water, she said, "I've pretty well decided to retire next June."

Helen looked at her, surprised.

"I haven't got the energy anymore. Besides, there's lots of young teachers waiting for old bags like me to move over."

"You should travel."

Gladie glanced at her sister. "Is that how you see me, Helen? Traipsing around the world, cat under my arm, toting all my possessions in matching luggage? I'd probably end up in a pensione somewhere, boring all the guests with reports on my gout and indigestion."

"You've been reading those old English novels again, Gladie. These days single women sunbathe on the Riviera in high-cut bikinis, and have affairs with muscular young men." Helen nudged her. "You'd have to get a bikini wax."

"That'll be the day, when I shave down there. Besides, I doubt Sea Queen makes a high-cut in size eighteen. And if they do, they shouldn't."

Helen laughed merrily, her small teeth white behind pink lips. "You have to plan, Gladie. Ted's taking a course at the high school this fall on retirement planning. You should sign up."

THE SECOND BATCH WAS READY for the sterilizer. The first, seven high-shouldered jars of golden fruit, stood cooling on the sideboard. Gladie scraped the peels and pits into the garbage.

Helen wiped down the checkered oil-cloth and rinsed the cloth under the tap. "I'll get the rest of the lids." Gladie bit into a fresh peach. The juice made her teeth ache. She gazed through the screen. Ted was cutting the front lawn, travelling back and forth on the riding mower, in and out of her line of sight. How satisfying it must be to have a man around, she thought. Someone to take care of things, repair a dripping tap or change a fuse.

A bee, momentarily confused by a breeze sweeping the sweet scent of peaches and sugar into the yard, bumped his nut-like body against the dark screen. Then he bumbled past, drawn to the hollyhocks at the corner of the house. Settling on the lip of a trembling blossom he abandoned himself to its moist pink-throated beauty. *Filament, anther, stigma, style, ovary.*

Helen appeared in the doorway. ''Can you believe this? We're out of lids. I was sure I'd bought enough.''

Gladie dropped the peach pit into the garbage. ''Maybe you put them somewhere safe.''

Helen smiled ruefully. ''They'll turn up at Christmas packed away with the cookie cutters. I'll call Carolyn.''

Gladie took another peach from the basket. Standing in the summer kitchen she could hear Helen on the phone chatting to Carolyn, who lived down the road. Although a dozen years separated Helen and Carolyn, they were close, closer than Helen and Gladie who had shared a lifetime. Gladie understood. Helen and Carolyn shared an outlook: Carolyn was beautiful, too. Her Grace Kelly looks had attracted a rich Toronto lawyer. To have Carolyn, he had changed his life. He divorced, sold his partnership, and moved his practice to Welland. He bought her a stone farmhouse with forty acres and an apple orchard, and each day he drove in to his office while Carolyn, the constant and domestic wife, baked bread, canned vegetables, and raised their four children. Gladie had decided Martin's appeal must be his charm; he certainly was not good-looking. All the bones of his face seemed to retreat from his thick blunt nose as though his profile had been moulded in the bowl of a spoon.

Helen returned. ''She's sending Sandra over on her bike. Want some lunch?''

Gladie followed Helen into the kitchen, leaned against the counter while her sister made sandwiches.

''Do you remember when we went to Stratford?'' Gladie asked. ''That young man we met? Kept following us around? Well, not me — it was you he was following, he was so smitten with you.''

''It's ten *years* since we went to Stratford.''

''You must remember him. He called himself a poet. 'You're eyes are like the stars that bind my soul to infinity,' or some such drivel.''

''Do you want mustard?''

''Come on, Helen. He stood out on the lawn under our balcony all night. For goodness sake, he had a rose in his teeth!''

''Oh, him.'' Helen laughed, crinkling her nose. ''Wasn't that funny?''

''You weren't very nice. I think you broke his heart.''

''He had no business pestering us that way. Call Ted, will you please.'' She carried the sandwiches to the table.

SANDRA RODE UP AS THEY WERE preparing to start the next batch. She leaned her bike against the tree and squinted, mole-like, at the house. She had the lids in a plastic bag.

As the girl pedalled back down the drive, Helen, watching from the door, said, ''Poor Sandra. She'll never be as pretty as her mother.''

''Helen, how could you say such a thing? Really.''

''What?''

Gladie spat out her sister's words. 'Poor Sandra. She'll never be as pretty as her mother.' You said it like a curse. Poor homely Sandra, doomed to the life of an old maid.''

"What foolishness! I was just stating a fact. Sandra will get a man if she wants one.''

"Ha!''

Helen faced Gladie, hands on her hips. ''You could have married, and you know it. Tom Heney would have married you in a minute.''

"That big softie. He didn't have an ounce of sense.''

"Frank Russell, too.''

"Marrying him didn't do Alice Wright any good, did it? Six kids and living hand to mouth all these years.''

"Well, you shouldn't have gone away to normal school.''

"I had to make a living. What did you want me to do? Live off Mother and Dad? Clerk at Elmore's Hardware?''

"Then spending every summer taking courses. You just got too high and mighty for this neck of the woods. No man wants a woman who's smarter than he is.''

"See what you've done, you've turned it all around.''

"Any woman can get a husband, Gladie. There's nothing to it.''

JUDY PULLED UP BESIDE THE CURB on Bay Street and Gladie scrambled out of the car, dragging her cotton shopping bag and purse after her. Behind them a driver honked the horn, then wheeled past, squealing rubber.

"Jerk,'' Judy snapped. She inclined her head to see Gladie through the open car door. Judy had recently quit wearing make-up, and Gladie thought her eyes seemed wary in her pale face. ''I'll meet you up at Bloor at four, Auntie. Okay?''

"Drive carefully, dear." As Judy turned left heading for University Avenue and Queen's Park, Gladie crossed toward Old City Hall and continued up Bay. The mid-morning heat, coming after the air-conditioned ride into Toronto, set waves of goose bumps travelling over her flesh.

At Dundas and Bay, in a scrap of parkland littered with mashed cigarette butts and hot dog wrappers, Gladie settled herself onto an empty bench in the sparse shade of a woody caragana. Two young couples, wearing shorts and T-shirts in ice cream colours, sauntered along the asphalt path. Their skin was fresh, supple and tanned, and their feet were bare in their track shoes. Summer people. They flopped down, laughing, and for a time the girls watched, amused, as their boyfriends wrestled extravagantly on the grass; then they tilted their faces and gazed at the bone-white sky.

Gladie took a peach from her bag. She nibbled around a dime-size patch of rot that marred its puckered skin. She smiled slightly as she thought of the jars of yellow fruit in the cold cellar, lined up beside the green tomato relish, waiting for winter.

The young men jumped to their feet, jogged to the hot dog vendor on the corner, and returned with four Cokes. Gladie glanced at her wrist and saw that she had forgotten her watch. Judy had turned up half an hour early and had stood in the porch jingling her keys while Gladie rushed about feeding the cat and clearing the table and gulping down her coffee. Then, outside of Grimsby, they had almost had a row. Judy had been proselytizing for hiring quotas, equal pay for equal work, parental leave, promotions for women.

"Where does that leave the men?" Gladie demanded. "They have their families to support."

"Aunt Gladie, how could you say such a thing? And you a career woman yourself?" Gladie had laughed out loud.

A career woman? Teaching was a job, a way to earn a living. Back then, what choices did a girl have? Nurse? Secretary? Teacher? Besides, whatever she chose would be short term, wouldn't it? Until she married. But a career? Hardly.

And what could Gladie say in her own defense — that life was a matter of expectations? That you grew up watching the people around you — parents, grandparents, aunts and uncles; attending weddings and christenings and anniversary parties (with Daddy always driving, and Mother in hat and gloves ensconced in the passenger seat); learning to cook, clean, can, sew, mend. Lessons of life stored away like the embroidered linens in your hope chest. Your future, accepted and believed in. Husband and wife, father and mother, the authority of men, the cleaving of women. *Man Woman Birth Death Infinity.*

Judy could never understand how it was. She'd grown up with bra burnings, co-ed dorms, the Pill.

Gladie smiled at the young man with dark hair. He grinned back, then crossed the grass toward her carrying a camera.

Gladie framed the two couples in the lens. The young men laid their arms territorially around the shoulders of their girlfriends. Smiles all around. As she clicked the shutter the girls turned in unison and kissed the boys on the cheek.

In the book stores, the teaching supply stores, the oriental shops along Dundas, Gladie shopped for decorated erasers and pencils, stickers and bookmarks — the bribes and rewards of her teacher's arsenal. The August air closed its fist around her body. Perspiration collected under the waistband of her navy cotton skirt, and between her breasts. As she

crossed Yonge toward the Eaton Centre, she tugged surreptitiously on her bra.

In Eaton's cafeteria she pushed her tray along the
aluminum track, selecting soup, a salmon sandwich, the fruit
cup, water, tea. While waiting to pay, she exchanged the
fruit cup for cherry cheesecake.

She sat beside the window at a table for four. She ate
slowly, glancing around the room occasionally at the other
grey heads who had come to eat and to kill some time. She
regretted not ordering fries and gravy even though she knew
the greasy taste would have spoiled the flavour of the cheesecake, which was not bad considering it was made with
powdered eggs.

Gladie took her blood pressure pill, washed it down with
water. She would save the last peach for the ride home.

Gladie heard her name spoken and looked up to see Herb
Davis, in permanent press slacks and blue plaid sport shirt,
standing over her carrying a food tray.

"Mind if I sit with you?" he asked.

"Oh. Herb. Hello. Yes. Here, let me get this stuff out of
your way."

Herb was an old friend of Ted's from their high school
days. Gladie had run into him and his wife on and off over
the years at Ted and Helen's, or in St. Kitt's when they were
down visiting his brother Alf. In her mind's eye, Herb is
always nineteen, draped over the front seat of Ted's old
Dodge, chatting up Gladie, her friend Flo, and Helen. Grinning at Helen. Gaping at Helen, while Helen plays her gay
saucy self. In those days, Herb had the looks of an English
choir boy — round eyes, plump rosy cheeks, stubby nose.
Now the nose seemed incongruous in his meaty face, and his
hair, gone the colour of putty, was sparse on top.

He had the Wednesday Special — hot roast beef sandwich with fries and gravy. "Do you want my coleslaw? I can't eat cabbage anymore. Bums up my gall bladder."

"Thank you, no. What are you doing downtown?"

"Blue Jays tonight. Against Boston." He cut his sandwich into triangles and forked it into his mouth. "I like to come down early and get something to eat. I'm no cook."

"I was sorry to hear about Winnie."

Herb wiped his mouth on his napkin. "I really appreciated your letter, Gladie."

He had married a girl from Gravenhurst, an interloper Flo called her. A sweet-smiling, sharp-eyed girl who cut Herb, like a heifer, out of the gang and steered him to Toronto where the opportunities were *so* much better.

"I sold our place in Scarborough. I've got an apartment up at Finch. I can hop on the subway and be at work in ten minutes."

Gladie imagined him returning every evening to an apartment crowded with photographs, record albums, chairs, table, bed; coming home to the tick-tick of the clock and the hum of the refrigerator, to microwaved TV dinners and TSN until bedtime.

He told her that he and Winnie had planned to buy a place in a trailer park in Florida when he retired in the spring. He speared the last piece of bread and mopped up the gravy on his plate. "There doesn't seem any point in retiring now," he said.

"You should have kept your house. A house keeps you busy."

"I miss the garden. Sometimes I even miss shovelling the damn snow."

"Canadian to the bone, aren't you, Herb?"

He laughed out loud, and it reminded her of long ago summer nights, pulsing with stars and promise. Every Saturday, after the community hall dance, they piled into Ted's car — boys in front, girls in back. They smoked and drank beer and felt deliciously wild. As they tore along the back roads, Herb would dangle his body recklessly out the car window and smash their empties against the suddenly bright road signs. Before summer was done, Helen was riding up front beside Ted (the sight of her ponytail swinging impudently over the seat had made Gladie want to reach out and snip it off). Herb was demoted to the back seat with Gladie and Flo; good old Flo, who always managed to maneuvre Gladie into the car first, then plumped herself down in the middle, next to Herb. Fat lot of good it did her, she was no match for Winnie.

Gladie showed Herb what she had bought for her students. She told him about a boy in her Grade Four class one year who was still reading at a primary level when he arrived in September. As she talked Herb rested his chin in his hand. Gladie realized she was aware of him, of the thin gold watch on his wrist, the plain wedding band, the knuckles fretting his man's broad hand.

"Anyway," she said, "I found out Stephen liked hockey cards, so every time he read me another book he earned a new package. By March, he'd caught up to the rest of the class."

"I'm going to get more coffee. Want some?"

She shifted his coleslaw to her tray. Against the opposite wall, where the light was dimmer, a woman sat alone at a table for two. She had dressed herself completely in shades of pink: a rose pleated skirt; a baby pink sweater adorned by three tiny pearl buttons stitched into the side seam; a pink chiffon scarf that trailed like Maypole ribbons from the ponytail on top of her head. Her feet, in pink patent slippers, were crossed delicately at the ankles. Her back was slightly arched, and she sipped 7-Up through a straw. She reminded Gladie of a girl from the soda fountain advertisements she used to see in the *Saturday Evening Post*. But her hair was white, and the skin around her eyes and jaw was slack and crumpled.

When Herb returned with their coffee, Gladie was tempted to point out the pink lady, half-hoping she would become their little shared joke. But the words held fast to her throat.

Herb hooked his elbow over the back of his chair and traced patterns in the sugar on his tray.

''Do you remember when we used to drive over to the bars in the States?'' he asked.

''No.''

''I guess you were already away at school then. Boy, did we have some times. We were taking a chance bringing Helen, but she wouldn't stay home. That one time she sure put a scare into us.''

Gladie sat back in her seat and stared past Herb toward the entrance. ''I watched *High Noon* on television Saturday night.''

''We'd gone over to Niagara. Ted got chummy with this American girl at the next table. It wasn't until we were ready to leave that we realized Helen was gone. The last anybody'd seen of her, she was talking to some fellow at the bar. We piled into the car and went looking for her. Didn't know *what* to do! Hell, we couldn't go to the police — we were carrying fake i.d.'s. And we sure weren't going to call our parents. Flo kept whining in that voice of hers'' — he imitated Flo in a Betty Boop voice: 'They're going to close the border, they're going to close the border. Oh my god, we'll be stuck here all night.' But we couldn't leave her, Helen I mean. We would have gladly left Flo. And Ted, he never said a word, he just kept driving around.''

"You're making this up. Flo would have told me.''

"Maybe it wasn't Flo then. It all happened that weekend they got engaged.''

And Gladie remembered being called from Sunday dinner, standing in the gloom of the boarding house hallway, gripping the worn telephone receiver — "I'm getting married, Gladie. Isn't it great? Ted just asked me.''

"So, did you find her?'' Gladie asked finally.

"Eventually we drifted back to the bar. The place was closed, and there she was sitting on the front steps, combing her hair and fixing her lipstick, as casual as you please. You would've thought she was waiting for a bus.'' Herb grinned and shook his head. "That Helen.''

Across the room the pink lady rose to her feet, slipped her small white bag over her shoulder and exited, holding the bag steady against her hip.

Gladie tilted her head to read Herb's watch. "I'd better get going,'' she said, pushing back her chair and gathering her things. "I'm meeting Judy at four.''

"I'll walk out with you,'' he said.

They headed toward the escalator, side by side, in silence. As they passed the luggage display Herb said, "Ya know, Gladie, I'm driving down home to visit Alf and Mary next week... '' Gladie stared straight ahead. What was he saying? She wanted to look at him, but she continued to fix her eyes on the Back-to-School sign at the end of the aisle. She wanted to say, to do, something. She had to, but what? What? Helen would know. . .

Herb stepped aside to allow Gladie onto the escalator. She hesitated; she felt suddenly light-headed. The treads and risers moved inexorably out of the floor and re-formed, counting off the moments as they fell away.

Gladie reached into her bag. As she took the top step she turned to Herb and, smiling, offered him the last peach.

A House in the Country
Bill MacDonald

IF AUNT LEONE HAD BEEN a man, she'd have been called a curmudgeon. Not that she was misanthropic, necessarily. Just easily bored. Tiresome people annoyed her, and she found many people tiresome. Her favourite expression was, "So-and-so doesn't have the brains God gave grasshoppers!"

She spent forty-two years clerking in the Mining Recorder's Office on Court Street, and during that time saw most of her contemporaries marry, have children and become grandparents. Though she herself did none of these, she gave no evidence of being resentful.

Except for funerals, she was not a frequent guest at family gatherings. She came to our house only rarely, such as for my parents' wedding anniversary and Easter Sunday. I remember feeling sorry for her, because she always seemed to be off in a corner somewhere, with no one to talk to, even in a crowded room.

For most of her adult life she occupied the ground floor of a house on Prospect Avenue. I have no idea what she did with her spare time, although my parents used to say that on weekends she never rose before three o'clock in the afternoon. I, for one, could never see anything wrong with that.

Winter and summer, she wore feathered hats and square-toed leather shoes, and took pride in the fact that in forty-two years she had never missed a day's work. I once questioned her on this, and she said it was true, but that, on occasion, because of snowstorms and unreliable alarm clocks, she'd been as much as four hours late!

I think what intrigued me about Aunt Leone was her self-reliance. That, and her honesty. If she liked you, she let you know; if she didn't, she ignored you. At her retirement tea, I overheard her telling her subordinates that in professional life you had to stand up for yourself, because if you didn't, who would? Deferring to male opinion, she said, and always kowtowing to other people, were pitfalls to be avoided. As a reward for forty-two years of meritorious service, she received a beautiful blown glass cockatoo, with which she seemed genuinely pleased.

WE WERE AMUSED, though not surprised, when Aunt Leone left Prospect Avenue and bought herself a rustic cottage on Arthur Street, out past Mapleward Road, on the banks of the Neebing River. She said she'd always wanted to live in the country, where she could cultivate raspberries and have a tortoise-shell cat.

"Won't you be lonely, Leone?" my father asked her.

"Not if I put up a birdfeeder," she said.

Before Christmas she informed everyone she was through with gift-giving. "All it does," she said, "is contribute to greed."

Nor did she see any point in coming all the way to town by bus to visit, when a telephone call from the snug comfort of her kitchen could accomplish the same purpose, at a fraction of the cost and bother.

"May we visit *you*?" asked my father.

"That depends," said Aunt Leone.

"On what, your horoscope?"

"On whether you bring me a bottle of Mogen David."

TRUE TO HER WORD, AUNT LEONE acquired a tortoise-shell cat named Zola and began cultivating raspberries. Her house was soon surrounded by tall, prickly canes, which, in summer, bore the reddest, most luscious berries imaginable. From her first crop, she ate raspberries at every meal, until, tiring of them, she decided to preserve the rest in quart sealers for the winter.

The following year she put up a sign, visible from the highway — RASPBERRIES - FREE FOR THE PICKING — and enjoyed sitting at her kitchen window watching people climb out of their cars and avail themselves of her generosity. On occasion, she said, if they were elderly, or infirm, she might even take out a pitcher of homemade root beer, or a pot of tea. But mostly she just liked to sit and watch, and only rarely did she have to rap a warning on the window at tempestuous children trampling the canes.

One sultry August afternoon, a young motorcyclist with greasy dark hair and tattoos on both arms stopped. She watched him dismount, eat a dozen handfuls of raspberries, then lie down and put a blue bandanna over his face and fall asleep.

"Zola," she said to the tortoise-shell cat, "I don't mind people partaking of my fruit, but I do object to them sleeping in my vineyard!"

And so she and Zola went out to accost this weary traveler, this insouciant stranger dressed in black. At first, she said, she intended to waken him rudely. But when she saw how soundly he was sleeping, and how defenceless he looked (despite the stubble on his cheeks and his tangled mane of hair), she hesitated.

He was not, after all, doing any damage. And Zola, who had intuition, showed no sign of alarm. So Aunt Leone let him sleep, and spent the afternoon pruning her canes with scissors and watering her peonies.

Later, a damp wind came down the river, and sandpipers appeared— usually a sign of rain. Aunt Leone says she was thinking about waking the motorcyclist and telling him to be on his way, when she looked up and there he was, standing in front of her. For a moment, she says, he reminded her of Cousin Dunstan, who was killed in the war. Something about the way he looked at you, with his head thrown back and a slight sneer on his lips. And the way he stood, full of bravado and self-confidence.

"Thank you for the berries, old mother," he said gruffly. "And for letting me sleep."

"I'm nobody's *old mother*," snapped Aunt Leone. "And the only reason I let you sleep was because I didn't know you were there!"

Confronting him, she says, she realized two things: first, how young he was and second, what a pleasant voice he had. Again, like Cousin Dunstan, who people used to say could charm the pants off a mannequin.

"What's your name?" Aunt Leone asked him.

"Parnell," he said, scratching Zola behind the ears. "I guess I'll be on my way."

"Parnell," said Aunt Leone. "I used to know a family by that name. They were in the bread business."

"I don't have family," said Parnell.

"There are worse things than not having family."

He was halfway to his motorcycle, she says, accompanied by Zola, when he turned around and came back and asked her for a drink of water.

"I have homemade root beer," she said.

"I'd rather have water," said Parnell.

And so she got him a glass of water, which he drank, and by then it was raining.

"I take it you're heading west?" she said.

"Red Lake," said Parnell. "I have a friend..."

"It's nice to have friends," said Aunt Leone.

They stood on her front porch in the rain, watching sandpipers dancing on the river bank. Two small boys drifting by in a punt, oblivious to the raindrops, held up a wriggling silver fish the size of a sardine.

"Would you like something to eat?" said Aunt Leone.

"If it's no trouble," said Parnell.

"Then come in and wipe your feet."

SHE SAYS SHE GAVE HIM TUNA FISH sandwiches and a plate of cold spaghetti, followed by raspberries in cream and a glass of buttermilk, and that during the entire meal, except to say he was still hungry, he did not utter a single word. Which was fine with her, because it gave her a chance to observe him, and try to figure out why he reminded her so much of Dunstan.

Finally he rose, and said he'd be on his way, because he wanted to make English River before dark.

And so she gave him a bag of mince tarts to take with him in his saddle bag, and walked to the highway with him, and watched him put on his helmet and mount his motorcycle and roar off into a drizzly sunset toward English River. Then she went back indoors, and was momentarily annoyed at herself for thinking the house felt empty. She stood looking out the window at her peonies, wondering what it must be like to be Parnell's age.

And then she noticed that her blown glass cockatoo was gone.

Her beautiful blown glass cockatoo.

Her medal of honour, so to speak; her badge of recognition.

It had been right there in the window, dangling on a thread, and now it was gone!

The only time he could have taken it, she reasoned, was while she had her back turned, making sandwiches. Or when she was down in the fruit cellar, fetching mince tarts.

What kind of gratitude was this, she asked Zola, when a guest to whom you had shown hospitality repaid you by stealing your blown glass cockatoo, which item, by the way, aside from your meagre pension, was all you had to show for forty-two years of meritorious service. To Parnell, it could only have been a trinket, of no more significance than a biker's tattoo. To Aunt Leone, it meant much more than that.

Despairing of human nature, she lay down in bed with a damp cloth over her eyes, and stayed there for two days.

DECEMBER WAS A COLD AND stormy month that year. Snow lay heavily on field and rooftop. In her rustic cottage beside the Neebing River, Aunt Leone spent a great deal of time gazing out her window at this white, featureless landscape. Schools were closed on three separate occasions, and one morning when she looked out she saw a station wagon upside down in the ditch at the end of her driveway.

Despite their confinement, she and Zola were far from unhappy. Though the berry patch was inaccessible, indeed *invisible*, they could still watch rose-breasted grosbeaks at the feeder and squirrels scampering up and down the evergreens. After supper they would listen to the radio, and sometimes, when skies were clear, they would turn out the lights and sit in the dark, watching the aurora borealis.

At Christmas time, Aunt Leone was spared the vexation of having to turn down well-meant invitations to turkey dinner, because nobody invited her. It may be that we all forgot whose turn it was, that each of us thought someone else had at least *asked* her. Put bluntly, a family oversight. Not that she would have come to town anyway.

On Christmas Eve, it snowed, and there was a cold north wind. On Christmas Day, she stayed in bed till noon, and only got up then because she knew the birds had nothing to eat. Looking out her window, she says, was like looking out at the end of the world. What was it they called it... *nuclear winter?*

At one o'clock in the afternoon, just as she was opening a tin of kippers for lunch, she says she saw the Greyhound bus go by, making heavy weather of it through the snow, and wondered who would be traveling by bus on Christmas Day.

But then she noticed that the bus had not gone by. It had in fact stopped, and let somebody off. Somebody wearing a dark overcoat and a billycock hat with earflaps. She says she wondered for a moment which of her various nephews it might be, come to visit her on Christmas. When the figure was halfway to her house, trudging through the drifts like Good King Wenceslas, she realized that it was Parnell. She says she had a good mind to lock the door and draw the curtains. What nerve, she thought — the thief returning.

When she peered out again he was standing there in the snow, looking rather pale and thin, it seemed to her, and she wondered if he was ill. And so she went and opened the door, and could see that he was in some difficulty, hunched over like an old man, and she thought to herself, "He'd better not have come here looking for succour, not if he's sick."

"I was afraid," gasped Parnell, lurching toward her, "that you wouldn't be here!"

"Then you should have stayed on the bus," said Aunt Leone.

Which slowed him down but did not stop him. "I only had a ticket to Kakabeka. The bus driver... "

"And if I hadn't been here?"

"I'd have broken down the door, old mother," he said, coughing. "As simple as that."

She stood aside as he staggered up the stairs, all covered with snow like a soldier exhausted from a long journey. Except that this time, she says, he did not remind her of Cousin Dunstan.

As THE SNOW FELL, AND IT became apparent that Parnell had no intention of leaving, even if he'd been able to, Aunt Leone says she put a tinned chicken in the oven and decided to make the best of it.

"I don't believe in Christmas," she told him.

"Nor do I," he said, sitting wearily on a chair close to the stove, as though anxious to absorb its heat.

"Christmas started out as a pagan feast," she said, noticing how gaunt he was, how hollow-eyed. "An appeasement to the gods of winter."

"Who can be very unkind," said Parnell, coughing.

Outdoors, a flurry of snow shook the house and scratched at the windows.

"It appears they've been unkind to you," said Aunt Leone, wondering who he was, and why he'd paid her this second visit.

"A slight congestion," he said, tapping his chest. "Nothing contagious. I'll be fine tomorrow."

Waiting for the chicken to heat, she learned that he had a stepsister in St. Catharines, that his motorcycle had been stolen and that, until recently, he had been third engineer aboard the bulk carrier, *Willowglen*. "At this time of year," he said, coughing, "it's no job for a man afraid of deep water."

"My father was a lake skipper," she said. "Back in the days of steam."

"The *Willowglen*," he started to say, but was interrupted by a fit of coughing. "The *Willowglen* has a triple expansion engine, and Scottish boilers."

Which meant nothing to Aunt Leone, but somehow made him seem less of an intruder. Seeing him shivering, she filled a pan with hot water and made him put his feet in it, and then she gave him a pair of woolen socks to put on, and the largest of her handknit sweaters, which almost fit him, but not quite. When the chicken was ready, she took it out of the oven and carved it as one would a turkey, with flourish, and poured them each a glass of Mogen David, with which they toasted Grampa Howlette, who had been a sea captain, and Zola, who had roused herself from hibernation, and of course the gods of winter, who needed appeasement.

According to Aunt Leone, it fell short of being a successful celebration, because during the meal, at which Parnell ate next to nothing, other than a bowl of preserved raspberries, he said it saddened him to think of people being alone at Christmas. Which was not something my aunt wished to hear, or even think about. Last year on the *Willowglen*, said Parnell, he and his mates had stuffed themselves so full of plum pudding they'd barely been able to stand watch.

"There are worse things than being alone at Christmas," said Aunt Leone.

"I know there are," said Parnell. "But may I tell you something, old mother? Tonight, I'm thankful to be here with you."

He dozed off, she says, sitting in his chair, with Zola curled on his lap, and she could not help remembering the first time she'd seen him, stretched out in her berry patch, with a blue bandanna over his face. He had finally stopped shivering, and in his ill-fitting sweater, with a faint smile on his lips, reminded her not so much of Dunstan, as of her own father. She was alarmed, however, at his laboured breathing, and at the waxy pallor of his cheeks, and knew in her heart, even then, that he needed medical attention.

The glass cockatoo, she says, didn't cross her mind until she was making up a bed for him on the living room couch. But since that would hardly have been the time to mention it, she decided to wait, and resigned herself to having him there overnight, or perhaps longer, if the snow continued and his "congestion" did not abate.

LOOKING BACK, I HAVE DIFFICULTY understanding her solicitude. But then, I had difficulty understanding her detachment, too, her *unsociability*, as my parents used to call it, and so the fault is probably mine, not hers.

She allowed Parnell to stay six weeks, during which time she nursed him as best she could, feeding him thin broth and preserved raspberries, which were inadequate, she knew, but it was all he wanted, or could keep down. Daily, she watched him grow thinner and more haggard, until his eyes were sunken in their sockets, his feverish brow and skeletal fingers the colour of faded parchment.

"Old mother," he said to her the day after Epiphany, "tomorrow, God willing, I'll be on my way."

"Don't be ridiculous," she said. "You're in no condition to go anywhere."

"I did not come here to die," he said.

"Then why *did* you come here?" she said, but immediately regretted having said it.

AT THE END OF JANUARY, old Mr. Papamichael, her next door neighbour, with whom she had a contract for snowplowing and who sometimes dropped in for a cup of tea, observed Parnell closely and diagnosed his ailment as hepatitis. But Grizelda Peacock, who drove the school bus and delivered mail, said as far as she was concerned Parnell had double pneumonia, just like her brother-in-law.

A travelling Amway salesman named Phineas, who came to the door flogging bath salts and cookware, said it was obvious to him that Parnell had AIDS, or possibly leukemia.

And so, in early February, as the days were lengthening and there was warmth to the sun, Aunt Leone telephoned my father and asked him what he thought she should do.

"Put the poor soul in an ambulance and send him to McKellar Hospital!" said my father. "It's what you should have done in the first place!"

And so Aunt Leone did. Not because she wanted to, but because my father told her if she didn't, she could find herself liable.

"Remember in the old days, Leone?" he said. "They used to come around and put quarantine signs on people's doors — red for scarlet fever, blue for diphtheria, orange for measles, yellow for chicken pox.''

Over Parnell's protestations, she phoned the hospital. She says she doesn't remember what she said, but later in the day an ambulance arrived, with two uniformed attendants, who, after coming in and looking at Parnell, put him on a stretcher and took him away. And when they were gone, and the house was silent, without the sound of his voice, or his coughing, she knelt beside the bed he had occupied since Christmas and wept.

THOUGH MY FATHER OFFERED to drive her, she insisted on coming to town by bus every day, even after Parnell no longer recognized her, or knew she was at his bedside. Which is where she was when he died in April, holding his hand, telling him for the hundredth time that he was not aboard the *Willowglen*, that he did not have to stand watch at midnight.

And because his step-sister in St. Catharines could not be located, it was Aunt Leone who made arrangements for his cremation, and sent a large donation of books to the Missions to Seamen at Keefer Terminal.

The day of the cremation she told us there were two things she regretted: never having found out what became of her blown glass cockatoo, and persuading Parnell that Easter was nothing more than a primitive observance of the vernal equinox.

IN JULY, SHE SOLD HER rustic cottage on the banks of the Neebing River and moved back to Prospect Avenue. Though she no longer has a berry patch, she does have space for a few peonies, and on sunny days she and Zola like to sit outdoors and watch the hummingbirds.

SPEAKING OF PERSUASION, I believe I've convinced her to have lunch with me next week at the Kestitupa. She says she's been thinking about Uncle Edgar lately, and is curious to see this hangout of his, this nefarious cafe, in which he spent so many convivial hours, and on whose walls, although she does not know it yet, hang portraits of cats who look like Zola.

"Do they welcome older ladies?" she said.

"With open arms," I said. "I'll introduce you to Finnish pancakes."

She thought about this a moment. "As long as they don't come with preserved raspberries. I have an aversion to preserved raspberries."

"We missed you last Christmas, Auntie," I said.

She thought about this a moment, too. "I was busy last Christmas," she said.

Which I took to mean that this Christmas, she might not be.

The Bridge
Jake MacDonald

THERE WAS ALWAYS THE BRIDGE. As long as anyone could remember, the bridge had been there, pre-dating even the beginnings of the town itself. The bridge was built in 1911, when there was nothing on either side of the river but unbroken forest. The first residents were railway navvies who lived in a chaotic tent city along the bank of the river and worked on the structure. The railway executives, admiring the glittering belt of blue river that seemed to stretch on forever, asked their Indian labourers what "Keewuttunnee" meant. The Indians, in the tradition of an old joke that their ancestors played on passing voyageurs, explained that it meant "good luck is coming." Like the voyageurs, the railway men eventually learned that "Keewuttunnee" referred to the fact that this channel of the river was a dead end, or cul-de-sac, but by then they had already decided that it was a pretty name for the town, and no one really cared what the word meant anyway.

The railway drew up grand designs for the future town of Keewuttunnee. Here you had a synapse of a major waterway and a railroad line. Surveyors went out and subdivided the bush for miles around; great sprawling maps declared the existence of East and West Keewuttunnee and the adjacent

industrial districts and thoroughfares like Pine Ridge Boul-
evard that funnelled the busy citizens in and out of residential
areas like Riverside Heights. In the ensuing years, while
investors waited for the town to catch up with the survey
map, many a brood of skunks was raised in the thickets of
those nonexistent avenues, many a scrawny wolf lifted its
leg against those rusted iron survey pins. The car and the
highway had been invented, and freight wasn't being hauled
by river anymore.

The town as it exists now is a random glittering complex
of wooden shacks, bare rock, Atco trailers, machine sheds,
prefabricated government bungalows, liquor store, gas station, CN station and derelict sockeyed log buildings, their
broken tin roofs sagging in the sun. At the time the bridge
was under construction the town proliferated in a ragged and
disorganized way, a ruff of tents and lacy walkways on
either side of the iron bridge's monstrous Victorian span.
Later, with the registration of deeds to property, the subtle
patterns of social hierarchy began to appear. High on the hill
on the east side of the river was the rockiest and poorest land.
This was inevitably set aside for welfare cases and Indian
reservation. Lower down, among the junk-strewn yards and
tethered huskies, were the shabby-sided wooden homes of
the non-status Indians and half-breeds and working poor.

Lower down on the hillsides, near the river, are today's
gaudy aluminum-sided bungalows with their shag-carpeted
living-rooms and satellite dishes in the backyard, the lot of
them occupied by schoolteachers, nurses, social workers,
police, small businessmen, Keewuttunnee's equivalent of a
ruling class. Along the riverbank, where the ancient broken
log cabins of the pre-settlement days crouch in the hum of
dragonflies and river, is real estate too choice for mere

residential purposes. Marina, fishing-lodge, government pier, float plane base and Keewuttunnee Bay Inn sit right along the waterfront, the most valuable property in town.

THE KEEWUTTUNNEE BAY INN features ten sparsely finished hotel rooms, a dining-room with bear rugs and moose heads, a snack bar finished in knotty pine and a beer parlour. The only item of decoration in the beer parlour with its formica-topped aluminum-legged tables is a large oil painting of the CNR bridge. In spring and summer the hotel is busy with American fishermen, who rent boats and clog the parking lots with their Winnebagos. In autumn the tourists leave, the summer people leave, and the river is silent and empty. Leaves rattle in the bare woods, and an outboard motor outside the hotel means Willy coming to shoot a game of pool, or an Indian on his way back up to the reserve. By Christmas the easiest part of winter has passed — there is less charm to the inexorable down-sift of snow, and the yellow beer parlour windows shine out into the endless winter night.

Lemon, the 30-year-old bartender at the Keewuttunnee Bay Inn, sees the winters come and go. He serves drinks to people like Bobby and Melvina, who sit around talking about Toronto and how they are going to do it right next time. He hears them debating keypunch school, pullout couches, the subway. He sees Bobby's new wardrobe — her scarf, tweed jacket, high boots — and sees Melvina hovering in the background, her shadowlike bovine presence almost completely eliminated by Bobby's vixenish good looks. Across the room from Bobby and Melvina he brings a round for Al Chaput, the off-duty cop, who comes in here like clockwork every Saturday night and pours down the

Cutty Sark until he's got that dull gleam in his eye, and then he sets them up for the Harrison boys, the regulars, who are in here every night in their blaze-orange MOTO-SKI jackets, boots flopping, talking loud like they own the place and banging the pool balls so hard that half the time they fly right off the table. Then Smelly Mike and Johnny No Cash, who steal the tips off the table if you're not quick to collect them, and old Joe Hudson, who's boring the pants off Al the cop by telling him for the umpteenth time about the day he threw the grenade in the window of the Normandy farmhouse and killed seventeen men and a dog, and all the other regulars with their habits and idiosyncracies and petulant little feuds; and then there's Willy, the ex-city boy, working for the CN, who with his curls, his sly wink and amiable Irish heart roves around the bar at will, the bridge between everybody, everybody's best friend.

ON THE MORNING THAT WILLY was killed, a Sunday morning in early February, Lemon was in the beer parlour cleaning up the mess of the night before. There had been only one brawl, not bad for a Saturday night, but there was still broken glass and dried blood on the floor and he was mopping it up when he heard the faint but distinct throbbing of a helicopter.

He leaned on the mop and listened. In the plexiglass front of the jukebox his gently potbellied, angel-haired reflection stared back at him.

A moment later there was a gloved thumping at the back door. Lemon lit a cigarette and unlocked the door. Swinton, or Swiny as he was called, stood in the brilliant cold, stamping his boots on the squeaking snow. Breath billowed from his contorted red face. "Will you hurry up and let me in, fer Christ sake? It's freezin' out here."

Swinton's moustache was mushy with frost under a snubbed, bulbous nose. "So . . . did you hear about Willy?"

Lemon felt something slip in him, cold as an icicle. Whenever someone said, "Did you hear about so-and-so," it meant bad news.

"He got killed. About twenty minutes ago. Over by the maintenance sheds. Got clipped by the train, I think."

Swiny, with grim deliberation, chalked a pool cue. He was seldom the bearer of important news, and he meant to use this opportunity wisely. Lemon moved to the window, shivered as he gazed out at the frost-rimed morning. He studied the bridge, then the far side of the river, as if his reaction might be located there. He buried his hands in his blue jeans pockets, stared out at the brilliant winter sun. Finally he shrugged and turned to Swiny. "I heard the helicopter."

"Yeah. We were real lucky that it came in. It was flying in spare parts for the railway, so the foreman says. Mind you, he was dead by the time it got here, but anyways... "

"What happened?"

Swiny broke the balls. "Uh... I figure he got hit by the train."

More steps came to the door, more knocking. It was Sonny Copenace, looking shaken. He'd seen it happen. "That, uh, steel strapping, eh? That they tie the lumber down with? Well, uh, one of them bust loose and was whipping around, hit Willy in the throat as the train went by. He was lyin' on the ground just flippin' there. Just flippin'."

Lemon shook his head. "That's bad."

Sonny Copenace sat down, lit one of Swiny's cigarettes. "Yeah, it's really a bummer, boy. One minute he's walking along there, the next minute, dead."

Then the Harrison boys arrived, announced by the tinny snarl of their snow machines, and they came in the door, now unlocked, and stomped the snow off their boots and strode automatically to the snooker table. Burt Harrison, his mane of blond hair still tangled from sleep, shook a fist emphatically and announced, ''There's going to be some serious goddamned drinking going on today.''

Then Bobby and Melvina arrived, both with tearful eyes, reeking of morning makeup, and confirmed that Willy was dead. They had just spoken to the cop. And then a moment later Al the cop arrived in person. His cheekbone was bruised from being punched in the face by a logger a few days ago and his hands were shaking from too much booze the night before, but that was normal. There wasn't much else to do on a Saturday night in Keewuttunnee in the wintertime but drink. Willy had been a close friend of his but Al chose to remain a policeman. Death was his department. As he peeled off his gloves the rakish tilt of his hat remained undisturbed. ''When somebody is that white,'' he explained, with a Gallic shrug, ''you can't do anything. You just lay a tarpaulin over them.''

There was a frown, a silence.

Al the cop sat on the edge of a bar stool and eyed the long glittery upside-down row of whiskey bottles.

Sonny Copenace, who had witnessed the accident, sat down heavily in a chair. ''Wow, man... I still can't believe it. I really liked that guy.''

''How do you think I feel? I was with him last night,'' Bobby said. Her eyes were smudged, and there was an unfamiliar hoarseness to her voice. Lemon glanced at her unsympathetically. Already she was playing it up, as if she and Willy had been tragic lovers.

"You mean he came over after I left?" inquired Melvina.

"Whaddya mean, Bobby, he was with me!" Swiny interjected.

Burt Harrison was shooting pool with his brother, talking quietly. "You should go see the blood, eh. It looks like a can of paint all over the snow. I almost horked."

"Well I still don't understand what happened," mumbled Melvina, twiddling her fingers uneasily.

"You know those steel bands that they wrap the lumber with on the freight train?" Al Chaput responded. "Well one of 'em was loose and whipping around, eh."

More people were showing up at the door.

"Listen you guys," announced Lemon, hoisting his hand. "We can't stay here. I'm not even supposed to be open. Let's go back to my place."

No one was listening.

"We might as well," Lemon persisted. "C'mon you guys, listen up, eh? Let's go back to my place. I got some food and booze and stuff and we can have a bit of a party. I think Willy would have wanted it that way. Whaddaya think? We might as well, eh? Hey Burt, you wanna put the damn pool balls down like I'm asking you? Okay?"

Lemon lived in an old cottage, winterized, that looked out onto the frozen river. It belonged to his father, as did the skewed, peeling row of light-housekeeping cabins behind, and in the summer his father came to Keewuttunnee and operated the whole thing as a tourist camp. Lemon, who had once taken twelve credits in Environmental Studies at the University of Manitoba, had lived for the last three years in Keewuttunnee, his hometown. His original plan had been to hole up in the vacant house for a year or so and save enough money to get out of the bush permanently, but one year had turned to three. Instead of banking money he was now in debt even worse than before, and his disgust with his own incompetence was vast.

BY MID-AFTERNOON THE PARTY at Lemon's house had become a local event. Everyone in town had heard about it, but not everyone came. As if cloven by an invisible flaw the town split into two halves: those who thought it proper to celebrate Willy's death with a party and those who didn't. Or so it seemed to Lemon, who had been off and on the telephone for the last hour trying to invite girls to the party, only to be greeted by the sepulchral tones of mothers who seemed chillingly disinclined to speak loud enough to be heard above the Rolling Stones on Lemon's stereo. Those who had proper homes with rec-rooms and carpeting and colour television sets stayed home with the curtains drawn. Daughters stared silently at Sunday afternoon homework while mothers' weary voices idled like engines in the kitchen. They disapproved of the party in Willy's honour. Those with no real homes, with only CN bunkhouses or shacks or overcrowded Indian Affairs prefabs to live in came to the party; those they partied with were their only real family, and when there's trouble in the family, Lemon thought to himself, you always immediately go home.

The afternoon passed quickly with the crowd swelling, then shrinking, then stabilizing around ten or twelve regulars who patronized the bar. The Harrison boys were in the kitchen, clomping around in their Kodiak boots, knocking over glasses and attempting to fry a huge mass of bacon in a cast iron pot. Lemon watched them uneasily, inclined to interfere but hesitant because of prior experience. Either of them, sober, was capable of being violently anti-social, and when liquor was involved, along with the death of a close friend, anything could happen. As Burt Harrison said, referring to the quieter mourners on the other side of town, "What do they think we're going to do? Just ignore it? Hah! Willy's dead, and I say there's gonna be some DRINKIN'!"

Lemon slipped out of the kitchen, detecting a whiff of war in the air. Bobby and Melvina were sitting by the fireplace, talking about the apartment they had already picked out, describing the wallpaper they'd decided on for the kitchen. Swiny, his head teetering like a boulder on the fatty stump of his neck, snuffled through his nose and guffawed. "You'll never cross that gaw-damned bridge till they carry you out in a box!"

Bobby showed him a contemptuous glance. "Go drink some more floor cleaner, teenage alky."

"Go hump a pig," he said, jerking a sip from his beer.

"I volunteer," muttered Al Chaput, who had finished his shift half an hour ago and now, in his SKI BANFF sweatshirt was drinking triples and making up for lost time.

Sonny Copenace, so drunk that he looked like he was staggering with fever, came up on Lemon from behind and grasped his elbow. He stared heavily into Lemon's eyes, breathing fumes of vodka and beer. "I wanna talk about Willy," he said. "To you. Jus' to you."

"There's nothing to talk about," said Lemon.

"That's right," declared Burt Harrison loudly. "We ain't here to talk, we're here to DRINK!"

Lemon felt like getting out of the house. He put on his parka and boots, went down the steps and outside into the winter dusk. The cold air rammed into his lungs and a cough tore out of him as he walked to the woodshed. He reached inside and threw two jack-pine logs on the snow, took the axe off the wall to split them. "Gonna be a cold night, Willy boy," he said.

The frosty steam of his statement hung in the air, proving he'd said it. He swung the axe listlessly and the block split into four. "Thanks," he said aloud.

He leaned on the axe and looked across the yard, across the blue fringes of shadow on the snow, at the smudged hemorrhage of sunset on the distant toothy ridge. Willy, or Will, as Lemon and a few others called him, had probably been his best friend. But then everybody thought that Willy was their best pal. He'd come here by choice; he'd liked it here. He liked the people, he liked the woods and he didn't have the split running through him.

Lemon halved the second block of wood, then straightened his back and looked through the yard. I'll never find it out here, he thought to himself. I never would have believed that my best friend could get killed and I wouldn't even feel sad about it.

IT WAS MIDNIGHT. Bobby's father had come to get her but she had made a furious speech and ended up crying. And Bobby's father had yelled that none of them had any respect for the dead and then he told Burt Harrison he was going to punch him in the face, and Burt only laughed. And then her father left and Bobby went down to the river to play ball hockey. Diana Highway, Sonny's wife, had come to get him but he was too drunk and started crying, so she had stayed, and now they were both down playing ball hockey on the slick black ice of the river. Swiny was in goal; he was using two cases of beer for goalposts. Sergeant McCandless had come looking for Al the cop, acting very grim and unfriendly because of some mistake that Al had made in the accident report, but Al, who had possibly been sentenced to the Keewuttunnee detachment for having a casual attitude in the first place, hid in the bedroom with Melvina and didn't come out for quite a while after the sergeant was gone. Now Al and Melvina were both down on the ice with the rest of the people playing ball hockey, adding their whooping and applause to the general tumult whenever someone heard an audible crack in the current-teased, treacherously thin ice. Occasionally Burt Harrison would jump up and down on the ice, claiming to test it.

Lemon, winded, clutching a stitch in his pot belly, climbed up the snow-packed riverbank and sat with his back against the foot of the bridge. He coughed into his mitt, and drew a bottle of brandy from his parka pocket. Mist billowed off the mouth of the bottle as he took a sip. Burt Harrison scrambled up the snowbank and sat heavily down beside him. "Gimme that," he said, taking Lemon's bottle. He guzzled, gasped. They exchanged cigarettes. Mist, sparks, smoke rolled upwards in the icy air.

"This party goes all night," decreed Burt Harrison. Lemon felt that there was an unspoken agreement among all of them that the party was cancelling out Willy's death. As long as the party endured, Willy was really there.

"You're a good shit, Lemon."

Burt Harrison seldom spoke to him, but earlier in a competition to see who could best fall headfirst down the stairs in the house, Lemon had made a number of superbly executed suicidal dives, surprising even himself and winning Burt's favour.

"I'll tell you, Lemon... how long have I known you for?"

"Uh, Grade One would you believe?"

"What, since that long? Well I don't care what anyone

says, you're not a bad guy.'' Lemon tapped his cigarette, watching sparks twirl down into the snow.

''An' when I get my dealership in Calgary, I want you to come and see me.'' He sipped again, expansively, at Lemon's bottle.

''Sure.''

Lemon leaned back on his elbows, scanning the deep starry night. Through the criss-crossed girders of the bridge he could see the Milky Way spill across the sky, and Cassiopeia, and the Bear. He remembered one night, at a campfire in late autumn, when Willy told him about a certain tribe of Celtic warriors who believed that the Milky Way wasn't just a random belt of stars but a bridge, a transparent crystal bridge across the night sky. And the bridge went from earth up to heaven, and when you died you crossed that great black bridge. And all those stars, all those legions of stars, were actually the torches of those travellers as they slowly crossed the bridge.

After they killed the bottle Burt and Lemon went down and rejoined the hockey game, on opposing teams. Right away Burt checked Lemon hard and Lemon fell down on his face, nearly breaking a tooth on the ice. Burt laughed, refusing to apologize, and Lemon shrugged it off, surprised that it didn't hurt. Then later Swiny hit Al the cop in the face with his hockey stick, yelling at him that he was a pig and get out of his crease, and then when Swiny saw the blood he started crying, but Burt punched him in the eye anyway, and Swiny apologized to everybody, tearfully lifting his arms as if he meant the entire town. Melvina took Al up to the house to fix his cut lip, and Lemon went back up on the snowbank and sat down while the game continued.

At one point Bobby came up and sat beside him, to see if

he would try to kiss her, and he did, so she went down and continued with the game and the night wore on. Whenever anyone was tired they would come up and sit on the snow beside Lemon, and the game would continue, and the shouts and yelling from the dire hockey game would lift like sacrificial smoke toward the bridge out of town.

The Authors

BONNIE BLAKE lives in Thunder Bay with her husband and two children. She writes a weekly column for the Thunder Bay Chronicle-Journal and works part-time as a teacher-librarian. Her poetry has appeared in *Tabula Rasa* and *Whiskey Jack*, and her first children's book was recently accepted for publication by Orca Books.

DOROTHY COLBY grew up in Battle Creek, Michigan, and in 1972 emigrated to Thunder Bay with her husband and three sons. She has been publishing her work since 1983. She is a swimmer, a bridge player and, in spite of her aversion to the long winters of northwestern Ontario, an avid skier.

HAZEL FULFORD is a member of the Thunder Bay Writers Guild and a graduate of Lakehead University. Her book, *When Trains Stopped in Dinorwic,* was published in 1990, and she is currently at work on a history of Gold Rock and Wabigoon, Ontario. She and her husband have two daughters and six grandchildren.

JOHN FUTHEY grew up in Chapleau, Ontario, where his father's family settled with the building of the CPR. Since 1964, he has been a professor of English Literature at Lakehead University in Thunder Bay. He takes pleasure in music, family, antiques, gardening and spurts of writing prose and poetry.

LEANDRO FRIGERI was born in Italy and raised in Thunder Bay. He teaches English at Hillcrest High School, and includes among his hobbies sailing, horticulture, and the age-old practice of tree grafting. Married, with two children, he lives in a restored farmhouse just west of Thunder Bay.

MARY FROST was born in Cork, Ireland, and is a graduate of the University of Ireland. She has worked as a teacher in England and Nigeria, and as an Education Officer with the WRAF. For the past fourteen years she has lived in Thunder Bay, where she is a member of the Thunder Bay Writers Guild and the Poetry Workshop. Her poetry has been published both in Canada and in Ireland.

ANNE KENT JOLLYMORE began writing as a child, by dictating stories to her parents. Her recent poetry and prose have appeared in several publications, both in Canada and in Ireland. She holds a Master's degree in clinical psychology from Lakehead University and attributes much of her development as a writer to the guidance of the late Bill Pendergrast.

MARIANNE JONES, like her fictional character Anja, spent her childhood summers at Surprise Lake outside Thunder Bay. She has written for newspapers, radio and magazines. She is a teacher, and she and her husband have two grown daughters, Jeni and Maureen. They live in Thunder Bay.

ELIZABETH KOUHI was born in Lappe, Ontario, a pioneer Finnish community near Thunder Bay. Her formal education began in a one-room school, led to McGill University in 1946 and the Ontario College of Education in 1963. In addition to teaching high school for nineteen years, she has published four books for children and a book of poems for adults.

DAVID LADEROUTE is a thirty-year-old geologist and military reservist who writes fiction and non-fiction in his spare time. Born and raised in Thunder Bay, he now lives in Kenora with his wife, Jackie, their three children and two cats.

CLAUDE LIMAN teaches American Literature and creative writing at Lakehead University. He has published two books of poetry, *Landing* (1976) and *Becoming My Father* (1988). A third collection, *Home-Made Hill*, is nearing completion. He feels honoured to appear in *The Wolf's Eye* with some of his former writing students.

BILL MacDONALD was born in Fort William and, except for three years in remote Arctic weather stations and a year at the Sorbonne, is a life-long resident of Thunder Bay. He holds an honours degree in French and English from the University of Manitoba and spent twenty-five years as head of the language department at Hillcrest High School. He has published four books: *Confessions of a Cornish Miner, Shaganash, Branches* and *The Whales of Superior.*

JAKE MacDONALD is a full-time writer of fiction, drama and journalism. His four books of fiction focus on the landscapes and people of the Minaki-Kenora area, where he lives for most of the year. During the summer, he works part-time as a fishing guide.

PAT McLEOD was born and raised in northwestern Ontario and lives in Thunder Bay with his wife Denise, son Brian and slightly brain-dead German shepherd. He started writing in 1983 and concentrates his efforts on short stories with horror/suspense themes. He enjoys the outdoors, particularly hunting and fishing.

ROSALIND MAKI has worked briefly as an editor and is the author of several short stories. Her first published fiction appeared in The Toronto Star Short Story Contest in 1990. Born in Thunder Bay, she now lives in Kaministiquia with her husband and their three children.

JOHN PRINGLE has lived most of his life in the Atikokan area, where he works in the forest industry. He has been writing short stories for several years and has published his work in *Grain* magazine. ''Slim Pike and the Windipogo'' is an excerpt from a novel in progress.

JEANETTE THOMPSON was born in outback Australia and earned a degree in Social Sciences before emigrating to Canada in 1983. She writes for radio and television, and has a keen interest in children's literature. She lives with her husband and young family in the Slate River Valley.

CHARLES WILKINS is the author of a number of books, both for adults and for children. His recently completed novel, *A Recollection of the Boneyard,* is based on a summer he spent working in a large Toronto cemetery. He is married, with one son, and is currently writer-in-residence at the Thunder Bay Public Library.

Date Due

PRINTED IN U.S.A.   CAT. NO. 24 161   BRO DART